A Match Made in Bed

"It doesn't seem right that we should be forced to marry because of last night. Nothing happened . . . except it might have helped if you had been dressed. I was shocked you don't sleep in nightclothes."

A wicked grin flashed across his face. He took another step toward her. They stood so close, she could feel his body heat. "There are other things I do that might shock you as well . . . at first. Does that make my offer more tempting? Or do you wish to spend the rest of your life playing safe?"

There it was, her choice. She could do what her father expected, which was safe. Or she could embrace what Fate had placed before her. Soren knew how to tempt her.

"In honesty, Cass, of all the heiresses in the world, I like you best."

"You don't know me, Soren. Not any longer. We are both very different than the children we were."

"Perhaps," he agreed, then added, "Perhaps not . . ."

And then, before she knew what he was about, he kissed her.

By Cathy Maxwell

The Spinster Heiresses
A MATCH MADE IN BED
IF EVER I SHOULD LOVE YOU

Marrying the Duke
A DATE AT THE ALTAR • THE FAIREST OF THEM ALL
THE MATCH OF THE CENTURY

The Brides of Wishmore
THE GROOM SAYS YES • THE BRIDE SAYS MAYBE
THE BRIDE SAYS NO

The Chattan Curse
THE DEVIL'S HEART • THE SCOTTISH WITCH
LYON'S BRIDE

THE SEDUCTION OF SCANDAL
HIS CHRISTMAS PLEASURE • THE MARRIAGE RING
THE EARL CLAIMS HIS WIFE
A SEDUCTION AT CHRISTMAS
IN THE HIGHLANDER'S BED
BEDDING THE HEIRESS • IN THE BED OF A DUKE
THE PRICE OF INDISCRETION
TEMPTATION OF A PROPER GOVERNESS
THE SEDUCTION OF AN ENGLISH LADY
ADVENTURES OF A SCOTTISH HEIRESS
THE LADY IS TEMPTED • THE WEDDING WAGER
THE MARRIAGE CONTRACT
A SCANDALOUS MARRIAGE • MARRIED IN HASTE
BECAUSE OF YOU • WHEN DREAMS COME TRUE
FALLING IN LOVE AGAIN • YOU AND NO OTHER
TREASURED VOWS • ALL THINGS BEAUTIFUL

CATHY MAXWELL

A Match Made in Bed

A Spinster Heiresses Novel

AVONBOOKS

An Imprint of HarperCollinsPublishers

A MATCH MADE IN BED. Copyright © 2018 by Catherine Maxwell, Inc. All rights reserved. Printed in the United States of America. No part of this book may be used or reproduced in any manner whatsoever without written permission except in the case of brief quotations embodied in critical articles and reviews. For information, address HarperCollins Publishers, 195 Broadway, New York, NY 10007.

First Avon Books mass market printing: May 2018
First Avon Books hardcover printing: April 2018

Print Edition ISBN: 978-0-06-265576-9
Digital Edition ISBN: 978-0-06-265577-6

Cover design by Patricia Barrow
Cover art by Larry Rostant
Author photo by Mary A. Behre

Avon, Avon & logo, and Avon Books & logo are registered trademarks of HarperCollins Publishers in the United States of America and other countries.

HarperCollins is a registered trademark of HarperCollins Publishers in the United States of America and other countries.

FIRST EDITION

18 19 20 21 22 QGM 10 9 8 7 6 5 4 3 2 1

For Sudie Todd and Sherri Farley Snovell
I am wealthy in my friends.

Acknowledgments

I'd like to express my gratitude to my editor Lucia Macro and my friend Teresa Kleeman. I may come up with the story, but a good editor and willing resources help hammer it out. If I got it wrong, the fault is mine alone. They tried their best to steer me!

Chapter 1

Soren York, Lord Dewsberry, was determined to marry the Holwell Heiress. He needed her money. Desperately.

The problem was, Miss Cassandra Holwell appeared equally tenacious in avoiding him.

And he didn't understand why.

Soren stood in the short hall located between the dining room and the reception room where the other houseguests were enjoying before-dinner banter and introductions. It was a good spot to observe Cass unobtrusively and plot his next strategy. He didn't think she knew he was here. He'd tried to keep his name on the guest list hushed. He was running out of time to find a rich wife and hoped to slip past her guard to present his case.

All he needed was a good listening to. A marriage to him would help Cass as well. She'd been on the Marriage Mart for at least three Seasons. She needed a husband as much as he needed a wife.

The other guests were from the very highest tiers of Society. They gathered at the invitation of the Dowager Duchess of Camberly for her annual country rout. An invite to this event meant one was important, and they were all very pleased with themselves, especially Cass's father, the bombastic MP Holwell. He had inserted himself into a group of lords where he was loudly conferring his opinion on anything and everything. His wife, Helen, Cass's stepmother, stood at his side, a look of importance on her sharp features.

Cass herself sat on a settee in the middle of the room, hands demurely folded in her lap. There was nothing to fault about her demeanor.

Or her appearance. Her hair, the color of a golden ale, was piled high on her head in artfully arranged curls secured with diamond-tipped pins. The expensive stones caught the light and winked mockingly at Soren as if daring him to come forward.

They alone would have been beacon enough to draw the eye to her. However, around her neck she wore the famed Bingham pearls, a long, lustrous strand that set off Cass's perfect complexion.

Her height also made her stand out. Cassandra Holwell was taller than the average man, although an inch or two shorter than Soren, he was pleased to admit. She was also a notable bluestocking, that sort of woman who valued her *own* opinion, who thought she was as intelligent as a man, and who had a decided preference for books. Fortunately, while she held strong opinions, she lacked her father's demeaning arrogance.

Nor did her proclivities deter Soren. He couldn't remember a time in their acquaintance when Cass hadn't had her nose in a book or had not known her own mind. Actually, he admired women who were bold and had something to say for themselves. They attracted him.

It also helped that he'd thought Cass Holwell one of the prettiest girls in Cornwall back in the day, and his opinion had not changed—

Huge hands clamped down on his shoulders from behind. "Are you ready to make your move?" the newly named Duke of Camberly said close to Soren's ear, lest they be overheard scheming. "You had best be. Minerva has squawked long and hard about my insisting she invite MP Holwell to her prize event, until she learned we were up to matchmaking. Now she is onboard with our plan."

Minerva was the dowager duchess. No one had been more surprised than she when a series of untimely deaths had left a grandson of a second son, Matthew Addison—who had been nothing more than a lowly tutor at Eton and a hopeful poet—the new heir.

To his credit, Matt had a poet's dark, handsome looks and a fine mind. He was also without guile and naïve to the wolves of the world. Soren both feared for him and envied him.

"Or," Soren countered, "the dowager could also just be relieved you are not considering Miss Holwell for your duchess." Camberly could use a marriageable heiress as well. The ducal estates were vast and in need of an infusion of money.

"That was her fear. She swears she could never abide being related to someone with the table manners of Holwell. Are his that terrible?"

"I've never seen him take a meal where he does not spit his food all over the place while he blusters away."

"Ah, so it is true what I've heard, that he is a fool."

"An *elected* fool," Soren emphasized. "The worst sort. Before every election, Holwell returns to Cornwall to ply the masses with barrel kegs of ale and spits of roast pork while greasing any palm held out to him. They vote for him again and again. It is a travesty. They all think he is a jolly fellow. Or, knowing the Cornish, they prefer him in London instead of as a neighbor."

"Are you certain *you* wish to be related to him? Didn't you tell me once there is bad blood between your family and the Holwells?"

"According to Holwell, we are sworn enemies."

The duke's brow lifted. "There is a story here. What did you do to them?"

"It is what they did to us. Or rather, what we did to ourselves. My grandfather had lost heavily at the card tables and needed money quickly. He borrowed it from Toland Holwell, using a prime bit of our land as security."

"Security?" Camberly said. "Wouldn't he accept your grandfather's word as a man of honor?"

"Miners don't accept anyone's word of honor when money is at stake. There was even a contract my grandfather had to sign."

"A miner?"

"Aye, Toland started off in the mines but he made his true money smuggling. He developed a smugglers' route between the Cornish coast and London. He claimed he could move ten barrels of brandy from Land's End to Edinburgh with nary a taxman being the wiser. He was a shrewd man, and the only one with the blunt who was willing to lend it to my grandfather. Supposedly, and I do not know if this is true, my grandfather gathered enough cash to pay back the debt. However, he discovered in the contract that Toland had charged him so much interest, he owed twice what he had originally borrowed. We took Toland to court, but the contract was ruled valid. Then, to add insult to injury, Holwell claimed a large portion of our estate when we couldn't pay, and built a fine house."

Soren's gaze strayed back to the golden Cass. "Since then, the Holwell fortunes have risen while ours have fallen, mostly through our own faults," he had to add. The trial of his life was his struggle to undo the damage his grandfather and father's foolishnesses had brought upon his family's estate, Pentreath Castle. "Marrying the Holwell Heiress would provide a certain poetic justice, don't you think? Miss Holwell is her father's only child. Eventually Toland's lands would be returned to my family."

"But won't she be suspicious of you?"

In the reception room, Cass leaned down to better hear what Lady Bainhurst was saying. Her Ladyship was around Cass's age and the wife of the influential Lord Bainhurst.

Sitting on Cass's other side on the settee was Miss Willa Reverly, the daughter of the banker Leland Reverly. Both Miss Reverly and Cass were known as the Spinster Heiresses. They were young women whose fathers knew their daughters were prizes and had yet to accept anyone's offer for their hands. The word was that both men held out for the best titles. They knew the power, and lure, of their money could ensure their descendants a rightful place among the nobility.

Soren drew his gaze away from the settee. "She might be. We were once friends," he added.

Camberly's interest picked up. "What sort of friends?"

"Childhood. Until I came to London several weeks ago, I hadn't seen her for ten years or so. I was warned to stay away from her back then."

"So, she was the forbidden."

"Forbidden? Aye, absolutely. My parents went to great trouble to be certain I knew that a York would never associate with a Holwell."

"And yet you were drawn to her."

Soren had to laugh. "Sometimes, you are too dramatic."

"I just enjoy a good story, especially one that relives the Capulets and the Montagues."

"We were far from that. I came upon her at a parish picnic. She was sitting inside the church reading while the rest of us were playing our games."

"How old were you?"

"I was thirteen. She was eleven. I remember she looked very lonely." A bit like she did now, he suddenly realized. She appeared at ease, and yet, something about the stiffness in her shoulders told him she was not. He understood her apprehensiveness in Cornwall. It could be a small society for a woman of her class . . . but this was a London crowd, and he sensed she was still not comfortable in her own skin.

"Well, you needn't worry about blood feuds," the duke assured him. "I asked Letty to mention your name several times and talk about what a stellar husband you would make."

"You didn't." Soren's reaction was part alarm, part embarrassment.

"We did," Camberly answered proudly. "We want to take full credit on your wedding day."

"Your Grace, first, I must do this my own way."

"Your way is not bringing the lady closer to you. Didn't you say you need to return to Cornwall soon?"

Soren had. It was imperative he return to Pentreath.

"We are helping," the duke assured him. "Just a bit of prodding. Letty knows what she is doing."

"Letty? Do you mean *Lady* Bainhurst? You sound too familiar when you use her given name, Your Grace."

Camberly's easy manner evaporated.

No, this was not the proper time or place for such a conversation, but Soren was not going to let this opportunity pass. His friend had become very secretive. He'd taken to disappearing from Society for days on end. Soren did not believe he went missing alone. Matt returned too pleased with himself. For all the loftiness of his title, Camberly was not a sophisticate or in any form jaded, especially to romance. God help him, he was a poet.

And what sort of friend would Soren be if he didn't warn him? "Your Grace, you'd best watch yourself. You may be a duke, but her husband prides himself on the power he wields. He is not one to share anything."

"He is twenty years her senior. He is too old for such a young wife."

"Still, she is his wife. And a man in his forties is not ancient."

"He doesn't appreciate her."

"He doesn't need to. He is married to her, Matt. I've known you for close to two decades. You are not one for playing games. *She is*. You are not her first lover."

That news tightened the ducal jaw. Camberly took a step away.

Putting a touch of empathy he did not feel in his voice, Soren cautioned, as he'd promised the dowager he would, "There is gossip. Letty Bainhurst is not discreet."

Camberly's mouth opened as if he would deny any connection, and then he closed it. His somber eyes strayed in the direction of his rumored paramour. "I can't. I love her."

"You are poaching on another man's territory. It will not go well if you are discovered."

"We are careful."

"Ah, yes, careful," Soren echoed. "If I had a pound for every man I've heard make that claim, I'd not need to marry money."

The response was a cold silence.

Soren leaned closer to his friend. "Welcoming smiles can turn to vicious tongues in a snap of the fingers. Bainhurst is notably pugnacious. He would proudly put his sword through you, and everyone would believe him justified."

"I'm not afraid of him."

"You are also not a fighter. You are a scholar. You know words, not weapons."

"Granted, I haven't been a soldier like yourself, but I'm not a coward—"

"I'm not saying you are."

"We are careful," the duke reiterated.

"You play with fire, you will be burnt. It is the oldest adage known to man. And the one continually ignored."

Camberly put his hands behind his back. He did appear a duke, even as he professed, "I've never met anyone like her. She has so much passion inside her waiting to be released."

"I'm certain you are eager to help," Soren murmured.

His friend ignored the comment. "I can't stay

away from her. It is impossible. What we have between us is stronger than mere human will." He turned away from Soren. "It can't be wrong. It isn't."

Soren shrugged, the movement straining the seams of his jacket. It was a bit too tight. He'd purchased his evening clothes from the widow of the man for whom they had been tailored. Another forced economy. He hadn't the money to go to a tailor. Once he won Cass, his first act would be to burn these clothes.

"I've done my duty," Soren conceded. "Spoken my piece. I'll say no more." Instead, life would have to teach Matt its lessons.

At that moment, Minerva, the dowager, came up behind them from the dining room, where she'd been checking last-minute details. The purple plumes in her hair bounced as she said, "My dear grandchild, what are you doing hiding here when you should be out amongst the guests? Circulate, Camberly. Circulate."

"Yes, Grandmother, of course," he said. "Especially since Dewsberry and I are growing disagreeable with each other." He marched into the room, not even bothering to go to the reception room's main doorway where the butler had been waiting to announce him. He set a direct course for Letty Bainhurst.

"You spoke to him just now?" Minerva asked,

referring to her concerns about the duke's love interest.

"As you requested of me."

"Did he listen?"

Soren looked down at her. "Do you see where he is?"

She stared bleakly at her late husband's heir leaning over the immoral Lady Bainhurst. "Yes. He is ogling her breasts." She sighed her exasperation. "Do you men not realize how obvious you are?"

"Apparently not. Then again, an idiot couldn't miss those breasts. They appear to be served up on a platter."

"And supposedly her husband doesn't notice."

"He enjoys his jealousy. How else would he have a reason to call men out?"

The color drained from her face. "The title cannot afford another death. You have been a good friend to Matthew, my lord. Please don't abandon him."

"If I can be of service, I will, Your Grace. However, I cannot save him from himself."

"He'd be wiser to pay attention to Miss Reverly and her thousands of pounds in funds, as would you. Aligning yourself with Holwell is folly." She shivered her distaste for MP Holwell.

"Miss Holwell will someday inherit land that abuts mine. Furthermore, she receives the Bingham fortune when she marries. The pearls around her neck alone would wipe away my debts and secure Pentreath."

"Yes, yes." She gave his arm a motherly pat. "And MP Holwell is an absolute troll of a man. Let me remind you, when you marry, you take on not only a wife, but her family as well."

Soren's gaze went once again to Cass's shining halo of hair. Was he being overly stubborn? Cass had rebuffed his every attempt to court her.

And yet, he reminded himself, they had been friends at one time—until she'd abruptly refused to speak to him.

The sudden recollection startled him.

He'd forgotten that incident, he realized. Memory was a funny thing. However, now he could recall her abrupt change toward him. They had been at a house party and she'd gone cold. Before he could learn what had created the rift between them, his father had informed him he would not be returning to school and had shipped him off to an uncle in Upper Canada.

Could whatever had set her against him years ago be behind her distance now?

He refused to believe so. He could not remember anything he'd done to upset her. Besides, Cass was a reasonable woman. She wouldn't carry a grudge for years . . . would she?

Either way, he would win her. Because otherwise, he'd lose Pentreath, and he was not going to give up his birthright easily. Not with his son's future in play.

"I'm willing to take MP Holwell on," he told the dowager.

"You and my grandson, both fools in love."

"I'm not in love. Lust, perhaps, but not love."

Her answer was a world-weary sigh. "Give me your arm, Dewsberry, and lead me in to properly welcome the guests, something Matthew is not doing. Unless everyone is tucked into Letty Bainhurst's bodice. If being in my company as a favored guest does not impress your Miss Holwell, then she isn't worth your attention."

Soren knew better than to argue with a duchess.

Chapter 2

He's here. I know he is," Cassandra whispered in the ear of her friend Willa, lest she be overheard by either Lady Bainhurst sitting on the settee with them or the very handsome, highly desirable Duke of Camberly. He stood by Lady Bainhurst but Cassandra felt he gave her and Willa most of his attention.

"Who? Dewsberry?" Willa managed around the smile spread across her face for the duke's benefit. She was far more interested in him than in Cassandra's sudden premonition that Soren York was close at hand.

Willa was as petite as Cassandra was tall and perfectly formed in every way. Her hair was raven black, and the two were dear friends— well, except when it came to their competition to earn the attention of the Duke of Camberly.

They'd even made a flirting game of it, attaching points for different actions of courtship—a point for an introduction, three points for each dance, five points if he called upon them. When a woman had been on the Marriage Mart as long as they had, she needed a bit of competition to sharpen her skills . . . not that either of them required the edge of a game when it came to Camberly.

He was young and amazingly handsome. He had broad shoulders, a lean jaw, and dark hair that emphasized the jewel blue of his eyes. What woman wouldn't want to become his duchess?

Cassandra was actually ahead in the game by one point. She'd been wondering how many points being invited to this weekend would earn her when Willa had made her appearance in the reception room. They had not known the other was coming.

And now here was Camberly, ignoring his other guests and spending his time focusing on *both* of them.

Everyone knew he needed to marry money. She and Willa were the only two marriageable women invited to the dowager's house party as far as Cassandra could see. Did this mean the duke intended to decide between the two of them? Perhaps even this very week?

The thought made her giddy. She wanted Camberly. He was "the one." The very embodiment of all her romantic dreams. No other could match him. And she was *not* going to let Soren York ruin this country party and her one chance for marital happiness with his presence.

Willa proved what a good friend she was by momentarily turning her attention from hanging on to the duke's every word to murmur, "I don't see Dewsberry."

"He's here," Cassandra insisted. She sat up straighter so that she could unobtrusively gain a better look around the room.

There had been someone lurking in the hall leading to the dining room. That was when she'd first experienced the suspicion that things weren't completely right. However, she'd been so distracted with Willa's presence and what it meant to her chances with the duke, she'd not been interested in concentrating on her inner sense.

Then again, the duke had come from that direction, making an appearance that had surprised everyone in the room by his lack of fanfare. Still . . . Soren was *here*.

The tingling of the hairs at the nape of her neck had never failed her, especially since she'd been exercising it more than she wished for the past month. Soren seemed to be everywhere she went in spite of her best efforts to avoid him because she knew what he wanted—marriage.

Dewsberry might be an old and respected title,

but the earldom was done up, ruined by generations of poor decisions and unwise gambling. Soren was hunting her because of the money she would inherit upon marriage and because her father's lands abutted his. He was that obvious. However, she thought herself safe here. Why would Camberly, who also needed a rich wife, invite a competitor?

Unless the duke thought to hand off whichever heiress he didn't want to Dewsberry?

The walls in the room seemed to close in around her.

She would not marry Dewsberry. She couldn't.

Her father would never allow it. The Yorks were his enemies. They looked down on the Holwells, and neither she nor her father would subject themselves to their high-handed treatment.

But also, Soren had betrayed her. She could recall perfectly the pain of what he'd done to her. It had been close to eleven years ago, and the hurt, the disappointment, was still surprisingly raw.

From the other side of the room, her father caught her eye. He was of average height, with bushy eyebrows and hair that had gone gray at a young age. Helen stood at his side as she always did. She had a short nose and a determined chin. Her hair had once been red but had faded to a dull brown. Her father had noticed Cassandra wasn't paying attention to the duke. With a scowl and a jerk of his head, he silently commanded her to focus on her business. His goal was for her to marry a titled man. He wanted his descendants to be "the highest of the high," such as a duke.

And he was right; she was not listening to Camberly.

She plastered a smile on her face and an expression of feigned interest. The duke was talking about friends. She pretended she understood the thread of the conversation. Apparently, he'd been at a horse race? Or riding in a park? She wasn't certain.

Fortunately, the duke and Lady Bainhurst liked to hear themselves talk so there hadn't been much call for her or Willa to offer a response. Besides, women in need of a husband were expected to listen more than "jabber," something her stepmother was always upon her about.

You have too many opinions, Cassandra, she liked to say. *We'll never find a husband for you. Two daughters I've easily married off, but you? I don't know. I just don't know.*

This Season, Cassandra was truly making an effort to be all that she should be. She'd had offers in the past, but her suitors had been penniless younger sons or worse, tradesmen. Her father had rejected them all—

The duke's next words snapped her out of her

worried woolgathering. ". . . Take my good friend Dewsberry. There are few men who are better riders. He has a gift for understanding horses."

Willa, bless her heart, dared to ask what Cassandra feared. "Is Lord Dewsberry here?"

"Of course," the duke answered. "Such a good man."

"Yes, he is," Lady Bainhurst chimed in brightly. "And quite handsome, don't you agree, Miss Holwell?"

So. There it was. Her intuition was once again correct.

Cassandra looked at the duke's classic male beauty and dropped her gaze to her lap before choking out, "I suppose."

It was a lackluster response but then, look at what she was losing. It was now apparent to her that the duke was more interested in Willa. Why else would he be hobnobbing with them in a room full of far more important people?

As for herself? Camberly was playing matchmaker.

At that moment, the butler stepped into the room.

Expectantly, everyone looked in his direction. "Minerva, Duchess of Camberly," he announced. "Escorted by the Earl of Dewsberry."

Willa leaned back toward her. "You are uncanny."

"I wish I hadn't been right," Cassandra answered under her breath as she and Willa rose politely with the others in deference to the duchess.

The butler stepped aside and Soren came forward with the aged dowager on his arm.

"Shouldn't you be the one escorting your grandmother?" Lady Bainhurst said to the duke.

"I'd much rather be right here," he answered.

Yes, here . . . with Willa, Cassandra thought.

Her friend must have sensed her bitter disappointment. Willa gave her hand a commiserating squeeze, a beat before shooting a dazzling smile up at the duke. And she did have to look up because she was so petite and he so tall; they would always appear the oddest of couples.

Yes, Cassandra was that jealous, and it was unflattering. Still, she couldn't control it . . . because she and Camberly would have made a far more handsome couple. They were both tall. He'd spend his life bending down to kiss Willa.

Lady Bainhurst added insult to injury by sidling closer to Cassandra. "You know Dewsberry is in the market for a wife? The two of you are both Cornish, are you not?"

"We are."

Cassandra could also add, *I'd rather be staked to a seven-foot-high stone pillar and let birds peck my eyes blind than wed Soren York*. But that would have sounded churlish.

She'd save those words for Soren.

He now escorted the dowager around the room so she could personally welcome her guests, but Cassandra knew they would end up here. She could admit that, as Lady Bainhurst had pointed out, Soren was not unattractive. Nor was Her Ladyship the first woman to say this about him.

It was true he lacked the duke's flair, but Soren bore himself well. He'd been a military officer, which, considering how adventuresome he'd been as a lad, seemed a proper career for him.

He had blue-gray eyes that often saw more than they should, and yet revealed nothing about himself. His hair had been white blond in their youth. Time had toned it down to a light brown, and someplace throughout his adventures, someone had broken his nose. It was obvious when he was in profile.

Cassandra could also concede that his shoulders were as broad as Camberly's . . . perhaps even broader—still, he was not the man for her. They had nothing in common save for both being from Cornwall, a place she hoped never to see again.

Her father was watching Soren, as well. Was he surprised a York escorted their hostess? These had been doors her father had knocked on and knocked on for years without admittance. His feelings were clear when, upon seeing the duchess and Soren close at hand, he moved so that he would not have to show respect to a York.

If the duchess noticed, she gave no sign. Instead, she tapped Soren's arm to direct him toward the settee. "And here we have three lovely English roses," she announced as she approached.

Cassandra, Willa, and Lady Bainhurst offered proper curtseys. Cassandra refused to make eye contact with Soren. It was the one thing she could do without being impolite, and she knew he would know he was being ignored. He was no fool.

However, Willa and Lady Bainhurst were under no such strictures. "How wonderful that you are here with us this weekend, Lord Dewsberry," Lady Bainhurst said, offering her gloved hand.

Soren gallantly bent over it. "It is my pleasure as well."

He had a deep voice with a distinctive sound. It was a bit gravelly, a bit husky, definitely masculine, and unforgettable.

Cassandra wished she wasn't going to have to listen to it for the next few days.

"Miss Reverly, how good to see you again," he said.

Willa bobbed another curtsey. "Thank you, my lord. It is a pleasure to see you as well."

And then he gave his attention to Cassandra. She could feel the warmth of it. Worse, the dowager, the duke, and seemingly everyone in the room watched them. Cassandra had no choice but to acknowledge Soren.

"Miss Holwell, I'm happy to see you as well."

She borrowed Willa's manners. "Thank you, my lord," she chirped, dignifying him with the barest of curtseys. Her father would be scrutinizing her every movement.

The dowager pursed her lips in a sound of satisfaction. "Why, I say, what a good couple you make. I'd not realized it before." She emphasized her words by pretending to push Cassandra closer to Soren. "So tall and equally fair. I wonder, can you both trace your ancestry back to the same Viking raid? Would that not be something?" she declared to the room.

Heads nodded agreement until Cassandra said, "I do not claim Viking blood." The words came out snippier than she would ever have intended.

Eyebrows were raised, especially the dowager's.

There was an awkward moment.

Soren stepped into the breach. "We Cornish, Your Grace, are not particularly proud of our raider history. Especially those of us who actually do have names that could be traced back to those days."

"Ah, yes, York." She smiled munificently at

Soren, letting him and everyone else in the room know she found him a favorite—and then her watery gaze slid to Cassandra. "I'm certain Holwell is not a Nordic name. It doesn't even have a particularly melodious sound."

As if York did?

Cassandra wisely kept her thoughts to herself, and a vapid smile across her closed lips.

Thankfully, the Camberly butler stepped into the room. "Dinner is served."

"Thank you, Marshall," the dowager answered. She looked to the duke. "Your Grace, you will escort me in."

"Of course, Grandmother."

"Ah, and Bainhurst, you have come for your wife," the dowager said to a hard-looking man in his forties. His hair was close-cropped with a good amount of iron gray among the black. He was of average height, with frowning lines around deep-set eyes. At one time he'd probably been quite handsome. That time had passed, to Cassandra's way of thinking. He was too full of himself now, too prideful. She could feel it about him immediately. This was a man one should never cross.

And he was especially pleased to have a young and beautiful wife. He staked his claim to her by placing a heavy hand on her shoulder.

For her part, his lady didn't flinch. Cassandra realized that the very pleasant Lady Bainhurst she'd been enjoying conversation with might also be a cold creature who could well take care of herself. There was no basis for the thought, just a strong awareness of an undercurrent of something Cassandra did not understand.

The dowager busily paired Willa to the overly plump and gossipy Mr. Bullock, who tiptoed when he walked. He was vastly annoying. Willa's father smiled his satisfaction because Mr. Bullock was a confirmed bachelor. Mr. Reverly probably thought, as Cassandra did, that this pairing was saving her for Camberly's attention.

And then the dowager announced what Cassandra had feared she would say. "Lord Dewsberry, will you please escort Miss Holwell in to dinner?"

"It would be an honor," Soren responded.

Cassandra had been aware of him moving into position behind her. He'd known.

She dared not look at her father. He would not kick up a fuss right here with everyone's eyes upon them, but she knew she'd be hearing his opinion later.

He had no need to fear. Cassandra had let down her guard around Soren once and he had wounded her in the cruelest way possible. A wise woman would gird her loins against him. And if

Cassandra was anything, she was wise. Without looking at Soren, she placed her hand so lightly on his arm, she barely touched his sleeve.

The dowager finished her assignments. They would all process in. They might be in the country; however, London rules would be observed, albeit an hour earlier for dining. She led the way to the dining room with the duke, followed by Lord Bainhurst and his lady, with all the pomp due a formal event.

Others fell in line. Soren moved and Cassandra went with him, almost tripping over the hem of her dress. She'd stepped wrong and would have fallen except for her hand quickly gripping his arm.

It was a humbling moment. Soren knew what had happened, and he knew that he had saved her.

She had yet to look at him, although from the corner of her eye she could see the hard line of his jaw . . . and a hint of a smile as if he was pleased with himself.

The thought struck her that he truly did need a haircut. What was wrong with him, or his valet, that he wasn't a bit tidier?

Then she chastised herself for even noticing.

At that moment, as the line entering the room slowed to a stop so that people could be properly seated, he turned and looked right at her with his all-too-knowing eyes.

She refused to give him the satisfaction of so much as a glance. She could feel the heat of his stare. Instead she focused on the bald patch on Lord Rawlins's head in front of her.

"You are welcome," he said quietly, a hint of laughter in his voice.

He's nothing to me, she began repeating to herself. *Nothing at all.*

She must keep those words in mind.

Chapter 3

The dining room was set for forty with gilt-edged plates and silver centerpieces. The light of what seemed to be hundreds of candles reflected off the place settings and glassware. Footmen dressed in forest green velvet and cream satin stood ready to pull out chairs. It was all a bit much, and yet emphasized the power of the House of Camberly and paid honor to the importance of the company.

Soren also knew this party was costing Camberly more blunt than he could afford to spend. He'd complained to Soren about his grandmother's extravagances. Apparently there was no reasoning with Minerva. She wanted what she wanted, and it was up to the Duke of Camberly to see she received it. Soren was glad his mother wasn't as reckless. She might be cold but she wasn't a spendthrift.

The guests flowed around the table searching

for their names on the place cards at each setting. The scent of cooked meats and breads was in the air, and the convivial atmosphere was enhanced by the fact that everyone in this room believed he or she had been invited as a Person of Importance. They mattered.

Cassandra had removed her hand from Soren's arm as quickly as she was able. All without so much as a *full* glance his way.

Soren watched her look for her seat. The duke was naturally at the head of the table, with Miss Reverly on one side and Lady Bainhurst on the other. Disappointment crossed Cass's face when she noticed. She acted as if she'd hoped she was nearer the head of the table and then realized that there was only one seat unclaimed, the one next to Soren.

She straightened her shoulders and accepted her chair assignment with the stoic grace of a French noble heading to the gallows.

Soren took it upon himself to pull out her chair.

"Please, allow me," he said.

She hesitated as if debating taking the chair or bolting for the door. The dowager and other ladies were already seated. The gentlemen now waited upon Cassandra. Even the servants, queued up in the doorway with trays of soup dishes in their hands, waited for her.

"Thank you," she murmured, and sat with the

weight of an anvil. As a matter of form, he tried to give the chair a little push toward the table. It didn't budge. She must have had her heels dug in. She was doing it on purpose, another silent message that she was not pleased he was one of her dinner companions, as if her iciness hadn't been enough.

Of course, once her bum hit the seat, the gentlemen at the table were free to take theirs and—finally!—all eyes were off the spectacle Cass was making of herself.

And of Soren, since he was the gallant performing a servant's job.

Why the devil had he thought to do a bit more than he should? She was making her feelings toward him very obvious.

Several raised their eyebrows at him and more than one smirked in a knowing way. Yes, all the world knew he was making a play for the Holwell Heiress. And her rudeness was ensuring they knew he did it because he didn't have any other choice. Damn it all.

Servants rushed forward with the soup course. Footmen began filling wineglasses. Good, because he needed a drink.

The eating started. He sampled his soup. "Ah, this is very superb, is it not?" He spoke to those around him in general.

Sitting on Cass's other side, Lord Rawlins nodded.

"Camberly always sets a good table." Across from Cass, the almost deaf Lord Crossley nodded as if he agreed. Soren doubted he'd heard a word.

"I think it needs salt," the widowed Marchioness of Haddingdon pronounced. She was seated to Soren's right. She had been quite the thing in her day. She still dressed the part in bold colors, a purple turban with jewels and two huge plumes, each the size of a full-grown ostrich. Her bodice was cut so shamelessly low her aged, ample bosoms threatened to spill over. "I need salt," she repeated, speaking to the air.

A footman stepped forward, picked up the salt dish that was right in front of her, and sprinkled her soup with a silver spoon. She peered down to see what he was doing, leaving Soren to change his opinion from thinking her too haughty to salt her own food, to suspecting she probably possessed a very strong pair of spectacles vanity prevented her from wearing.

"Is it better, my lady?" the footman asked.

She tasted the soup with a smack of her lips. "Yes, that is fine. Much better." The footman stepped back.

"And what do you think, Miss Holwell?" Soren asked, keeping his tone formal and polite. "Is the soup to your liking?"

She wanted to ignore him. For the briefest

moment, resentment flashed in her expressive eyes. She looked away. "It is good."

Well, at least she'd acknowledged him.

But then her nose wrinkled. She took a sniff. "Do I smell camphor?" She looked at Soren's jacket, her brows puzzled together.

Lady Melrose, a birdlike woman who was the dowager's sister and seated across from Soren, tested the air. "I don't smell anything."

"I don't, either," Lady Haddingdon agreed before taking another slurp of her soup.

But Soren could smell it.

When he'd first purchased the jacket, it had reeked of camphor, a popular agent against moths. He'd given it a good airing out and had already worn it to several balls and dinner parties without complaint, and yet he'd always been aware of the slightly medicinal odor. Especially the day after an event. Camphor had come to symbolize his bloody empty pockets.

Then again, that Cass had noticed might be a sign she paid more attention to him than he thought?

Perhaps Camberly and the dowager's plan did have some merit.

The hard-of-hearing Lord Crossley said to the people on either side of him, "What? What are they saying?" No one answered him.

With a last quizzical glance, Miss Holwell turned her attention to her meal.

Lady Melrose spoke up. "I understand you are recently returned from the war in America, Lord Dewsberry. What do you make of all that is going on there?"

"Here now, were you in the military?" Lord Rawlins asked. He had been surreptitiously ogling Cass's admirable breasts in such a way that Soren had been tempted to thump him on the head.

"I was for a time," Soren said.

"A time? What does that mean?" Rawlins barked. He motioned for this wineglass to be refilled. The footman also filled Soren's.

"I sold my commission several years ago."

"And why?"

"I had other opportunities."

"What sort of opportunities?"

"I embarked on business," Soren answered. That statement was met by several blank stares.

"Do you mean trade?" Lady Haddingdon queried. "You sold your commission to work?"

Soren knew their generation would think him odd. His generation would as well, although things were changing. If they knew the complete truth of his life in Canada, they'd be horrified.

He wondered if Cass would be as well. The girl she had been wouldn't have blinked. But the woman she had become apparently followed the pack.

Or did she? She'd been known for thinking for herself. Now, behind a veneer of bored sophistication, she pretended to be uninterested, but he sensed she listened.

For that reason, he elaborated. "I have investments in Canada. I own a trading post, a store for general supplies, and a tavern. I also started a small shipping company on Lake Huron."

He was proud of his accomplishments. To his knowledge, he was the first York to make money instead of squandering it. Hence he could set aside his pride to purchase another man's clothes and not run up more debt. Of course, finding a tailor willing to extend him credit had also been a challenge. Tradesmen were wary of the York name.

"Why would you need to ship things on a lake?" Lady Melrose wondered.

"Lake Huron is larger than the Channel," Soren explained. He understood how difficult it was for the average Englishman to grasp the vastness of Canada.

"But you are a storekeeper?" Rawlins questioned.

"I HEARD HE IS DONE UP," Lord Crossley said to Rawlins, indicating with a nod of his head he was speaking of Soren.

"You are speaking too loud," Lady Melrose chided him.

"WHAT?"

"BE QUIET," Lady Haddingdon said, a comment that was heard up and down the table. There were twitters here and there. Glances were exchanged.

Soren could have cheerfully wished them all to Hades.

Lady Melrose proved she was indeed attempting to be his angel by saying, "My late husband was good in business. It is one of the things I liked most about him. Tell me, Dewsberry. Are your businesses lucrative?"

"There is the rub. They were starting to do well when I was there to oversee things. Then my father died. I had to return to England and took on a partner." He kept his story simple. "He is overseeing matters for me; however, with the war . . . well, one never knows."

"Your man could be robbing you blind," Rawlins predicted.

"Possibly." With Soren's luck of late, he probably was. Or bankrupting the businesses. "I pray not."

"Did you see any savages?" the blunt Lady Haddingdon demanded. It was a question all Londoners liked to ask and the one Soren detested the most.

"I knew many natives," he answered. "I find them intelligent people."

"I hear they run around half naked. Is that true? Are they all naked?"

"No, they wear clothes."

"Oh," was her disappointed response. "I'd like to see one. I hear they are frightfully ugly."

"You 'hear' a great deal," Soren countered. "The truth is, the natives are not ugly. They are a handsome people who have the same concerns and cares as you or I."

"It sounds as if you admire these Indians?" Rawlins said.

"I do," Soren answered. "I've worked with them for years. They are our closest allies in the war we fight right now and I respect them. No," he said, correcting himself. He'd attended too many dinner parties where he'd been "polite," a condition that was starting to annoy him about himself. "I *admire* them." If they knew the whole truth, they would be truly shocked.

Even so, that statement killed conversation. Rawlins pulled a face at Lord Crossley, who hadn't heard a word of what had been said. "What? What? What?" he repeated, albeit more quietly than before.

Lady Melrose shushed him while, beneath the table, Lady Haddingdon placed her hand on Soren's thigh.

At first, he thought she'd made a mistake. He looked askance at her. She smiled at him with her squinting eyes. He took her hand and moved it back to her lap, warning her with a pat to keep it there. Her response was an unrepentant burp into her napkin and a signal to the footman that she needed more wine.

She might not know where the salt dish was, but she could unerringly find both his thigh and her wineglass.

With a shake of his head, Soren looked away from her and found himself face to face with Miss Holwell. She had witnessed the bit of lap play. The corners in her mouth curled with disapproval. Coolly, she gave him her shoulder. That momentary interest in him and his life had been dismissed. She had moved her stiff, unyielding attention toward—

Camberly?

Her gaze had gone right to the duke. A look of such heartfelt longing crossed her face that finally Soren understood.

Cassandra Holwell had set her cap for the duke. She'd thought she'd been invited to Mayfield this weekend because Camberly was interested in *her*.

And she was interested in *him*.

Jealousy was an uncomfortable emotion, one Soren had rarely experienced. He felt it now with a vengeance.

Cass was a fool if she thought a miner's granddaughter could become a duchess. Then again, his mother had always claimed the Holwells were more arrogant about their money and standing than the Yorks could ever have imagined being. Cass's father had never ceased reaching far above himself. The man's gall was legendary.

It was also obvious that if Cass had a duke in mind, well then, being a countess would be meaningless.

Soren drained his wineglass and glanced down the table at her father. The man was talking with his mouth full of bread and gesturing wildly with his knife as he declared the Tories were wrong on the agriculture question. He spoke almost as loudly as the deaf Lord Crossley but with the puffed-up consequence of a man who believed his daughter could and should marry a duke.

Camberly was not the man for Cass. Matt needed seasoning. He was a lamb, a dreamer among the *ton*'s wolves. He didn't need a wife who could do nothing for him save give over her fortune, any more than he needed Letty Bainhurst for a lover.

But how to tell Cass those truths? How to stop her from sending furtive looks in Camberly's direction? Had there once been a time when he'd been so vulnerable? Or foolish? If there had been, then life had pounded any memory of it out of him.

He wondered what she would say if she knew about Letty? Would she still make adoring calf's eyes at her duke?

As he remembered, the Cass he'd known in his childhood had been a bit of a stickler when it came to rules. She had delighted in lecturing everyone on manners and good behavior—himself especially. That Cass would never have approved of adultery.

Before he knew what he was about, he leaned toward her. "You know Camberly is not for you."

Her response was to pretend he hadn't spoken . . . just as she'd pretended he hadn't escorted her in to dinner. Except there *was* a slight stiffening in her shoulder blades. She set her soup spoon aside, folding her hands in her lap and looking anywhere but at him.

The game was on. He hated being snubbed, especially since there was no reason for her to have any more pride than he had. Yes, he was practically penniless. But she was the daughter of a buffoon. They were on equal standing in his mind.

"I mean, it is true Camberly needs to marry money, but he has his choice of candidates," Soren observed conversationally. "He also must be very particular. He will want someone young."

That comment broke her stony reserve. She swiveled in her seat to look down her nose at him. Her eyes flashed their disdain, and he couldn't help but smile. He had her. She would not ignore him now—

"Bread, my lady?" A servant offered the bread basket between them, breaking the moment.

She nodded. The servant put a piece on her plate. She busied herself with knife and butter.

Once again, she refused to look at Soren, but she was also not paying attention to Camberly. As far as Soren was concerned, that was a mark for his side.

The servant offered him bread. "Please. Thank you," he said cheerily and broke his bread apart.

Her eyebrow lifted. "When did you start speaking so familiarly to servants?" Her tone could have cut glass. God, he prayed her pomposity was a veneer. He suddenly realized that perhaps it was his mission to snap her out of it.

"Always have. I'm one of the little people. How about you, Miss Holwell?"

"The little people, my lord? How can that be true? You have 'lord' in front of your name. You come from *the* family in our parish."

"Our *humble* Cornish parish," he answered. "Humility is an attitude, Miss Holwell. An openness. Besides, aren't you trying to have 'duchess' in front of yours?"

She faced him. "That is the second time you have referred to the duke and myself. Let me assure you, I don't have any such expectations."

"Liar."

Her face flushed red. She drew herself up and then gave him her back, fiercely engaging Lord Rawlins in conversation about the hare in cream sauce being served.

Lady Haddingdon's hand returned to Soren's knee. He shot her a look. She was unrepentant. "I won't ignore you like she is, Dewsberry. It has been a long time since I've been seated by one as handsome as you."

"And I know why," he assured her, moving her hand back to her lap. She cackled her amusement.

The hare dish was placed in front of him. He had no appetite. Instead, he listened to Cass laugh at something Lord Rawlins had said as if he was the most clever man in the room.

Leaning toward her, Soren said, "Who would have thought that at one time we'd spoken easily with each other?"

She turned and considered him. "Easily?" She shook her head to deny his words. "There can be nothing *easy* between a Holwell and a York."

THERE, CASSANDRA HAD let Soren know exactly where he stood, and *it felt good*.

And how dare he appear to woo her on one

hand and then mock her on the other as not being suitable—or attractive?

The last was a loaded word. Especially from *him*.

Oh, there was so much she wanted to say, including how hard it had been to hold her tongue ever since the marquis's ball when he'd started asking her to dance and pretending that they had a friendly acquaintance.

The sight of the food on her plate made her ill. There was no way she could eat. There was no room for simple nourishment. Not when she was filled with so much bile.

The difficulty was that Cassandra prided herself on her composure. She'd spent years going through the humiliating exercise of being trotted out for men to ogle and judge with dismissive or snidely clever comments. She had managed to keep control over her emotions, to appear serene.

But right now, she discovered she didn't have the will to continue to be silent. In this moment, she couldn't sit next to Soren York and *pretend*.

Not when everyone in the room, save for her father and stepmother, was apparently thinking that a match between them would be a good thing. After all, Soren wasn't first quality. He came from a line of gamblers who'd left him with empty pockets. They wouldn't want *their* daughters to marry him.

But it would be perfectly fine for *her* to be his wife . . . because they didn't consider her first quality, either. Her father was boorish and his manner crude. Yes, Cassandra knew what *they* whispered. Her father did as well. He took great pride in pushing himself upon them.

Whereas she sometimes wished she could disappear . . .

"Excuse me," she said to the table. She tore her napkin from her lap and tossed it beside her plate. Before anyone could comment, she pushed back her chair and walked away from the table.

Did the conversation miss a beat as she left? She thought not. She didn't even hear a pause.

A footman opened the door to the hall. She walked through it and then stopped. *Where* could she go?

She wanted to go home to London, to stop pretending that she could fit in—

"It is down the hall, my lady," the footman whispered. "The third door on the right."

"Down the hall—? Oh, yes, thank you." He had assumed she was interested in the necessary room set aside for the ladies. There was another one for the gentlemen. It was a quick, convenient place as any to escape. At least it gave her an excuse for having abruptly risen from the table and taken her leave.

She moved down the hall and opened the appropriate door. She was pleased to find she was alone. The maid who had been in there earlier had obviously been pulled to the kitchen to help with the serving of so many guests.

And at last, Cassandra felt free to think.

The tension in her shoulders eased. She was away from *him*. She raised a relieved hand to her forehead.

Confound it all, she'd been completely content with her life knowing that Soren York was on the other side of the world. Why had he returned to England?

More important, why was he hounding her? Why was he placing himself in *her* path?

Oh, she knew he wanted her money, but she would never marry him. *Not ever.*

For one thing, he was too honest. Brutally so. She knew he was right, Camberly was not interested in her. Willa would make a better duchess. She wasn't as rich in her own right as Cassandra but she had money enough. Yes, there was the height difference—and Cassandra still believed as a couple, it would make them look silly—however, her friend was beautiful.

Even Willa's father had been given a position of honor at the table, whereas her father and stepmother were located at the foot of the table. She also realized that the only thing that had saved her from ignobly being seated with them was

Soren, the duke's good friend. Indeed, he was probably the reason the Holwells had even been invited to this party.

And that annoyed her most of all.

Everyone in that room believed she should marry the penniless Lord Dewsberry and consider herself fortunate. Even grateful.

How little they knew him. Or her.

She wasn't some dull bookworm. She'd make a brilliant duchess. With Camberly by her side, she'd host a literary salon that would rule London. She'd thought it all out. It was her favorite dream. Everyone of importance would desire an invitation, but she would be very choosy. Only those with ideas of merit or who had great talent would be invited. Lord Rawlins and Lady Haddingdon were definitely off the guest list.

At her salon, the conversation would sparkle with wit and great ideas would be discussed. Minds would be changed. And she'd feel she had something meaningful in her life.

Oh, she'd attempted to hold a salon on her own merit. Her father had humored her and allowed her to host two. They had not been well attended. Her friends Willa and Leonie had been the only guests to show to both of them. Cassandra had tried to convince some scholars to come but they had politely declined. In the end, the program had been several readings by poets more interested in the food that was served than in presenting their work.

The salon was her big dream ... however, Cassandra had smaller, *secret* dreams as well. She called them secret because she rarely voiced them. They were too simple for a woman of her intelligence, but truth be known, she did want her own home and a husband she admired.

Soren did not pass that muster.

She would also like children. When she visited her stepsisters, she enjoyed her nieces and nephew. Their growing minds intrigued her. She found them fascinating.

And she would be involved in her children's lives. Amanda and Laura depended upon nurses and governesses. Cassandra fancied teaching her children herself. She'd talk to them about geography and literature and mathematics and help them understand why such things were important to know—her daughters as well as her sons.

She herself had been most fortunate that the local vicar in Cornwall, Mr. Morwath, had encouraged her to read. He'd loaned her books and had even pushed her father to hire good tutors. Otherwise, her father and Helen would have been happy to keep her ignorant of science and other topics they considered "unsuitable."

But no one told a duchess what she could and couldn't do . . . except it appeared Cassandra had lost Camberly's interest—

No, she'd never had it. His interest had been a ruse to match her with Soren. And now, who knew if she would realize any of her dreams? Especially the secret ones?

Cassandra went to the washbasin. She poured lukewarm water into a bowl, wet a cloth, and pressed it to her neck and heated cheeks. It felt good. She shouldn't have let Soren goad her.

Nor could she hide forever in the necessary room. She was going to have to return to the dining room and resume her seat, but first she would enjoy a moment's more respite from—

The door opened . . . and Soren York walked in, destroying her privacy.

Chapter 4

*S*torming the ladies' necessary room was not the best idea Soren had ever had; however, it served the purpose. He had her where they could have a moment of straightforward conversation.

Cass obviously did not agree with him. "*Leave this room immediately*," she ordered. She actually quivered with outrage.

It was a bit overdramatic.

His response was to walk around the room, listening at the screens set up in one corner for privacy. "Good, we are alone."

"No, *you* are alone." She began walking toward the door. "*I am leaving.*"

"Not yet." He hooked his hand in her arm, circling her away from the door.

She yanked her arm away. "You would stop me? Don't think I won't scream."

Soren raised a conciliatory hand. "Cass, you

are not a screamer. We need to talk and here is as good a place as any—"

"I have nothing to say to you."

"Obviously you do or you wouldn't be so huffy with me."

"I'm not huffy—"

"Cass, you are huffy—"

"*And I am not 'Cass.'* My name is Cassandra. Miss Holwell to you."

"Yes, Miss Holwell," Soren repeated, mocking her with meekness. And why not? She was being unreasonable. "I used to call you Cass. You didn't correct me then."

"But I did not *like* it. I've already corrected you more than once this Season. Especially the evening when you referred to me as 'Cassie.' "

She had.

Soren was unapologetic. "If you truly didn't like my calling you Cass, why didn't you say something in the beginning? Back when we were children?"

His logic appeared to stump her and then she said, "Because. Now will you leave?"

" 'Because' is not an explanation," he argued.

"It is all you are going to receive." She edged away from him as she spoke, moving as if preparing to physically defend herself.

At last, the thought occurred to Soren that something was very wrong between them. He attempted diplomacy. "I'm not trying to intimidate you."

"You have followed me into the ladies' necessary room—"

"I wish a moment's private conversation with you. Something I haven't been able to have because you have been avoiding me, haven't you?"

She didn't deny the accusation. Instead, she announced, "I will not marry you. I have no desire to have anything to do with you."

Her bluntness annoyed him. "I've received that message," he assured her. "What I don't understand is what I did to set you off. Put the whole idea of marriage aside—" He'd have to work on that issue later. "We were friends once, Cass." Almost too late he remembered to use her full name. "—andra," he added.

"Until you *betrayed* that friendship."

Now *there* was an accusation that surprised him.

"Betrayed our friendship? What are you talking about?" He searched his memory. "You are the one who changed everything. You stopped speaking to me."

"I gave you the cut direct," she declared rather proudly. She referred to the social weapon of rudely ignoring an acquaintance. It was a fierce thing to do . . . if one paid attention to ridiculous etiquette. Soren did not.

"The cut direct?" The words didn't even taste good in his mouth. "You were thirteen. Children don't do the cut direct."

"*I* did."

"Ah, well, you have me there." He shook his head. Back in those days she was always claiming the silliest of ideas, usually gleaned from books. "Of course, if I wasn't aware that I'd received the cut direct, it loses its power, doesn't it? It can't truly be a cut direct, if I don't know I've been cut. Or that you are being direct. Which you weren't, by the way, because I didn't know I'd received it."

Her answer to his logic was a haughty glare, one he easily ignored.

Soren was glad for this conversation. Jesting aside, he wanted the air cleared between them. "Very well, you delivered the 'cut direct,' " he conceded. "And you did this because I 'betrayed' you?" Now, there was another overburdened word. "You will pardon my ignorance. What exactly did my fifteen-year-old self do?"

"You mocked me. Just as you did at the dining table this evening."

Soren already regretted his blunt comment when he'd told her Camberly would never marry her. It was the truth; still, he could have been gentler, less confrontational . . . although he would hardly consider his honesty a "betrayal."

In truth, he'd always pushed her a bit. Some would say that it was the natural inclination of a York wanting to best a Holwell, but he knew differently. He'd wanted Cass to notice him. He did not like being dismissed. Her opinion had always been surprisingly important to him. He'd valued her approval. He still wanted to have it, and more. He would like to have her in his bed.

Marrying Cass Holwell would be no chore at all. She had everything that attracted him to a woman. She was fiercely independent and un-afraid, two qualities he hadn't seen in any other woman in London. He teased her about books but he admired her intelligence. He'd learned long ago a woman without wit could make for deadly dull nights. And she was very easy on his eyes. How could he not be interested in her?

"I didn't mean to tease you," he said. He didn't like the word "mock." "I don't know what came over me at the table." He wasn't about to admit to jealousy. "Why shouldn't you be a duchess? You could." There, he'd apologized.

She was not mollified. "I *don't* demand an apology for our dialogue at the dinner table, al-though you *were* rude. What you said to me in there is nothing less than what I would expect of you." She sounded like the stuffiest of govern-esses.

"Oh. Well, then I'm sorry I apologized. I can't

seem to keep from offending you." Yes, he was *mocking* her, and rightly so. She was throwing his apology back in his face—and she was the one who had wanted it.

Her hands clenched into fists at her side. "You think you are so clever. Or that I am so desperate for marriage I'd lower my standards to your level—"

"Wait a minute, Cass. Now you are the one growing very personal here," he warned.

"*Cassandra*," she barked.

"*Cass*-andra," he fired back. Her picking on the nickname didn't make sense to Soren. Who wanted to go around being Cassandrrrraaa? The name was a mouthful. But a bit of honesty between them was refreshing. He pushed for more. "*And*, because I can't read your mind and you obviously have been nursing a grudge against me for, what? Say, ten years and more—?"

"*You called me a dog.*"

The words flew out of her, and once spoken, she pulled away, covering her mouth, as if to deny them.

"A dog?" Soren frowned. "I've never said anything of the sort about you."

That brought her back. "Oh yes, you did. It was at the Burfords' house party."

"Which one? They had one every year."

"It was the last one you attended." Her voice

was accusing, as if he was being deliberately provocative.

"Right before I left for Canada?"

"Yes."

Soren searched his mind. Why would he call her a dog, especially since she was anything but ugly or four-legged? "I don't remember saying anything so offensive."

"You don't recall trying to be clever for the other boys?"

"I recollect the other lads. I also remember that suddenly, you refused to have anything to do with me." He'd forgotten that day in general until this moment. "You went off in a huff. That was your cut direct?"

"Because you called me a dog," she insisted.

He was genuinely puzzled. "Cassandra, I'm sorry. I have no memory of saying such a thing."

She walked right up to him then. "We were up in the schoolroom, the lot of us. You picked up a slate and drew something. The other boys snickered over it. Do you not remember now?"

"No."

She looked as if she could not, *would not* believe him.

He held up his hands as if to show her he was hiding nothing, and then the details of that day came into focus.

That morning, on the way to the Burford party,

his father had informed Soren he would not be returning to school. He was behind on Soren's board and the headmaster was becoming threatening.

Instead, his father had decided to send Soren to his uncle in Canada. *You can finish your schooling there*, he'd said. *We'll purchase a commission for you when you are of age. You'll do well.*

Soren's stunned surprise had quickly escalated to fury that everything he'd known was going to be stripped away because of his father's recklessness with money. In a fit of rebellious anger, he had nipped a bottle of port when no one was looking. He and the lads had escaped to the schoolroom to drink their bottle in private. That day, he had felt he was being thrown away. His friends would continue their schooling and go on to Oxford and he would be in Canada, wherever that was.

And then Cass and some of the girls had come into the room, disturbing the masculine bond a stolen bottle had given them . . .

He looked to her. "Tell me again what I did?"

"You drew a picture of a dog on one of the slates in the schoolroom. You wrote my name on it." Her chin lifted in justified anger. She sounded grievously offended.

This was apparently what she wanted an apology for, and Soren should give it to her.

But he couldn't.

From deep within came that selfsame desire to revolt that he'd experienced the day he'd stolen the port. He did not remember drawing a picture of a dog or even holding a slate. Could he have done it? Yes. It would have been a foolish, rude thing to do, but that day, he'd been in a mood.

So, he said what he truly felt. "You've been nursing a grudge against me all these years because of some childhood piece of nonsense?"

"You were fifteen."

"I was an idiot at fifteen. All boys are idiots at that age."

"Except *you* have apparently not improved," she countered crisply, and would have marched around him for the door, save for his arm going up to block her way.

"What does that mean?" he demanded.

"Exactly what I said," she returned.

He could have put his fist through a wall in frustration. "You are carrying on this way because of some silly drawing I did on a slate when we were children, and you believe *I* am immature? Do I understand you correctly?"

"I was hurt," she replied primly.

"I see. And in your 'hurt,' do you feel you have the license to behave like the lowest class of person toward me? There are draymen who have better manners than you have, Miss Holwell."

She did not like that at all. Her brows knit together sharply. "I believe you are overreacting."

"I believe you don't know what friendship is."

"A friend doesn't call another one a dog."

She was right. Still . . .

"I was fifteen. I was a stupid, rowdy boy. We do things like that. It means nothing—"

She cut off his dismissive words by raising her arms in the air as if to block them. "You didn't do it to the boys around you or to the other girls. You did it to me. You *said* you were my *friend*— and I didn't have many. I trusted you."

That sobered him.

"You made the others laugh at me. And now?" She lowered her arms. "Now, you are supposedly courting me for my fortune and act confused that I'm not overwhelmed by your attention." Her voice took on a simpering tone. "Oh, my dear Lord Dewsberry." She batted her eyes and fanned her cheeks as if they were overheated.

Now, who was mocking whom?

"All I've done is ask you to dance a time or two and escort you in to dinner," he countered tensely.

"But what you really want is money. My money; anyone's money. You don't see me, Soren. The dog incident brought home to me that my friendship didn't mean anything to you. I was a novelty, nothing more. We'd both been warned to stay away from each other and, of course, how could we? We were both too curious for our own good. And the idea of a friendship between us? It was all a sham, just as a marriage between us would be nothing more than a charade."

She wasn't right about the friendship, but she was dead correct about the money.

He'd marry Beelzebub if the devil had the blunt he needed. Pentreath Castle was at stake. Soren had returned to England to learn that his late father had mortgaged the estate to the hilt. The man's body had barely been cold before creditors had come knocking on the door.

Soren was determined not to lose his birthright. What he had once been willing to walk away from had taken on more meaning with the birth of his son. He would not fail Logan or future generations the way his father and grandfather had. Therefore, since any money he had was tied up in his Canadian businesses, he'd made a pact with one Jeremiah Huggett, the most ruthless of the moneylenders—but what choice had Soren had? None.

Now a payment was due and Huggett was looking for his money or Pentreath.

Soren's motive for marrying was a time-honored solution. However, it would come across as shallow to an overly moral woman.

There was a long beat of silence between them.

Soren broke it first. "So, where are we? Friends? Enemies? Passersby? I never intended to hurt you."

The heat left her.

Her hand reached out to touch the wooden top of the washbasin. She rubbed a finger along the grain as if in deep thought. Her whole being softened with sadness, and he realized she wasn't as set against him as she pretended.

"Cass—" he started. Yes, he sensed an opportunity in his favor, and he was desperate enough to mine it.

She cut him off. "Our friendship was a long time ago," she admitted. "I was quite naïve then. The picture you drew on the slate, it didn't really matter, Soren. I've been called worse names, especially back then. But what hurt was your callousness. I thought you understood what your friendship meant to me. You see, everyone liked you. They thought I was odd. I didn't fit in. And all of the parish believed my family had unfairly taken your grandfather's lands. Even now, they don't like the Holwells overmuch. I try never to go back Lantern Fields." She referred to the house Toland had built on York lands.

"Nonsense. How many elections has your father won?"

"Three, and that is only because no one runs

against him. They don't have the money, even though they distrust him."

She *was* more perceptive than he had imagined. "I'm certain you are admired," he offered.

"And I'm certain you are mouthing meaningless flattery. How is that for plain speaking? There are few in Cornwall who have use for an outspoken, headstrong woman. And I return their feelings. When my father was first elected, I was happy to escape to London. It was freedom to finally be myself. I have a good life in the city. I shall not return to Cornwall. Ever."

Well, that was that.

What was left to be said between them?

Honesty.

"I'm sorry for my rude drawing. You are right, it wasn't kind of me. I can only say in my defense that I'd just learned Father was sending me away to Canada. He hadn't paid my school fees. My education wasn't as important to him as a good hour in a gaming den. Then, again, I wasn't, either. It didn't bother him that I'd been asked not to return, that his gambling had once again humiliated me." Now *he* was the one to take a step away. "That day, I was angry at everyone and unfortunately acted out in an unsuitable manner."

She frowned at the top of the washbasin as if digesting what he'd said. He wished he could read her thoughts. She seemed so distant—and so much like the lonely girl who had first caught his interest.

And then she looked up. "Thank you for your apology."

"Then we are fine with each other?"

"I won't marry you," she answered.

"I haven't asked you."

Annoyance flashed in her eyes.

"I won't lie, my father left nothing in his estate," he admitted. "However, even worse would be having a wife who doesn't want me."

He'd already learned that lesson. Marriage was tricky business.

She nodded as if agreeing he was right—she didn't want him.

A keen stab of disappointment shot through him . . . but he would survive. He always survived.

She moved toward the door. This time, he didn't stop her.

However, instead of leaving, she paused, her hand on the door handle. She glanced back at him. For a moment, she had the appearance of an exquisite porcelain model of a true English Rose with her blond curls and her blue eyes dark and considering.

Oh, there was depth to Cassandra Holwell. There always had been.

"It is not that I don't believe you wouldn't be a good husband," she said.

"Are you going to give me that Holwell and York nonsense again?"

She had the good grace to blush.

"Then what is it?" he prodded. She had opened the topic. Let her finish it.

"I want greater things for my life, Soren."

"Such as being a duchess?" There was that touch of jealousy again. It shamed him.

If she noticed, she did not give an indication. Instead, she said, "I want the power to do something important. Something that matters. I can't do that in Cornwall."

You are wrong, he wanted to tell her, but then her mind was set.

"Ah, Cass, you just want a poet for a husband." He kept his voice light.

It was the right touch. Her eyes lit with humor. "It is the bookworm in me. Or perhaps I just want poems written in my honor."

"I can write poetry."

"I can't imagine it, Soren."

"If I can draw a dog, I can certainly write a poem. Let's see . . . *I called you a dog because I'm as dull as a log*," he recited. "*But you are actually very pretty, and now I'm trying to be flirty.*"

His poor attempt startled a laugh out of her,

and he was charmed. He'd forgotten how special her laughter was. She was usually too cautious and conscientious to be completely herself—until she laughed.

What he was thinking must have shown on his face, because she sobered, but she did not run . . .

Perhaps there could be something between them—?

The turning of the handle beneath her palm broke the spell between them. The door opened on Cass. She stepped back just as Lady Haddingdon attempted to enter the room.

The first person Her Ladyship laid eyes on was Soren.

"Why, Lord Dewsberry? Am I in the wrong room?" She looked up to squint at the hand-printed sign on the door and Cass used the moment to slip past her.

"Excuse me, my lady," she murmured, and made her escape.

"I'm not in the wrong room," Lady Haddingdon said. "I believe you are, my lord."

"I am indeed," Soren agreed with a short bow. "With your leave?" He didn't wait for an answer but moved past the woman to chase after Cass.

And what would he do if he caught her? She'd made up her mind.

Nor was she in the hallway. He walked back into the dining room. They were on the beef course. He moved to his place at the table, expecting Cass to be there.

She wasn't.

Her seat was empty.

Nor did she return.

Down the table from him, Soren saw MP Holwell smile his satisfaction.

OF COURSE, CASSANDRA could not return to the dining room. If Soren's purpose had been to rattle her, his confrontation in the necessary room had done the trick. She would not be able to sit beside him for the rest of the meal in peace.

For years, she'd proudly nursed her grudge against Soren. It was what had made her a Holwell, she'd told herself. Yorks were not to be trusted, even though at one time Soren had been her ambassador. Because he'd befriended her, everyone else had included her as well, until the day he'd left without saying good-bye. He'd just disappeared.

Now she knew he'd been as surprised to be sent away as she'd been to lose him.

Seeking solace in the bedroom assigned to her, Cassandra sat on the bedside chair and tackled her own culpability in the incident in the schoolroom. She had jumped to some conclusions. Silly ones, she realized . . . and yet, at the time, it had been as if he'd broken her heart.

During that same period, she'd acted out quite a bit herself. Her father had recently married Helen. Cassandra had found herself with two stepsisters who treated her as if she was of no consequence.

When she'd first met them, she'd thought them perfect. They were of average height and had average-sized hands and average-sized feet, something they often pointed out to her as if hers were gigantic. They rarely discussed ideas because they were more interested in what Helen referred to as "feminine" pursuits—handwork, gossiping, primping. They studied art and music and practiced dance steps.

In contrast, Cassandra could not even stitch a button on a piece of clothing. The whole process, as simple as it was, annoyed her. And she had a terrible voice. Music lessons had been wasted on her. Helen had said as much repeatedly. Cassandra was also not particularly concerned with household matters. Helen had accused her of being too willing to rely on a housekeeper, which sounded like a perfectly good idea to Cassandra.

Running her fingers absently over the perfect pearls around her neck, she thought of her mother's legacy. After all, once she married, she would be wealthy enough to afford whatever she wished. She'd be free of others' opinions and she could hire the best housekeeper in the world and let her sing while she sewed on buttons.

Nonetheless, it had not been easy to have step-sisters who laughed at her—that is, on all matters save Soren. They thought he was the most handsome, most daring lad in Cornwall and had ceased purposefully irritating her. Other girls started to include her. She hadn't been considered an odd goose, and that had felt good.

Then there was the slate incident, followed by Soren seemingly disappearing from her life, and she'd been forced to soldier on alone. She had been miserable. The best thing that had happened to her was her father moving them all to London. In the city, she met Willa and Leonie and began to thrive.

Cassandra sat for a long time mulling over the past but with a different lens. Perhaps she shouldn't have blamed him for everything—

A knock on the door sounded before it opened. Her father and stepmother entered the room.

"Here you are," her father said with his usual blustery good humor he wore for appearances' sake. It was a sign that he was happy with her. "We have been looking for you everywhere."

"Is dinner over?" Cassandra asked, rising. She'd been so preoccupied with her thoughts, she had lost track of time.

"Oh, yes," he answered. "In fact, most are already to their beds."

"Has Maggie been here yet?" Helen wondered. Maggie was Helen's lady's maid, whom she and Cassandra shared when they traveled.

"No, she has not," Cassandra answered.

"When I'm done with her, I'll send her to you. I'm exhausted. Traveling today and then enduring that endless feast downstairs has taken its toll. Do you mind if I go off to bed, Thomas?"

"Not at all, my love. And this will give me a chance to speak to my daughter alone."

"That is what I thought you wanted. A private moment. Good night, Cassandra." There was no kiss on the cheek between them. Theirs was not that sort of relationship.

"Good night, Helen," Cassandra dutifully answered.

Once they were alone, her father placed his thumb on her chin to pull her head down for her to look at him. "What did Dewsberry do to you? Did he say something?"

Yes, Papa, he said he wants to marry me.

Those words never left her mouth. She held up a dismissive hand. "He barely spoke to me for the short time I was at dinner. And even if he had, I would not have paid him any attention."

"I saw him trying to talk to you." He released

her chin. "I know he's interested. He'd take any woman who had money. He's done up, broken. He barely has two shillings to his name." He laughed his pleasure. "You missed what happened after dinner. The Marchioness of Haddingdon followed him around all evening. Made a complete cake of herself."

"She's at least thirty years older than he is," Cassandra protested.

"What is age when money is involved? She's rich. That is all a scoundrel like Dewsberry is interested in. I should tip off her son. He'd horsewhip Dewsberry if he knew."

The suggestion horrified her. "You sound happy that one of our Cornish neighbors is in trouble."

Her father laughed. "I am, because I don't want him for a neighbor. He's finished, Cassandra. All those York pikers who have looked down their arrogant noses at the Holwells can kiss my arse. I might buy Pentreath myself—"

"Buy Pentreath?"

"Aye, the rumor is that it will be on the chopping block soon. I have my lawyer studying the matter. But enough of this. What of the duke?"

It took a mental pivot for Cassandra to overcome her shock that Soren could lose his ancestral home, to her father's interest in the duke. "I don't think Camberly is interested."

This was not the first time she'd had to give her father this news. He was ever hopeful and always encouraging. He obviously didn't see her the same way gentlemen of his choosing did. Those who did offer for her rarely met his standards. He was very particular.

"I don't know about that," he countered. "Yes, I was confused when he paired you up with Dewsberry and sat the two of you halfway down the table out of his and my reach; however, I believe he was being clever. I wish you'd been in the reception room when the gentlemen joined the ladies after dinner. You might have been in for a surprise."

"What do you mean?"

He tapped a finger against his nose. "Before dinner, His Grace set a straight course for you when he entered the room."

That was true.

"I watched him during the meal." Her father paced as he spoke, a parliamentarian presenting his case. "Willa Reverly may have been sitting beside him but he had his eye on you. He noticed you had not returned. He appeared worried."

"He did?"

"Oh, yes. He asked about you."

"Really?" Cassandra felt her spirits lift.

"Aye."

"What did he say?"

"Not much. What could he say? *You* were not there. But he didn't pay another moment's attention to Miss Reverly. Perhaps he had been attempting to make you jealous?"

Camberly had asked about her. That was startling news. She had thought him lost to her.

She had a momentary thought of Soren, and dismissed it. Her father was right. The Yorks had mishandled the gifts of their birthright. Even though Soren seemed different from his grandfather and father, a wise woman would not turn over her fortune, or her life, to him.

"So, tomorrow!" Her father clapped his hands and beamed approval. "Dress your best, look your prettiest. You have a duke to catch!" On those words, he wished her a good night and left the room.

Minutes later, Maggie knocked and helped Cassandra undress, plaited her hair into one long thick braid, and set out her clothes for the morrow. To be honest, the ivory, white, and pale shades that were the wardrobe of an unmarried woman did not suit Cassandra. They washed out her features. She could well imagine herself dressing vividly like Lady Haddingdon. She'd look better. In the end, she chose an ivory cambric with a thin stripe of green, her favorite color. It was hung on a wall peg for the next day.

"Good night, Maggie."

"Good night, Miss Cassandra."

Alone, Cassandra took out her traveling valise. It had a false bottom. She lifted the panel to reveal a velvet-lined compartment. She placed the precious pearls and the diamond-tipped hairpins carefully beside a set of garnets the size of a robin's eggs. At home in her dressing table was a necklace and bracelet of sapphires. These jewels and vague memories that time worked hard to rob from her were all she had that was personal of her mother. She guarded the jewels carefully.

When she traveled, which she rarely did, she protected her jewelry in this secret compartment. At home, she'd devised a special hideaway and told no one about it. She didn't know what she'd do if her mother's jewelry was ever stolen, especially the pearls. They were her favorites. Her father had told her that the king had once begged her grandfather Bingham for them and been refused.

Cassandra blew out the bedside candle, climbed beneath the covers, and waited for sleep. It did not come.

Her mind was too busy. Furthermore, Mayfield's lumpy mattress must have been as old as the house. Nor did the sheets smell fresh. And the bed ropes needed to be tightened. They were stretched to the point that between them and the mattress, she could not be comfortable.

She struggled to sleep for a good hour and more. Outside her door, she listened to other guests find their rooms until there was silence.

Staring up at the ceiling, Cassandra knew there was no hope for her. Her usual nighttime ritual was to read a chapter or two. Reading settled her mind and body; however, in the excitement of arriving at Mayfield, she'd left her book in the coach.

There was supposed to be a small reading room at the end of the hall outside her door. When she'd first arrived, a maid had told her about it. There must be a book there.

Cassandra rose from the bed and donned her dressing robe over her nightgown. The robe was a sensible garment of soft wool in a green the color of the deepest forest, because no one cared what a debutante wore to bed. She should dress if she was going to leave her room, but that would call for far more effort than she wished to expend. Her hope was to find a book and return to her bed without anyone being the wiser. Picking up the candle in its holder, she slipped her bare feet into the kid slippers she had worn to dinner and left the room.

Several wall sconces lit the hallway. All was very quiet. She walked toward where she thought the reading room was.

In truth, Mayfield was a bit of a rabbit warren.

Apparently, earlier dukes made their mark on the house by adding wings to create a maze of hallways. Her parents' room was down another hall from hers.

As she hurried toward the reading room, she noticed how actually shabby the house was. Downstairs, there was a semblance of stately wealth, but here were discolored rectangles on the walls, signs that a portrait had once proudly hung there and was now gone. Cassandra didn't understand why someone hadn't applied a brush and paint to the problem. Or hadn't seen to the tightening of bed ropes before important guests arrived.

The reading room was dark, the door partly ajar. Cassandra took a moment to light her candle off a wall sconce. She expected the room to be full of books. Why else call it a reading room?

So she was a bit surprised when she saw empty bookshelves.

However, the room was set up for reading. In front of the cold hearth were tall, upholstered chairs and a rug. Deeper in the room was another chair, larger than the fireside ones. On a small table beside it was a book. One lone book . . . with *all* of these bookshelves.

Cassandra could weep. If there had been other books in this room, they had apparently been sold off.

Curious about what that remaining book was

titled, Cassandra quietly closed the door and crossed to it. She set the candle down and picked up the book. *Plutarch's Lives.* If someone was going to hold fast to a book, this was a good one to keep. It would also help her sleep.

She picked up her candle and was about to leave when a weight or a body slammed against the door from the outside. A woman giggled—and, in a panic because Cassandra had no desire to be caught in her nightclothes walking about, she blew out her candle, plunging the room into darkness.

Barely a beat later, the door burst open. Lady Bainhurst and the Duke of Camberly, wrapped in an amorous embrace, tumbled into the room.

Chapter 5

*C*assandra wasn't certain what to do. She was too stunned to make her presence known, and then it quickly became obvious the moment to do so had passed.

Not only that, but the duke and Lady Bainhurst were too involved in themselves to politely interrupt.

She lowered herself back into the chair, trying to be as inconspicuous as possible. She thanked the Lord she was wearing forest green. Perhaps she could blend into the room's deep shadows.

There was moaning, fervent promises, puckering and kissing. Camberly, the poet of her dreams, kicked the door closed behind him, or so he thought. It hit the frame and then bounced open, the light from the hall highlighting his mouth on Her Ladyship's ear and his hand cupping her rear as her fingers tore at his neck cloth.

"You didn't close it," Lady Bainhurst chided between wet-sounding kisses.

"I don't care," he answered, his voice guttural and demanding. He carried her down to the floor. "No one is up anyway. There is just you and me . . ."

And me, Cassandra could have added, if she'd had the nerve.

She sat in the haven of the chair and put her hands over her ears. She wasn't that much out of sight. If they weren't so preoccupied with each other, they could see her. She looked toward the door for escape. It was not that far away. Should she risk sneaking by them?

The sounds coming from the rug evaded her best efforts to shut them out. Lady Bainhurst was making small giggling, yipping noises. Camberly was growling. He sounded much like a rooting pig.

Cassandra didn't want to peek to see what they were doing, but she found she must. Curiosity had always been a besetting sin.

Lady Bainhurst was on the floor. She lay on her back, her arms flung out over her head. Her hair was loose from its pins, her bodice undone, and her skirts pulled up well above her waist.

The duke was nowhere to be seen.

Cassandra could hear him but couldn't place where he was—until she realized he was partially hidden by one of the chairs and that he was busy kissing parts of Lady Bainhurst's body that Cassandra had never thought anyone would kiss.

And Her Ladyship actually liked what he was doing.

Why, she was gasping and sighing and cooing as if in the throes of some great satisfaction—until the moment when her voice took on a keening filled with desire. She brought her hands down as if to reach for Camberly, *confirming he was where Cassandra thought he was.* Frantically, she whispered, "Don't stop. *Please,* don't stop."

Cassandra didn't know what to do or think. She now understood what it meant to be paralyzed. She couldn't even breathe—and then Lady Bainhurst turned her head in Cassandra's direction and their gazes locked.

Horrified to be caught spying, Cassandra didn't know why Her Ladyship didn't shriek or shout a warning.

Instead, she smiled at Cassandra, the expression reminiscent of the cat caught in the cream. Her voice turned silky. "Take me, Matt. Have me. I'm *yours.*"

Shock moved Cassandra's feet. She no longer worried about being discovered. She ran to the door. She didn't dare look back. She didn't need to. The image of the two lovers was burned in her mind. She hoped to slip away and she was almost successful. No cry went up, until she made the mistake of shutting the door behind her.

She always shut doors. It was good manners to do so, but this time, her reflexive politeness did not serve her well.

On the other side of the door, Camberly said, "What was that?"

Cassandra didn't wait for Lady Bainhurst's answer. Instead, she lifted her hems and began running for her room. She was halfway there when from around the corner at the far end of the hall, she heard the march of boots.

"This way?" a male voice boomed in the stillness.

"Yes, Lord Bainhurst," came the answer. "They were seen in this hallway." Someone had tattled to His Lordship about his wife. There was about to be a scene.

Cassandra's panic doubled.

She did not want to be a witness to the duke being caught with his pants down. Nor did she want Camberly to piece together that she had been the person in the room when he was doing unmentionable things to Lady Bainhurst. She didn't even wish to be discovered roaming about in her dressing gown.

Instinct took over. She opened the nearest door and jumped into the darkness, shutting the door behind her, but she'd been a second too slow to react. She'd been seen.

"*There, that door,*" Lord Bainhurst shouted. "*Letty.*"

"Not that room—" the tattler countered, but it was too late.

Cassandra grabbed the door handle as it began to turn. She tightened her grasp, using both hands and all her strength to prevent the door from opening.

Behind her, she heard movement.

"*What the devil*—" a male voice said. Wait, not just any male voice—*Soren's* voice. She recognized him immediately. She'd sought refuge in *his* room.

Everything happened at once.

"They are down the hall, my lord," the tattler tried to explain.

"*They* are in here," Lord Bainhurst declared right outside the door. "I saw Letty run inside."

How anyone could mistake Cassandra for the shorter Letty Bainhurst, she did not know. She also didn't have time to consider the matter before the full force of Lord Bainhurst's body slammed into the door. The door withstood the blow, but Cassandra was no longer worried about Bainhurst, not when strong hands roughly grabbed her and turned her around.

"Soren—" she started, releasing her hold on the door and raising her hands to warn him—

Another blow bounced the door open. It hit Cassandra, who fell forward into Soren's arms, and he was *naked*. The man did not have a stitch on him.

Light and Lord Bainhurst's body spilled into the room.

Soren's reactions were swifter than her own. To her surprise, he physically lifted her, something that had never happened in her adult life, and swung her out of the way of harm. He positioned his body as a wall between her and Lord Bainhurst. It was a gallant gesture, and would have been more so if he'd been clothed.

"Aha—!" Lord Bainhurst declared, finding his balance right before Soren cut him off by grabbing him by the lapels of his jacket. Soren shoved him back into the arms of a group of men who had accompanied him and now gathered in the doorway.

However, Cassandra wasn't as concerned with them as she was at the sight of *all* of Soren.

She'd never seen all of a *living* man before.

Certainly, she had admired the male form with vague intellectuality when she'd studied sculptures of it. But those had been art.

Soren was flesh and blood, and he looked better than any sculpture she had ever seen. The light from the hallway emphasized his buttocks, his back, his thighs. They were muscular and strong. Well-formed. Impressive. She couldn't judge all of him, the "bits" so to speak, because he had his back to her, but what she could see was most admirable.

Unfortunately, everyone else could witness he was naked as well.

And Lord Bainbridge was so worked up in a jealous rage, he had not yet registered that Cassandra was not his wife. He jumped to the worst of conclusions and he did so at the top of his voice.

"*Dewsberry?* You scoundrel. *Hand over my wife.*" Doors up and down the hallway began opening as Lord Bainhurst's shouting woke the other guests.

Cassandra had to do something to save Soren's dignity. She noticed his breeches hanging over a chair and she reached for them. How humiliating this must be for him. As it was for her. She truly felt overheated.

She offered his breeches to him.

In the face of Bainhurst's blustering, he felt her gentle nudge and reached for his clothing even as he blocked with one strong forearm Lord Bainhurst's attempt to run into the room again.

"*Bring her out here,*" His Lordship demanded. "Let us all see her for the scheming adulteress she is."

"My lord, return to your bed." Soren's voice was steel-edged. If he had used that tone on Cassandra, she would have obeyed him instantly.

However, Lord Bainhurst was not of a like mind. He was frothing with anger. Two gentlemen attempted to reason with him but he shook them off. *"I call you out, Dewsberry,"* he shouted for all to hear.

"Oh, I will happily meet you, Bainhurst," was Soren's cool reply.

"And I will *happily* run my sword through *you*. You blackguard. You wife thief. You *coward*."

He was beyond reason, and Cassandra realized there was only one solution. She knew Soren was trying to protect her identity from prying eyes, but if she didn't act, the scene would grow worse, if that was possible.

She stepped away from Soren's protective presence and presented herself to Lord Bainhurst. "I am not your wife."

It took a moment for the furious lord to change the direction of his anger, but everyone else in the hall—and she was quite shocked at how many had gathered—was startled to see her. They stood in their night caps and bedclothes, their sleepy expressions giving way to salacious curiosity.

"Where's Letty?" Lord Bainhurst demanded.

"I don't know," Cassandra answered with a calmness she was far from feeling. Indeed, she was close to tears.

He scowled and looked past her. "Dewsberry, where is my wife?"

"She is not here, you fool." Soren stepped forward to stand beside Cassandra. He had, thankfully, found an opportunity to put on his breeches. However, he was still naked to the waist. And his feet were bare. She knew imaginations around them were jumping to the worst possible conclusion.

Slowly, the knowledge that his wife was not in the room sank into Lord Bainhurst's thick skull. He looked back and forth between her and Soren and then glanced at the man on his right. "You said—?" He broke off as if just now noticing with alarm the crowd in the hallway.

The man, a weaselly sort, lowered his voice. "I tried to tell you this wasn't the room."

"You did not," was the swift rebuttal. "I wouldn't have crashed into Dewsberry's room if I'd heard you. You should have stopped me."

Before there was answer, a new voice joined the hullabaloo.

"*Cassandra?*" Her father spoke as if he could scarce believe his eyes. He pushed his way through the crowd toward her.

BEFORE CASS HAD run into his room, Soren had been in a sound slumber, and he had needed the sleep. The worry over his family's debts and the doubts that he'd struggled to keep at bay had come up against the knowledge that he would not be winning the heiress. Cass believed herself too good for him, and she was right. She could do better than him.

It was a humbling admission.

He could find another heiress to marry, except he found his heart wasn't in it. First, he didn't know if that was possible. Heiresses were not plentiful this Season.

Secondly, Cass's rejection had hit him surprisingly hard. He'd be lying if he said he wasn't disappointed. He'd discovered he actually wanted her for a wife.

He didn't know why. They barely knew each other. A childhood friendship was not a good basis for determining a wife. He'd known Mary for a year before he'd married her and it had soured in a blink. They had turned out to be two completely different people. Then again, he had apparently been wrong about her character. When he'd asked her to marry him, he could never have imagined Mary would leave him, taking with her the knowledge that she carried his son.

She'd kept Logan from him and it was only upon her death that he'd learned he had fathered a child.

Now, *that* was a betrayal.

At least he and Cass had cleared the air between them, something he and Mary had never been able to do.

Either way, the truth was that, this night, he was damn tired of fighting to keep his birthright. He was ready to turn his future over to Fate. If he lost Pentreath to the moneylenders, well, he'd manage. He must. His son was counting on him. He'd not be the first landless lord and probably not the last.

His final thought before falling into asleep was perhaps, in the morning, he'd find his will to fight again . . .

And then Cassandra woke him and he found himself involved in Bainhurst's insane accusations that were the certain ruin of Cassandra's standing in Society. Soren also knew that Bainhurst was entitled to his jealousy. Camberly was a fool in love with the wrong woman.

Now Cassandra's father was involved.

God help him.

MP Holwell pushed his way through the guests ogling Soren and Cass's state of undress. He took it all in himself, his scowl deepening. His mousy wife stood right behind him. Like Cass, she was in her dressing robe and a lace night cap. Many of the other ladies gathered around them wore the same. However, it was Cass they damned.

All color had drained from Cassandra's face.

To Soren's surprise, she took an instinctive step toward him. "Father, it isn't what you think."

"It is what I see," Holwell declared. "You've shamed me, girl. You've shamed all of us—"

"Now wait a minute—" Soren started.

Her father cut him off. "I'll hear nothing from you, Dewsberry. Everyone knows you would like nothing better than to destroy my reputation. Well, you've done it. You've made a mockery of my family name."

"Father, listen to me, please. It isn't what you think—"

He grabbed her roughly by the arm and shoved her toward her stepmother. "*Enough*," he barked.

Soren lost all reason. A parent should stand up for a child. Not join in her humiliation. He towered over the shorter man. "I wish to marry your daughter."

Soren didn't know who was more shocked with his statement, Holwell, everyone in the hall, or himself. The moment the words were out, he had a fleeting desire to call them back, but wouldn't.

Cass would never recover from this night's business. Marriageable young women risked everything if they were caught in a man's room. Even if he and Cass could explain that this was all a misunderstanding, chattering minds would dismiss the truth.

Soren, too, would pay. He would be branded the rascal she'd been dallying with, but all the world adored a rake. His name would be relatively unscathed. While hers would be unsalvageable, save for marriage to him. It was the only honorable option.

His declaration was met with a collective gasp of appreciation from their avid audience. The one thing Society adored better than a scandal was a grand romance.

Lady Haddingdon, decked out in a purple robe and night cap, clapped her hands gleefully. "I knew something was afoot when I caught them in the necessary room together over dinner."

"The necessary room during dinner?" a man standing behind Bainhurst repeated, his tone putting a lewd twist to the words.

Soren dismissed all of them. His focus was on Cass, who stood with her hands clasped in front of her like a penitent, her head lowered in humiliation. *Stand tall*, he wanted to tell her. *There is no reason for shame.*

However, Soren's answer to his offer came from her father. In ringing tones, Holwell announced, "No child of mine will marry a York."

"I'll not accept an answer from anyone but Cass," Soren challenged.

"*Cassandra.* Her name is Cassandra," Holwell

answered. "Although the likes of you do not have permission to use it."

Her father's rudeness only made Soren more determined to free her from him. The feud between their two families was nonsense. Dewsberry was an old and respected title—or it had been until his grandfather and father had disgraced it. But Soren would see it shine again and, in that moment, he knew with complete conviction he wanted Cass by his side. That desire was not based upon her fortune.

No, his certainty that she alone could help him meet the challenges of his life, and there were many, came from a place deep within him. He knew he was making the right decision.

Besides, even if he was wrong, she did have a fortune.

Holwell was in politics. He valued public opinion. So, Soren played to the public. He went down on one knee in front of her, a half-dressed swain intent on baring his soul.

Cass stared at him as if he had lost his wits. Perhaps he had.

"Miss Holwell, will you do me the honor of becoming my wife?"

"*Bah!*" Her father's sharp exclamation robbed the moment of any sincerity. "Refuse him, daughter," he ordered. "Put him in his place."

The hallway grew quiet. People held their breaths as they leaned in for every second of the drama. Even Bainhurst.

Cass looked to her father, then back to Soren kneeling before her. Her brows gathered, but no words left her lips.

Her father was at her ear. "Accept his offer and you will be no daughter of mine." He then turned and shouldered his way through the crowd. His wife followed as if she was his shadow.

Cass blinked as if in hurt surprise. Soren took her hand, bringing her attention back to him. She looked down at him.

"We'll be good together," Soren promised.

For a moment, he believed she was going to say yes to him. Her palm was warm, her fingers long.

And then she pulled her hand free. "I can't," she whispered. *"It is too much to decide right now."*

On those words, she chased after her parent.

She was gone.

What the devil?

Soren couldn't believe he had been rejected. Did she not realize her life as she'd known it was over? Rightly or wrongly, circumstances had conspired to label her damaged goods.

Then again, wasn't she the one earlier who had warned him a Holwell and a York could never be together?

Except she didn't believe it. He knew for a fact she was not reacting to the feud. Something else spurred her. Something he didn't understand.

Nor was he the only one surprised by her reaction. The silence in the hall told him that everyone was shocked she'd refused him. It was a foolish move.

Soren rose.

His movement stirred the others. They began creeping toward their rooms as if embarrassed for him. Here and there was a murmured "Good night, Dewsberry," but most were very quiet. He had no doubt they would find their voices on the morrow.

However, he was not through with this evening's business.

"Lord Bainhurst," Soren said.

The jealous lord had been conferring with the two men who had been with him when he had attacked Soren's bedroom door. He looked up.

"There is a challenge between us, is there not?" Soren said.

Everyone who had been quietly dispersing now turned back to Soren.

Bainhurst shot a quizzical glance to his companions. They shrugged their answers. He took a step toward Soren and gave a congenial laugh, as if the two of them were friends. "I did issue one, but that was when I believed you were with my wife. I was overwrought, Dewsberry. I ask you to beg pardon."

"I will not."

"But you should," Bainhurst countered with a self-deprecating chuckle. "The grievance I had, well, apparently I jumped to a conclusion."

"So you did."

"Which means that I no longer require satisfaction. *And*, I offer my most abject apologies for ruining your sleep, my lord."

"Your apology is not accepted."

Bainhurst was not laughing now. "But there is no reason to duel."

"Actually, I find there is a very good reason to duel. You have interfered with my life."

"I apologize—"

"You have disturbed Miss Holwell's life—"

"I apologize to her as well," Bainhurst quickly assured him.

"Your apology is *not* accepted," Soren repeated. "I find myself with a strong desire to—how did you phrase it? 'Run you though with a sword.' Yes, that is what it was."

The deference dropped from Bainhurst's voice. "There is no need, Dewsberry."

"Oh, I have need, Bainhurst. A strong one." Soren noticed Camberly standing on the edges of the onlookers. He appeared as if he had just stumbled on the scene and wasn't completely certain of what was going on, or of the unwitting role Soren suspected he'd played. Something had driven Cass to jump into his room and it had been more than Bainhurst. Had she caught Camberly and Letty doing something they shouldn't? Or had it all been a coincidence? Stranger things had happened. "You will serve as my second, Your Grace." It was not a question.

The duke mumbled, "I am happy to be of service."

"Thank you, Your Grace," Soren said. He looked to Bainhurst. "Let us not let this matter linger. We meet tomorrow at dawn. I'm certain the duke can provide the weapons."

"Ah, yes, I can," Camberly dutifully answered.

"Then we are all done. I'll see you in the morning, Bainhurst."

"But it is so soon," he protested. "Surely we should consider the matter a day or two?"

"I've already considered. I know what I want to do." Soren returned to his room, slamming the door on a sobered Lord Bainhurst.

Chapter 6

$\mathcal{O}$nce out of sight of the gossips, Cassandra slowed her step as she walked to her parents' room. Her father had never publicly repudiated her before. Then again, she'd never given him cause. She'd always done as he expected. She believed she could soothe his anger, but she'd learned over the years it was always best to tread carefully when his pride was hurt.

As she turned the corner onto their hall, a door opened and a woman in a nightdress backed out of the room still kissing her lover. Cassandra stopped in her tracks. There was nowhere to hide, and she wasn't going to make the mistake of jumping into a convenient room again.

Male arms tried to draw the woman back but she broke the kiss with a giggle. "Tomorrow," she whispered, and the promise must have been enough.

The door shut and the woman turned, alarmed at the sight of Cassandra.

The woman was Dame Hester, Admiral Sir Denby Clark's wife and a woman as old as Cassandra's stepmother. She was also one of the moral prioresses of Society. Many a young woman had been coldly dismissed from the ranks of being marriageable because of this woman's yea or nay.

Having met the admiral on several occasions, Cassandra knew those strong arms did not belong to him. He was so slight of stature, he looked comical in his uniform jacket and wig.

Dame Hester's eye took on a frozen stare as she moved forward. She walked right past Cassandra as if she wasn't there. Nor was Cassandra going to do anything to call attention to herself.

She waited until she could no longer hear a footstep from the older woman. Only then did she look back. Dame Hester was gone, vanished around a corner in this labyrinth of a house.

Cassandra released the breath she was holding. Now she realized why everyone was so quick to jump to conclusions about her and Soren. Didn't anyone stay in their rooms?

Or with their mates?

This house party appeared to be nothing less than an opportunity to hop from spouse to lover, and it was confusing to someone like herself who had always believed in honoring vows and moral codes. The image of Lady Bainhurst and the duke rolling on the floor would be burned into her mind for eternity. Camberly had known Lady Bainhurst was married. He obviously didn't care.

The infatuation Cassandra felt for him died a quick death. Her poet hero was fatally flawed. He didn't value the sanctity of marriage, and she was disappointed. Yes, most of the poets of her acquaintance were rascals. They wouldn't pledge fidelity to anything. However, Camberly was a *duke.* He had been a scholar. Shouldn't he be held to a higher standard?

Meanwhile, Soren York, the man she'd dismissed as shallow, had performed with the gallantry of a true gentleman.

Cassandra was not naïve. Her fortune would have greatly compensated Dewsberry if she had accepted his marriage offer. However, few would have stepped up as he did on her behalf.

She reached her parents' door. She drew a deep breath, released it, and knocked lightly in case they were not awake.

Immediately, her father's voice said, "There she is. I told you she would come to us." The door opened.

Her father stood in his nightshirt and stockinged feet as if he'd quickly risen from the bed. The hairs on his head went this way and that as if he'd been pulling on them.

She felt as if she was six again. He was her

family, her blood. They were the only two left who remembered her mother . . . although she was rarely mentioned.

He motioned her inside and shut the door. "Did you refuse his offer?" His voice was cold.

"I told him I couldn't make a decision."

"But you will reject him," Helen said, sounding surprisingly anxious. She sat in the bed, the covers pulled to her waist.

Cassandra looked from her stepmother to her father. In spite of Soren's poverty, Dewsberry was a respected title. Wasn't marrying a nobleman what they wanted her to do?

She tried to choose her words wisely. "If I don't accept this offer . . . then what future would I have? Everyone believes the worst of me."

"As they should." Her father sat in a bedside chair. "What the deuce were you doing in *his* room?"

"It isn't how it looked. I couldn't sleep without a book to read. There was a small library on that floor. I just wanted a book. You know how I am."

"And then?" His expression was unrelenting.

"Well, I couldn't find one. The shelves were bare except for one book in the whole room. It was on a table at the far end. I went to see what it was and then this couple came in and started—" Heat rushed to her cheeks, making her feel slightly faint. "They were very indiscreet."

"I told you she acted as if she was afraid," Helen said.

"Was Dewsberry part of that couple?" her father demanded. "Did he force you into his room?"

"Force? Oh, no, absolutely not," Cassandra hurriedly assured him. "I escaped the library, hopefully without that couple detecting who I was." Another wave of heat crept up her neck. She hated how easily she blushed.

"Was one part of the couple Bainhurst's wife?" her father asked.

Cassandra thought it an obvious question considering the way Lord Bainhurst had been carrying on. She didn't wish to answer it. Her father had a taste for gossip, especially when he could use it in politics, but she would not lie. She nodded.

And then, as she feared, her father leaned forward with interest. "Who was the man she was with?"

"I couldn't see his face." That part was mostly true.

"You didn't recognize him?" There was doubt in his voice. "He had to be one of the guests here."

"The library was dark," she answered, making herself meet his eye. "I was also worrying about how I could remove myself from the situation. I did not want to be involved."

"How long were you there before you could

leave?" He believed she was lying. He'd always been able to tell.

"It was a bit."

"Then why couldn't you tell who the man was?"

She hated this questioning. "Because they went down on the floor. The man was hidden behind a chair."

"But you could see the woman was Letty Bainhurst?"

"Yes."

Silence met her answer, and then her father shocked her by throwing his head back and laughing. Her stepmother appeared as confused as Cassandra until she made a gasp of understanding and laughed as well.

Cassandra frowned. "Where is the humor?"

Her father leaned toward Cassandra. "My sweet, naïve little birdie." Birdie had been his name for her from as long as she could remember. "Bainhurst will not want this story making the rounds. And if he can't figure out who the man was, he's a fool."

"I'm surprised we didn't see it immediately," Helen agreed. "Camberly was by her side most of the evening except we thought he was paying attention to Cassandra or Miss Reverly. He kept one of them close to him at all times. Our young duke is clever."

"But not clever enough," her father answered.

"Not for us," Helen agreed. "But tell me, Cassandra, how did you end up with Dewsberry? Everyone was whispering you were found in his room?"

"I was returning to my room when I heard Lord Bainhurst approaching. He was in a high tear. I panicked. I didn't want to be part of the scene so I opened the nearest door and jumped in. I wasn't thinking."

"And it was happenstance that you chose Dewsberry's room?" her father asked.

Cassandra nodded.

"What a bloody mess," her father said with disgust.

Hope surged through her. "Then you believe people will understand that everything was very innocent?"

Her stepmother spoke. "No, Cassandra, you are ruined. It is through no fault of your own. This one night will give you a reputation. However, you needn't fear being alone. You will be with us. My daughters, their husbands, their children, we will all gather around you." She looked to her husband. "This is a good solution to our 'predicament.'"

"Yes, yes, you are right. This is very good." Her father stood and faced Cassandra, his arms opening to her in loving benevolence. "You were wise to reject Dewsberry's offer. Everyone knows he made it under duress. It is actually a humiliation to you."

"It is?"

Gentling his voice, her father informed her, "He wouldn't have offered if he wasn't being forced to do so."

But Soren had made his intent clear, she could have said. Earlier. When they had their confrontation during dinner. He wanted to marry her—

No, she corrected herself, he wanted to marry her money.

"Don't worry about your future," her father continued. "As Helen said, you have your family. We'll take our leave on the morrow. We'll be gone from this place and these people. We'll go directly to Cornwall and return you to Lantern Fields. The more I consider the matter, perhaps this *is* all for the best. You were never cut out for married life, birdie. You are too tall and too independent thinking."

He wanted to return her to Cornwall? Cassandra challenged him. "Why send me to Lantern Fields? And how can I be too tall for marriage? You always told me to be proud of my height, that it wasn't a deterrent."

"Not to me, it isn't. Your mother was taller than I was, God rest her soul."

"And you just said that this whole incident to-night was not my fault." Cassandra rejected his logic. "I don't want to be buried in the country."

"You won't be buried," her stepmother said, rising out of the bed to come around to her as if from maternal concern. "You can still plan your little literary salons. They will be traveling ones. Doesn't that sound fun? You can go up to Manchester to see my Amanda and to Devon to visit Laura." She spoke of her daughters, Cassandra's stepsisters who were married to industrious young men.

"You will be in the bosom of your family," her father said enthusiastically.

But Cassandra didn't want to be in their bosoms. "What of my fortune?" It would come to her only upon marriage. Until then, her father managed it for her, sometimes asking her opinion on expenditures such as using a portion for her stepsisters' dowries. "If I don't marry, I will never claim it. Isn't that the terms of my mother and grandfather's wills? I'll be penniless and a burden."

"Nonsense. You needn't worry about money. We will take care of you. Isn't that right, Helen?"

Something was not making sense here, but Cassandra too overwhelmed to work the problem through. They spoke as if it was fine for her not to inherit her mother's money.

"Nothing happened between Lord Dewsberry and myself."

"That is a relief. We wouldn't want any York by-blows," her father said cheerily.

"But why should I be branded by this whole incident? Why, less than fifteen minutes ago, I saw Dame Hester leaving the room of a man who is not her husband. No one will punish her."

"Dame Hester, eh?" She could see her father squirrel that bit of information away.

However, it was Helen who brought home the truth. "My dear, it pains me to tell you, but your life as you knew it is over, whether the standards are fair or not. There are rules for when a woman can do as she pleases. You broke the rules—"

"I was only searching for a book," Cassandra insisted.

"Well, that is what comes from reading," Helen breezily answered. "As your father said, you are fortunate to have the loving arms of your family."

"Helen is right, my dear. Dewsberry did you no favors. In fact," he continued, his temper flaring, "I wouldn't be surprised if that *blackguard* hasn't orchestrated the whole sequence of events. Yorks are crafty that way. My father saved old Lord Dewsberry's hide and we've been paying for it ever since."

Cassandra couldn't imagine how. To her, it seemed as if the Holwell fortunes had risen while the Yorks had suffered over generations of bad decisions.

Helen sat Cassandra on the edge of the bed. She raised a hand to smooth Cassandra's hair. The gesture was comforting. When Cassandra was younger and Helen new to her life, she had yearned for her stepmother's touch. It was rarely given.

"I know this is hard," Helen said. "Your father and I had great expectations for you. As you did for yourself. What we need to do now is make the best of things. We will see that you have a good life."

"But I wanted to marry." Cassandra's words sounded plaintive even to her own ears. "It isn't just that I wished the status to improve my literary salons . . . I want children."

Her father clasped his hands behind his back. "Ah, birdie, that is what I wanted more than anything else for you. But now, you are beyond redemption."

Cassandra frowned. On one level, her spirit challenged such a verdict. On another, she realized he was right. The story of her being flushed out of Soren's bedroom would be standard gossip once the other guests returned to London. With Bainhurst involved, there were too many juicy tidbits.

Tears stung her eyes. "I'm sorry, Papa. I—" She

broke off, almost overcome with bitter disappointment and regret for the role she'd played in her own demise. Why had she thought she could wander around the halls of a strange house? "I feel ashamed."

"Oh, here now." Her father put his arms around her. "You don't need a husband. Not when you have a father who loves you as much as I."

Cassandra nodded. "I just don't want to return to Cornwall." She'd never fit in there. Ever.

"You'll need to be there for a bit," he regretfully informed her.

"Will you and Helen be with me?"

"Parliament is in session, birdie. You know I will need to be in the city. Can't be a thorn in the high and mighty if I'm rusticating."

He relished fighting for the common man, even though he'd wanted his daughter to marry a nobleman. He'd wanted his grandchildren to be titled, and now Cassandra had failed him. "I'm so sorry," she whispered, taking the blame on herself.

"Here," he said, rising, "you need to be off to your bed. Tomorrow, we will pack up for Cornwall. Your life will be good. As Helen said, her girls and I will do all we can to see you are included. Don't forget, you will have your books. Now come, I'll walk you to your room." And so he did. They didn't say much. He seemed to understand that Cassandra needed to process this unexpected turn of events.

Alone in her room, and once she was in bed, especially on a mattress as uncomfortable as this one, a hundred scenarios of what she *could* have done, what she *should* have said played in her mind and kept her awake.

Why had she panicked over the appearance of Lord Bainhurst and run into the first available room? Or why hadn't she just stayed in her corner in the reading room? She could have been quiet. Yes, Lady Bainhurst had seen her, but she doubted if Her Ladyship would have brought her presence to the duke's attention. Even if she had, this whole affair would have been between them.

And why did Soren York sleep naked?

Perhaps if he'd been wearing a nightshirt, people would not have drawn the wrong conclusions. She knew it was silly to believe the other guests wouldn't have put the worst possible slant to the incident. Still, decent people wore clothes to bed. Even now she was suitably clad. What was wrong with him?

By the time that dawn was approaching, an overwrought Cassandra had herself convinced that her father was right. Her life had been ruined, and Dewsberry was completely to blame.

In a few hours, her family would leave Mayfield. She'd be trundled off to the country, where she would live the role of a relation who had embarrassed her family. She would die alone, an eccentric who would serve as a warning to new debutantes of the danger of being caught in gentlemen's rooms. She would be the odd setting at a table, the one that family members would shake their heads over, wondering what to do with her.

She would also not know the marriage bed.

For years, she'd read poetic allusions to it. It was a rite of passage that would not be hers, even though all the scandalmongers would believe she'd already reveled in it.

As for Lord Dewsberry—well, he'd probably find an heiress to marry. He was handsome, and very well built. She had seen that with her own eyes. The image of his naked buttocks had been burned into her memory. She'd never thought overmuch about male bums. Now she couldn't stop thinking about them.

He would go on with his life to the acclaim of all, while her dreams, her hopes were ended. She would not inherit her mother's fortune. She'd lost it all through her own gullibility. In fact, she had no doubt that once her father put her in the family coach bound for Cornwall, Society would rarely see her again.

Soren deserved to know what his ill-thought actions, including his supposedly honorable proposal of marriage, had done to her. In her frantic state of mind, she found herself believing that he had known her father would never let her marry him. He'd been saving his own face when he'd made the offer.

She threw back the covers. It was almost dawn. Good. Hopefully those tiptoeing around the hallways had finally settled down to whatever bed they chose. With the sense of indignation born from having her life turned inside out and very little sleep, she threw on her robe and slipped her feet into the kid slippers, just as she had the night before. Soren's room was only a few doors from hers. She could have her say and be back in bed before anyone was the wiser.

Cassandra placed her hand on the door handle and then stopped, hearing male voices in the hallway. She cracked the door.

The Duke of Camberly and Soren stood in front of his room. Both were dressed for the day. The duke handed Soren a sword. Soren removed it from its scabbard and tested the weight. He made a few experimental parries. Cassandra remembered he had seen military service in Canada. Watching the ease with which he used the weapon, she certainly believed the stories true.

"Good, eh?" Camberly said.

"Excellent." Soren held the blade up to the light.

"A dueling blade is different than what I am used to but this is nice." He balanced the sword between two fingers as if testing its weight and then threw it up to catch it by the hilt. He thrust forward and smiled.

"It will cut though silk. My valet spent an hour sharpening both of the swords. I gave the other to Bainhurst's second so he could test it."

"Your man did a fine job," Soren answered. He slipped the sword back into its scabbard. "Are we ready?"

"I should also tell you, Bainhurst *again* wishes you to accept his apology. He believes there is no reason to duel."

Duel? The word alarmed Cassandra.

"Miss Holwell's reputation is reason enough. You turned him down?"

"Of course."

Soren's response was a chilling smile of satisfaction. This was not the acquaintance of her childhood but a man unafraid to kill. "Let us go."

Cassandra took action. She threw open the door and planted herself in their path.

"You will not duel on my account," she declared.

The duke was startled but Soren behaved as if he'd expected her to jump out and make a statement. Level gray eyes met hers. His gaze dropped to take in her forest green robe. Her hair must certainly be a mess. The once meticulous braid was loose from a night of tossing, turning, and running through the halls.

"Good morning, Miss Holwell."

He sounded calm.

As for herself? She had a disquieting mental image of his naked back. She quashed it from her mind. "Good morning," she returned, barely civil because of the errant direction of her thoughts. "What are you doing?"

"You know what I'm doing. You just told me not to do it."

Such reasonableness was annoying.

"And I meant those words. I will not allow a duel to be fought on *my* behalf. Dueling is *barbaric.*"

"Cass, return to your bed." He started forward.

"I'm not some child you can order about. And my name is *Cassandra.* Cass-an-dra."

Soren gave a small salute acknowledging his error, and then he and the duke walked right around her, one on either side, and continued down the hall. She took a step after them, and then realized she couldn't go anywhere in her current state of undress. They turned the corner and went out of sight.

Her temper exploded. A rage the likes of which she'd never known gripped her. How dare he patronize her? Did her desires, her wishes account for anything? If there was any "defending" to be done, she would defend herself. Modern men—rational, intelligent men—did not resolve differences by carving pieces off each other, especially in her name.

Meanwhile, she was being shuttled off to the country to be a nobody. And Soren believed he was doing her favor?

He was wrong.

Nor would she leave it be. At this point, her reputation was in tatters. Her convictions were all she had and they were worth the fight.

She rushed into her room, tore off her nightclothes, and scrambled into the dress hanging there. She didn't even bother to fuss with her hair. She was going to stop a duel. Artful curls were unnecessary to such an endeavor.

Chapter 7

*O*f course Cassandra had ambushed him in the hall.

Soren had almost expected it.

He'd also known they needed to hash out what had happened last night. He was not put off by her anger this morning. That seemed to be the way she was most comfortable communicating with him . . . and he didn't believe it was because of some childish insult.

No, there was something else between him and Cass—

"Miss Holwell is certainly fetching *en déshabillé*," Camberly observed. "Perhaps I should rethink this idea of marrying an heiress."

They were going down the stairs heading toward the front door. He spoke half in jest, but the stab of jealousy Soren experienced brought him to halt. "Cass Holwell is not for you."

"Cassandra," Camberly corrected. "Like the seer warning the Trojans."

"You are full of nonsense," Soren shot back, sorely conscious that Cass would have known what he was talking about. Soren hadn't been one to pay attention in school.

He marched down the remaining stairs uncaring of whether the duke followed him or not, although he knew he would.

"You are quite testy this morning," Camberly said. "One would sense you are angry with me. And for what? I've been up all night in your service."

Was he truly that obtuse? "If you wish to play fast and loose with women, that is your choice. However, you *will* leave Miss Holwell alone."

"I don't play fast and loose with women."

Soren gave him a look of disgust.

"I don't," Camberly insisted. "You are talking about Letty, aren't you? Soren, I worship her. She is my goddess. I'm not interested in your Miss Holwell."

Soren liked hearing those words. He walked on. A footman opened the front door for them.

Once outside, the duke continued, "The problem is that Letty is married to the wrong man. Bainhurst cares more for his pride than his wife."

"Funny how pride is all a man has when his

wife is cuckolding him," Soren said under his breath, but he was heard anyway.

"Is it cuckolding if one has found love?"

"Do you hear yourself? How would you feel if you were in Bainhurst's boots?"

Camberly did not answer. Instead, he changed the subject by catching Soren's arm. "The park is this way," he said. The side path led them to an expanse of green lawn. Fog drifted like dragon's breath through the clearing.

Under the branches of a spreading oak, Bainhurst and his second waited along with a few men interested enough in the contest to disturb their sleep.

Soren began mentally preparing himself for the coming venture, only to be interrupted by the duke's weak logic. "She would be better off without him."

"We all would. That doesn't mean you ignore the vows made before man and God."

"Says the man who has challenged him to a duel."

"*He* challenged me." Soren stopped when they were some twenty feet from the other men. He faced Camberly. "And if I don't do this, then all the world will believe I dishonored Cassandra Holwell. I'll be damned if I let that happen." He began tugging at the knot in his neck cloth.

"But didn't I hear people say last night that you

proposed marriage to her? And she turned you down?"

"As is her right." He handed his neck cloth to Camberly. "Besides, she didn't say no. She said she couldn't. Her father is behind that decision."

"She hasn't acted all that interested in you when I've been around the two of you."

That statement annoyed Soren. He removed his jacket and handed it to the duke. "Cass is an independent thinker. She has queer notions."

"Such as?"

"She reads prodigiously."

Camberly shrugged. "I believe everyone should read prodigiously."

"You are not female. Cass will have an idea in her head and then she is hard to dissuade once she has reasoned her way into it."

"Such as her distaste for dueling?"

"Exactly."

"Then you had best be ready because here she comes now."

Camberly was looking past Soren toward the house—and there she was, making her way toward them, her whole being bristling with indignation. She had dressed hastily and had not appeared to have touched her hair. Her braid swung with her determination. Soren had no doubt she intended to the stop the duel.

Well, Cass-an-drrraaa was about to learn she

could not always have her way. He reached for
the hilt of the sword Camberly held in its scabbard and pulled it out. He hadn't bothered re-
moving his boots for this match. He didn't expect
the swordfight to last long.

The sharpened blade caught the first rays of
the morning's sun. "Come, Bainhurst," he called.
"Let's do this." In an aside to Camberly, he said,
"Make certain she stays out the way." He walked
to the flat section of field in front to wait for his
opponent.

Bainhurst was a surly soul on a good day. This
morning, he appeared positively grim. Mayhap
someone had mentioned that Soren was more
fighter than gentleman. That would work in
Soren's favor.

"What is she doing here?" Bainhurst said by
way of greeting, nodding in Cass's direction.

"Observing," Soren said. "Don't worry. The
duke will stop her."

"I do not believe Camberly is a match against
the energy of her nature," Bainhurst rightly suggested.

Soren sliced the air a few times with his sword.
"Then we'd best begin."

A germ of an idea had begun to form in his
mind, and he liked it. He had a trick of his own
to play, one that would serve both Bainhurst and
himself.

CASSANDRA KNEW SOREN had seen her approaching. He'd looked right at her. He also knew what she was about. However, instead of waiting, he'd stepped out into the dueling field.

One of the things that had always annoyed her was how men, including her father, dismissed her very right concerns for the flimsiest of reasons. Her father's favorite response was that she didn't understand a man's world and should keep her opinions and her questions to herself.

Well, she had every right to interfere now; when someone was fighting a duel using her name, then it was her concern.

The Duke of Camberly approached her. She held up a hand. "Do not come an inch closer, Your Grace. I will *run* over you."

He did not obey. "You shouldn't be here."

"You shouldn't test me, Your Grace," she answered without missing a step.

He spread his arms as if to block her way. "I implore you. This is no place for a lady."

Cassandra came to a halt in front of him with a glare that could have scorched him to the ground.

Because of his amoral, dishonorable behavior, two men were about to face off, and one could lose his life. She would never forgive herself if something happened to Soren. It was suddenly that plain and clear to her. "*Move* out of *my* way."

Camberly blinked as if astounded by her directness, and then he moved, chastened. "Good luck, Miss Holwell."

"*I'm* not the one who will need luck, Your Grace." She honed her sights on Soren.

He had his back to her. He held his sword up and ready, waiting for his opponent. He was aware of her. She knew that all the way to her bones. Bainhurst hadn't even lifted his sword. He watched her with a wary eye.

"I wish to speak to you, Lord Dewsberry." Her voice rang clear in the dawn's air.

He didn't turn or lower his sword. "I'm busy defending your honor, Miss Holwell."

She came to a halt. "You may stop doing *anything* on my behalf *this instant*."

He sounded almost bored as, without bothering to turn, he answered, "I'm sorry, Miss Holwell. Your insistent innocence about how the world works has made this duel a necessity."

Her temper snapped. "What *swill*."

"Should I leave the two of your alone?" Lord Bainhurst suggested.

"No," Soren said, even as Cassandra replied, "*Yes*."

His Lordship stood as if undecided which one he should obey, and Cassandra considered that a win for herself.

Apparently, so did Soren. He lowered his sword and faced her. "Are you going to marry me?"

That suggestion surprised her. She could not hide her amazement. Her mind was going in one direction and his apparently in another.

"It is the only other option," he informed her. "I either lop off both of Bainhurst's ears, which I can do rather easily—"

"Here now," Lord Bainhurst protested. "It will not be easy—"

With a lightning quickness, Soren raised his sword, flicked his wrist, and nicked His Lordship's sleeve.

"Damn," Lord Bainhurst swore with a twinge of admiration, and took a cautious step back.

"I didn't scratch him," Soren said to Cassandra. "Although I could have. I am very good at this."

His offhand manner annoyed her. She crossed her arms. "Ah, so this isn't your first duel?" She parodied his matter-of-fact tone so that he understood she found the situation reprehensible.

"In truth, it is. However, Bainhurst would not be the first man I've killed."

That uncrossed her arms. How did one respond to such a statement? For the first time in her memory, Cassandra found herself speechless, while he watched with guileless eyes and an air of profound patience.

"You've killed men before?" she repeated, wanting him to deny it.

"Several. I was in the military, Miss Holwell.

After that, well, a man set on making his fortune in the wilds of Upper Canada should know how to use a weapon. I have excellent tomahawk skills."

Cassandra didn't know what a tomahawk was, but it sounded dangerous. "You seem almost proud of that fact."

"I am. We each have our talents. You read; I fight. Both serve a purpose."

"But I don't want you to *fight for me.*"

"Then stop making it so damn difficult."

And she realized they weren't talking about the duel.

As did Lord Bainhurst. "I will wait over there," he said, indicating his group of friends, "while the two of you hash this out."

Neither of them answered him. He could come or go as he pleased. They had something more important to discuss—themselves.

Soren took a step toward her. "I know you have been raised to believe every York is a wastrel but damn it all, Cassandra, I've worked hard to be a better man. I have businesses in Canada. Or, I had them. They were struggling when I was called home to take over the title and care for my mother. What with the war, I could be even more of a pauper than I am now. How is that for honesty? But you, too, are not without faults. For one, you are more pigheaded than your father."

"Pigheaded—?"

"Yes, stubborn, obstinate, ridiculous even."

"I know what pigheaded means—"

"Then stop fighting me. I'm not the one who made the rules but here they are—if you refuse to marry me and I don't duel with Bainhurst, then there isn't a soul in London who won't think you a fool. They will pity you because you ruined yourself."

He was right, both about what would happen to her, and her pigheadedness. She resisted accepting the truth even as he rationally laid it out to her. It was all unfair.

Soren sensed his advantage. "What choice will you make, Cassandra? Will you marry me and save Bainhurst's miserable life? Or should I run him through?"

"It would be unwise to kill him. He is a powerful man."

"I'm in a powerful mood. And he has lost all sense of judgment over that adulterous wife of his."

"You know." The information caught her off guard. She'd not told him what she'd witnessed the night before.

"That Letty Bainhurst is ready for a tumble in any man's arms? Oh, yes. The person who doesn't know is Camberly. He is besotted with her. But then, so is her husband."

"Are your debts bad?" she asked. After all, she did have a practical mind.

"I could lose Pentreath," he answered soberly. "I'm doing everything I can to save it. The castle isn't just my birthright, but my son's."

His son. If she married him, she would be the mother of his children. She would not be alone or the object of scorn and pity. "I don't want to be the unmarried relation," she murmured.

"I imagine it would be like being buried alive for a woman."

He was right, and no matter what her parents said, that was the truth of it.

Lord Bainhurst called out, "Dewsberry, shall we move on with it?"

"No," Cassandra called, even as Soren said, "Yes."

She frowned at him. He shrugged his answer. "I am going to do what is honorable. One way or the other."

"It doesn't seem right that we should be forced to marry because of last night," she insisted. "Nothing happened . . . except it might have helped if you had been dressed. I was shocked you don't sleep in nightclothes."

A wicked grin flashed across his face. He took another step toward her. They stood so close, she could feel his body heat. "There are other things I do that might shock you as well . . . at first. Does that make my offer more tempting? Or do you wish to spend the rest of your life playing safe?"

There it was, her choice. She could do what her father expected, which was safe. Or she could embrace what Fate had placed before her. Soren knew how to tempt her.

"In honesty, Cass, of all the heiresses in the world, I like you best."

She rather liked him as well, when she wasn't exasperated with him.

Still, for the sake of argument, she had to say, "You don't know me, Soren. Not any longer. We are both very different than the children we were."

"Perhaps," he agreed, then added, "Perhaps not . . ."

And then, before she knew what he was about, he kissed her.

He didn't ask permission. There was no fanfare or fancy words. Just his lips on hers as if it was the most natural thing in the world to do.

In fact, he'd probably been two steps ahead of her from the moment she had confronted him. This had always been his objective.

Cassandra had been kissed before. At one of her literary salons, one of the poets, seeing they were momentarily alone, had seized upon the opportunity to plant a kiss on her mouth right there under her father's roof.

It hadn't been an easy kiss. Roger Edmonds had been far shorter than she. She'd been sitting in a chair, instructing him on what would happen at her salon when he'd taken advantage of the opportunity. It had been decidedly awkward. He kept bumping his mouth against hers as if she should be doing something.

When he was done and found her unmoved, Roger had insisted he could do better. He'd wanted to call on her the next day and spoke of "loving" her. She'd known better. He'd wanted her fortune.

Soren wanted her fortune as well—except he knew how to kiss.

He was also taller than she was. He didn't need to sit her down.

And his lips must have had some sort of magnetized property because not only did the kiss pull her to him, their lips fit together very well. There was no sloppy wetness. No furtive probings. He kissed like a man who enjoyed the art of it—and how could any woman resist opening to him? It was as if he breathed her in.

The kiss broke too soon.

He was the one who ended it, and she found herself leaning against his chest, his sword arm around her waist.

Dazed, she looked in his eyes. They had gone very dark. She marveled at the laugh lines that shot off from them, small indicators of his character.

"I knew there was something between us," he whispered. "We will do well together, Cassandra. All you need to do is say yes."

"Yes."

The word flowed out of her. *Yes*—to not being shuttled off to Cornwall. *Yes*—to having all life could offer. *Yes*—to what that kiss only hinted at.

Soren didn't waste a beat. He took her hand and held it up, announcing to the gentlemen, "Miss Holwell has agreed to be my wife."

The Duke of Camberly cheered while stifling a yawn. Lord Bainhurst called, "Are you satisfied? May we go to our breakfast now?"

Lacing his fingers with Cassandra's, Soren walked toward Bainhurst and his friends. He offered the sword to the duke. "I am satisfied, my lord."

"You didn't have to prick my coat," His Lordship complained. There was little heat in his voice.

"How else was the lady to know I was serious?" Soren countered.

Lord Bainhurst ignored him. Instead, he addressed Cassandra. "I am sorry that my rash actions ensnared you in all of this, Miss Holwell. Especially since you will be marrying this scoundrel. Oh, come now, I'm jesting. Dewsberry is a good man. Far better than his sire. We've all been worried about him. Make his rickety estate a home, give him babies, and may God's grace shine on you."

The truth struck her. She was going to marry. She would be a bride, a wife . . . someday, a mother. Her dream of a literary salon lingered a moment around her. Yes, it was something she wanted, but she had a sense that she was standing on the precipice of a bigger adventure, of grander dreams.

It was disconcerting to see the duke and Lord Bainhurst standing side by side. After Lord Bainhurst's pretty speech, she felt sorry for him. And she was overjoyed she was not marrying Camberly. He was no longer "the one."

In fact, after that kiss, she saw Soren with new eyes. And she had not forgotten his naked bum.

"You are wealthy now, Dewsberry," the duke said. There was a note of jealousy in his voice.

"That isn't what is important right now," Soren countered. He tugged on Cassandra's hand. "Come, let us find the breakfast room and we can make plans."

He began leading her toward the house. The men fell into step around them. The experience of being included in their number was a heady one for Cassandra. She was very conscious that she was now under Soren's protection.

The concept made her feel ladylike, vulnerable, and remarkably feminine. It was nice to be surrounded by men. She liked their energy.

Mayfield's breakfast room overlooked the back garden. It was a cheery yellow room. The breakfast dishes had been set up here while most of the guests were eating in the dining room, where there was a longer table and more chairs.

Given the earliness of the hour, Cassandra was amazed at how many of the fashionable set were up. Dame Hester was eating with her husband and there were at least a half dozen of the others who had witnessed the scene with Soren last night. The dowager was bustling about giving instructions to both servants and guests.

Soren took charge. He announced, "If I may beg your attention?"

The room quieted.

"Miss Holwell has made me the happiest of men. She has agreed to be my wife."

All eyes turned to her, and then the room seemed to explode with good wishes. Cassandra was suddenly self-conscious. She was aware that her hair was not done, that she hadn't even polished her teeth before she had charged out of the house to stop the duel. She thought to excuse herself to properly dress except the guests would not let her leave.

They acted as if she looked perfectly fine. The

hugs from the ladies felt genuine. The handshakes Soren received made Cassandra feel as if she had made the right choice. Lord Bainhurst and the duke acted as if they had played a part in matching the couple and they did so with great pride. She looked around for Willa, who was not at the table yet. Her friend enjoyed her sleep.

However, Letty Bainhurst was present. She rose from her breakfast, her hair and dress perfect, and whispered to Cassandra, "See? I knew you and Dewsberry would be excellent for each other."

People acted genuinely pleased for Soren. It was obvious that he was well-liked among the men. Of course, this was a crowd that if they'd heard the duel had taken place and one of the duelists had been injured, they would be equally forgiving. Such was the nature of this set.

And she would be one of them. Lady Dewsberry. Her Ladyship. My lady. *His* lady.

Cassandra glanced over to Soren and her heart did a funny thing. It actually seemed to grow a little.

The sensation was extraordinary. She didn't know that hearts could do that. She also found herself watching him and thinking about that kiss.

Yes, things could be good between them. She understood that now. This was not a mistake—

The room fell silent.

Heads turned to the door where Cassandra's father and stepmother had appeared.

Stepping forward, the dowager called in greeting, "MP Holwell, you are joining us just in time. You lucky man, you are going to have son-in-law. Your daughter accepted Dewsberry's offer."

Chapter 8

Soren knew the dowager was aware of the impact of her words. He could only believe that she'd decided to attack the matter head-on and consequently, give the marriage her blessing, almost as if in defiance of Holwell's disapproval.

He didn't care what the man thought. But he did worry about Cass. She seemed to change right before his eyes. A second earlier, she had appeared as happy and adorably rumpled as a woman who had set out to stop a duel should. Now, she became a shadow of that woman— especially when her father shot her a look of pure malice.

Soren placed his hand on the small of her back, a light touch to let her know that he was beside her. They were together.

Holwell's narrowed eyes noticed the movement. "You bloody bastard. Take your hands off my daughter." He raised a fist.

Soren's response was to circle her waist with his arm. He said, "Your daughter has paid me the honor of agreeing to become my wife. Our families will be joined. I want things to be good between us, for her sake."

"If she marries you, she is *no daughter of mine.*" On those hard words he left, his mousy wife scampering to catch up. It was exactly what he'd done last night, except this time when Cass started after him. Soren grabbed her hand.

"I must talk to him," she offered as if apologizing.

"Then I will go with you."

"It is best you don't."

"Cass—"

"*Please*, I must do this myself." This time when she tugged on her hand, he let her go.

"Well," the dowager said, breaking the silence after Cass had left the room. "He is unpleasant."

"Did you expect him to be something different?" Admiral Sir Denby Clark said. He motioned for a servant to fetch him another sausage.

The dowager answered, "I would expect some grace. He's lucky to have a son-in-law like Dewsberry. He acted like a buffoon."

Bainhurst spoke up. "Buffoons don't show appreciation."

"He didn't have to make a scene," Camberly countered.

"He's angry," the admiral said. "He marries her off, his fortune goes with her."

Wanting to be close to Cass in case she had a need for his support, Soren had been about take his leave of the room, but that statement stopped him. "What do you mean?"

Cutting into his sausages, a fork in one hand, a knife in the other, the admiral said, "I knew Miss Holwell's grandfather. We belonged to the same club. A nabob, he was. Made a bloody fortune and he didn't have much family. Everything went to his only child, although he was not pleased when his daughter married Holwell. He did not like him."

"Few do," the dowager said.

The admiral nodded. "I thought it odd Bingham let the marriage happen. Always wondered why, but he wasn't the sort you would have a conversation with . . . until one night. It was in my club. We were the only two in the room and I asked him to have a drink with me because he appeared in low spirits. He told me his daughter had died. She'd caught a fever and there had been no saving her. He himself was in ill health and he feared his death was imminent."

Everyone in the room was listening now.

"He'd settled a substantial dowry on his daughter when she married. It made Holwell a rich man, except he quickly ran through all the money. He was always in need of funds."

Soren understood that situation all too well.

"Bingham worried that once he died, Holwell would have guardianship over his granddaughter's inheritance until she married. He told me that is how he'd set up his will. His hope was she would choose a good man. But with death facing him, he feared Holwell could not be trusted with the money."

"But the Bingham fortune is rumored to be a vast one," the dowager said. "And Holwell is a MP. He has some money of his own. I'm not defending him but pointing out what I've noticed."

"Did you have a look at the coach he arrived in?" the admiral asked. "Does even the Regent have a coach that fine? Or any of the other MPs? That night, Bingham confided in me that he suspected Holwell would line his own pocket with his granddaughter's inheritance, and when I laid eyes on that coach, I think he is. He is also slipperier than a dockside eel. Both Bingham and I agreed upon that. Marry your heiress quick, Dewsberry, and claim the money immediately. That is my advice to you. Because if you don't, Holwell will do everything in his power to keep it. I'm surprised he is letting his daughter marry at all."

His last statement struck Soren.

There was no reason for a woman as vibrant as Cass to have been languishing on the Marriage Mart—unless Holwell was deliberately manipulating the situation. Would a father be so callous as to let his daughter believe he was acting in her best interests while perhaps furtively doing all he could to undermine her?

He would if he was greedy.

Bainhurst muttered, "You still will be a *very* rich man, Dewsberry. The pearls she wore last night were worth a fortune."

But Soren wasn't thinking of money. His concern was for Cass. "Excuse me." He set off to find her.

CASSANDRA FOUND HER father in the front hall with a footman and his bags. He was pulling on his gloves. Helen was already out the front door and walking toward the coach that had been brought round.

"Father," she said.

He looked up, the lines in his face deep with disapproval. "Are you leaving with me? Or are you going to disgrace your family and marry a scoundrel?"

"He has done nothing to earn that name."

"He is a York. They despise us. And now he's going to marry you, spend your money the way his father and grandfather went through theirs, and leave you to rot like a ship that has been beached after a storm."

"I don't believe that," Cassandra said, and she didn't. "I know he needs my inheritance—"

"And it is all right with you that he is only marrying you for your money?" Her father stepped closer. "Because I'll tell you, birdie, he will treat you worse than one of his servants. He will bury you in the country so that he can gamble and fritter away your money until you have nothing, including the respect of your family."

"Papa—"

"You will be *dead* to us."

He was so forceful, so certain. Cassandra placed a hand against her abdomen, overwhelmed with the decision she had made. What if her father was right? What if she found herself caught in an unhappy marriage? One where she was not valued as a true helpmate?

And then she remembered years ago when a bold lad had looked at her at the parish picnic where she'd hidden herself in the sanctuary with a book and had asked if she wanted to be his friend. *We can't tell them*, he'd said, meaning their parents. *They won't like it, and yet I can see nothing wrong with you.*

She'd valued that friendship. Cherished it. Because she hadn't been like the other children.

She'd lost her mother. Her father was not well liked. She'd picked that up even as a child.

Soren had been her first friend and, until now, he'd never asked for anything. Meanwhile, it seemed her family demanded more than she could give. Her father expected her to hold his grudges, she realized. And she'd never been close to her stepmother or stepsisters. They had been jealous of her money. Well, until they needed it for their dowries. Then they had included her, but they didn't *like* her.

Could she truly live out her days at their beck and call with no life of her own?

"Papa, I don't want to anger you."

"Then do as I say."

"I can't." The statement had come from a place inside her she hadn't known existed. She'd always been the dutiful daughter. "I'm ready to start my life," she tried to explain. "There is so much I have yet to experience."

"I've given you everything you have wanted."

"You have been more than generous, Papa. However, I want to understand what it means to be a wife." And a lover, she could have added. She wished to know this mystery between men and women. "I want to be a mother. I want to raise a child."

Ah, yes, here was the greatest question of her life. What had she missed by not having a mother's love as a guiding force in her life? Helen did not count. She and Helen had always been wary of each other.

"Then I will find you a husband," her father said. "We'll find a suitable man for you. But don't trust Dewsberry. You know nothing of him. He's like his father, secretive and conniving."

Her father was right. She did not know Soren well. Still, there was something she couldn't explain between them, and it was deeper than the pleasure of his kiss. It made her bristle at her father's accusations. It helped her find her voice. "I've made my decision, Papa."

"Very well then." He turned on his heel and walked out the door.

His abruptness startled her. Cassandra had always tried to please him. They were all the blood family either of them had. She believed he had her best interests at heart—and yet, he was wrong about Soren.

She moved to the door. Helen had already climbed into the coach. Her father joined her. The Holwell coach was as fine as any prince could boast. The cab was lacquered red and the wheels had yellow spokes. Her father had designed an emblem to go on the door. It was not a crest, but anyone seeing it would know this was a symbol of MP Holwell. He prided himself on the picture of a tree with deep roots and a miner's pick. The coach was pulled by a set of matched grays that would have any lord jealous.

With a knock on the roof, he ordered Terrance the driver to go. The coach pulled away. Her father sat stiff and unrelenting, his face in profile in the window. He did not even glance at her, and for a second, it was as if someone pulled her in half. She wanted to please him and please herself . . . and it could not be done.

Cassandra crossed her arms tightly against her waist and watched him go. Did he think she would chase after him?

After all, she was her father's daughter. She had pride as well.

Soren's voice said behind her, "He will come round."

Without turning, her gaze still on the coach as it grew smaller in the distance down the drive, she said, "No, he won't. He will expect me to go to him."

"Will you?"

She faced him. He needed to shave. After all they had been through this morning, she just now noticed that. And she herself was not all together. Her braid was a shambles. Why, she was not wearing stockings—and she felt drained.

"Are you saying you won't have me now?" She spoke half in jest. Or was she testing him?

"Camberly said we can say our vows in the family chapel. I will procure the special license."

"When will we marry?"

"If I send for the license immediately. I'm certain I can have it by tomorrow morning."

Tomorrow.

In her life, she'd never done anything rash or foolish. She was an heiress to be watched over and directed. The only choices she had ever had in life were for her reading material. Even her clothing had been carefully monitored by Helen and her father.

But they had left.

"Tomorrow?" she repeated, a bit dazed. She'd always thought she'd have a big wedding breakfast. She didn't know what to expect now.

"Easily."

She looked to Soren. He was going to be her husband. Her father's words echoed in her ears— *He's like his father, secretive and conniving.*

Soren didn't appear as if he was plotting anything wicked. In fact, she didn't know him well enough to know *what* he was thinking.

And she was hitching her future to his. "That sounds good."

"Come," he said, holding his arm out as if to shepherd her. "You need breakfast. And there are plans to make."

Cassandra didn't even know what plans needed to be made. Fortunately, the dowager did.

The entire female half of the company jumped into the wedding planning. "This will be grand fun," the dowager assured Cassandra. "A wedding, especially a controversial one, will make my country party the talk of the year." The other women agreed, and ideas and suggestions began flowing freely while Cassandra pecked at her breakfast.

Her stomach was uneasy. She felt as if she'd made a decision to walk off a pier. Her father had always been with her.

Willa took the chair next to hers. "Congratulations. This is exciting. I believe you are marrying a good man. He's certainly a handsome one."

"Our families are enemies." Cassandra didn't understand why she made the statement. Everything was jumbled in her mind. She'd disavowed such nonsense herself several times, but now, since she was severing all ties with her father, it sounded different.

Willa laughed. "Enemies? Isn't that rather medieval?"

"Not in Cornwall."

"Fortunately, you are not in Cornwall."

This was true. Cornwall was the last place Cassandra wished to be. "I haven't been there in years." She thought a moment and then said, "We will live in London."

"Of course," Willa agreed, although she sounded a touch distracted, and Cassandra realized she'd been so wrapped up in her own problems, she hadn't thought of anyone else.

"Is something the matter?" she asked Willa.

"Did you think the duke is interested in me?"

It seemed a lifetime since Cassandra had fretted over whether the duke paid attention to her or not.

"He sat with you at dinner. How many points would that be?"

"That silly game." Willa looked away a moment as if needing to compose herself. "I told myself it was all right that I haven't married. After all, you and Leonie were in your third Season. Now, well . . . my closest friends are gone."

Cassandra abhorred hearing Willa, who was lovely and talented, talk this way. She also understood the feelings of being left behind all too well. "Camberly isn't worth your interest."

"Oh, I know."

"You do?"

Willa nodded. "He is taken with Lord Bainhurst's wife. He had me sit next to him at dinner as a ruse. What they were doing under the table with their hands was silly."

"Under the table at dinner?" Cassandra was shocked. "With Lord Bainhurst at the table?"

"Can you believe? I had to pretend I didn't notice anything. They were so rude. Meanwhile, my father has hopes up that I have attracted his attention."

Willa frowned. "What sort of man takes up with another man's wife? Especially when that man is a guest under his roof? My skin crawls to think of it. Oh, wait, Father is signaling me to join him. And he is standing by the duke." Willa sighed. "I wish I *was* married. Then I'd be done with all of this nonsense." She looked to Cassandra. "And scoring points is not fun without competition." She left to see what her father wished.

Cassandra excused herself when the dowager and her friends had talked themselves out on the subject of her marriage and were, instead, discussing starting a game of cards.

Her valise sat on the bed. Maggie, the maid she and Helen shared, must have packed it. Cassandra was fortunate it had not been put on the coach. She removed her clothing and checked the false bottom. Her jewels were still there.

She began putting her things away. Only then did she reflect on everything she was losing. Abby, her personal maid, was at the London town house. Cassandra could contact Abby to see if she would accept a position with her once she and Soren decided where they would be living.

Where *would* they be living? Would Soren let her choose the house? What expectations did he have of her?

He's like his father, secretive and conniving. She pushed her father's words from her mind.

Instead, she stretched out on the bed and surprised herself by quickly falling asleep. A knocking on the door woke her. "Miss Holwell, the company is gathering for dinner," a maid said.

Alarmed by how deeply she had slept, Cassandra called, "I will be down presently. Please give the duchess my apologies." She hurried with her toilette, performing it herself. She shook a lace-trimmed dress in a light blue from the valise and styled her hair into a neat chignon at the nape of her neck with curls around her face. She wore the pearls again. She appeared fine in the looking glass.

"When I am married, I will wear bold, bright colors," she promised. That made her feel a bit better.

Soren was waiting for her at the foot of the stairs, looking every inch the elegant gentleman. He'd shaved, and she liked the spicy scent of his shaving soap. She'd noticed it before, she realized, during those times when she'd attempted to avoid him.

He escorted her into the reception room. "Are you all right?" he asked.

"I was just tired." She didn't want to think about the falling out with her father. She put on a brave face and plunged into the conversation and good humor of the esteemed company. Whereas the day before, the other guests had been rather dismissive of her, now everyone treated her as if she was one of them. Lady Melrose patted her on the hand and assured her, "You are making the best choice. A married lady lives a far better life than an unmarried one."

During the meal, Cassandra noticed other details about Soren that she'd not noted before. Her eye watched the grace with which he touched his glass and raised it to his lips. His nails were clean, his fingers tapered. He had a swordsman's hands. He'd killed men with them. He'd said as much to her.

Whenever she could, she covertly studied his lips. This morning's kiss had been the first thing she'd thought about when she woke this evening . . . and how well her lips had fit with his.

They would fit together well in other areas as well. He was taller by a few inches; however, her hips and his were about exactly right.

This man would guide her in the mysteries of sex. A poet at one of her literary salons had spoken of "the passion flower of ecstasy" between a man and a woman. Cassandra dearly wanted to know what he had meant.

Later, after dinner, when the gentlemen finished their port and joined the ladies, Cassandra could not help but admire how fluid his movements were as he crossed the reception room to her. Some men stomped, others minced, and then there were the bounders. Soren was none of those. He walked as if he was confident of his place in the world.

And yet, he'd known setbacks. Life had not been easy.

She believed she could respect him—*if* she could trust him. *He's like his father, secretive and conniving.*

The party started to disperse. Cassandra was surprised at how tired she was, even after her afternoon of sleep. She'd felt as if she was on a stage all evening.

"Let me escort you to your room," Soren offered.

She barely murmured a response.

"I have the license," he said as they walked up the stairs. "The rider returned shortly before dinner."

"Oh." She didn't know why she was so nervous, but "oh" was the only word she could manage.

"Camberly has offered a special suite of rooms in the family wing for tomorrow night."

"Hoooo." This was "oh" spoken while one was blushing. Did he notice? He wasn't looking at her. Perhaps he was a bit shy on the topic as well?

"Then I thought we would go to London."

That was a relief.

They had reached her door. "I will call on your father when we are there."

Cassandra found her voice. "He will not see you."

"He will. We must discuss your inheritance."

"Of course." She felt strangely deflated. What had she expected his reason for calling on her father to be? To mend fences? That would have been a waste of effort.

Still, she found she wanted to hope.

He seemed to glean the direction of her thoughts. "I know this is not the way you would have chosen to marry. I'm sorry it is this way."

"It is not your fault. Father is wrong to be bull-headed. How about your family? Will they be angered by this news?"

"Only my mother; however, she doesn't like anything I do. I ceased worrying about her approval years ago."

"So, we are both defying our families."

His lips curved into a reluctant smile. "Apparently. But it will be a good marriage, Cass. I know it isn't what you would have wanted, but we will make it work."

"And how do you know what I wanted? I do like you, Soren. If our regard for each other can survive a dog drawn on a slate, well, then, we might be happy."

"That is my hope." He barely acknowledged her attempt at humor. Instead, his gaze had moved from the doorframe—and to her lips.

He hoped for something more, too. He wanted to kiss her, and yet he held back, something he hadn't done that morning.

Just the thought of the kiss they had shared brought heat to her blood. Her breasts seemed to press against the light material of her dress—

Cassandra kissed Soren before he could kiss her. She sought to control the moment. She didn't aim for his mouth but for his cheek. She kissed him the way one would a cousin. A quick buss and nothing like the morning's kiss—because after an evening of knowing looks and talk of a "special suite," she was overwhelmed.

Then, before he could respond, she opened the door and slipped inside, shutting it firmly behind her. She collapsed against the door. Her heart raced as if she'd taken a great dare.

Seconds turned into a minute and then two. He was still there on the other side of the solid wood. She could sense his presence.

She rested her ear on the cool wood. She could swear she heard him breathing. Was it her imagination or did she catch a whiff of his shaving soap?

He spoke, his voice quiet and close to the door. "The hardest part of the future, Cassandra, is leaving what is known and trusted to move forward with courage. I know this is not the way you expected your life to unfold, but sometimes, expectations should be abandoned." He walked away.

She listened to his booted steps echo on the hardwood floor and wondered what he meant. Was he talking about the kiss? Or did he sense her deeper turmoil?

Soren was no poet, and yet his words had perfectly captured the conflict inside her.

Or was he speaking of himself? Did he, too, wonder if he was making the right decision? After all, he was selling his title for money.

They would soon know, because, on the morrow, they would both be stepping into their futures.

Chapter 9

So, she hadn't wanted him to kiss her the way he had that morning.

That was the reason she'd taken the matter into her own hands. Soren understood her motive as clearly as he knew his own name. What puzzled him was what she was afraid of. What she was thinking. Cassandra never acted without fore-thought, sometimes too much forethought.

For his part, kissing her had been all he could think about over dinner.

The kiss they had shared on the dueling field had made a difference. She'd responded to him. She'd not been experienced, but she had not held back. He wanted to believe her natural curiosity extended to the bedroom. This was a good thing, because Soren had no desire to be a monk and he wanted his wife to be his lover.

He understood the dangers of marriages of convenience. His parents had had one and they had come to detest each other. His mother had been from a good family of modest fortune. They had scraped together a sizable dowry to launch their daughter into Society. Soren knew it had been hard on her to watch her lazy albeit noble husband invest her money in silly schemes or gamble it away.

Meanwhile, his father had discovered he'd married a woman who was doomed to be perpetually disappointed. She was never satisfied, something that increasingly weighed on Soren.

He was their only child although he had a bastard brother and two bastard sisters. He wondered if Cass knew? It seemed to be a big secret in Cornwall, a place where secrets never stuck.

His half sisters were suitably and happily married. His half brother had a commission and served on the Peninsula. Soren had seen to their successful prospects. Not his father.

But there were things he needed to discuss with Cass, and they were topics that might not please her—such as his first marriage and his son.

Soren had no doubt Cass would find his mother a trial, just as he did. However, he hoped she bonded with his son. He'd mentioned Logan that morning to her. He'd told her that he wanted to save Pentreath for his son and she'd not made a comment . . . except now, on reflection, Soren wondered if she had fully understood what he'd meant. She might have thought he was speaking about *a* son in general, such as *their* son once they married.

He'd been preparing for bed. He now sat on the edge of the mattress, working over this new problem. It was quite possible Cass hadn't registered much of anything that was said, what with the duel and the proposal.

Absolutely, now that Cass had agreed to marry him, he must speak to her about Logan before she heard any rumors. His son was his sole motive for doing what he must to save Pentreath. He was also the reason Soren needed to return home soon. Considering he'd had no choice but to leave Logan in his mother's care, he'd already been gone too long.

So, when to talk to Cass?

There would be no time before the ceremony. Nor would he run the risk of Cass crying off. She was that independent-minded.

Should he have mentioned Logan before? Perhaps. But Cass had been so cold to him, there had not been an opportunity for private conversation.

He was also aware that she'd have a few questions about his late wife, Mary. And what would he say?

Soren lay back on the bed. Should he admit his bitterness toward Mary? She had attempted to rob him of Logan. He understood her justification. She'd decided she did not want their child to be raised in a white world. She'd been Lenape, and after he'd give up his commission, had suggested several times she wished him to return to her tribe with her. Soren had refused. He believed then, as he did now, their best opportunities were among his people.

Mary had disagreed and so she had never told him she was pregnant. She'd left and kept their son secret from him.

Soren stared at the ceiling, remembering the confusion, anger, and, yes, hurt he'd felt to return home and find his wife gone. He'd been away for a few days meeting with some gentlemen who wanted to help him open a trading post. She'd even instructed a neighbor to tell him not to come after her. She'd returned to her people.

He'd tried anyway. Mary had refused to see him—probably because by that time her pregnancy would have been showing—and it had made him very angry. He'd sacrificed everything for her.

However, time had calmed his temper. He could now blame himself for some of what happened. He'd been gone too often for a new bride. He'd left her in a culture that she understood but had not fully embraced. He should have understood how hard life was for her in the settlement.

And now he had a second chance at marriage.

He realized he truly wanted Cass. Even when she was prickly, and that was quite often. She knew her own mind, and she was exactly what Logan needed. She understood the manners and expectations of English Society. As MP Holwell's daughter, she'd also been an outsider. She would give Soren good advice concerning his son. He also believed Mary would have liked her.

For a moment, he imagined Mary and Cass facing each other. It would be hard to place odds on which woman had the most resolve.

And that was his curse, wasn't it? He didn't enjoy women who had little between their ears and brought nothing to the table. He liked them spirited and vibrant. Cass was a strong woman. Their children would be healthy. Her fortune would set their future on a good path.

Her fortune.

How many times today had someone made mention of it? Many had cheered his good luck at marrying an heiress. Others had made comments cloaked in jealousy. A few had wondered if he was interested in a business venture they were exploring or could he advance them a small loan? His answer to both was no.

Soren was going to secure Pentreath Castle for his son and his children by Cassandra. He was determined to put the lands around it to good use and to be an upstanding member of the House of Lords. He was not going to waste Cassandra's wealth. And he was going to take the admiral's advice and meet with Holwell with all haste.

The time to tell Cass of his son and first marriage would present itself. He just needed to wait for the right moment, and before the wedding would not be it.

That night, he wrote two letters. One was to his mother informing her of his marriage. The other was to Deborah Fowey, his father's mistress, who, after his death, had married the local wainwright. He was more honest in the second letter than the first.

Soren was happy to finally find his bed, but he did not sleep well. Instead, he had dreams of taunting a lonely girl who had trusted his friendship. Only, in the dream, she turned the tables on him. She'd drawn a picture of him as a "liar and sneak."

The accusation rolled around in his head even when he woke to greet his wedding day.

CASSANDRA HAD SLEPT well, and her natural optimism was revitalized for it.

She was picking up the reins of her life, she realized. Her father might not be happy, but she would not be trundled off to some corner of the world to be ignored. Instead, she would be experiencing life to its fullest.

With a husband came a place in Society. She vowed not to be passive and meek the way Helen was to her father. She planned on being a partner in marriage. She would help Soren manage his social affairs and become a famed hostess. Just as Society coveted invitations to the Dowager Duchess of Camberly's house party, everyone would desire the opportunity to attend one of her literary salons. She would host only the most important people and join them in discussions of great ideas. They would listen to her opinion, something her father never did.

She and Soren would have beautiful, golden-haired children. Cassandra could picture them. They would have lovely manners, and she would see the girls were educated as well as the boys. Most important of all, her son would someday be the Earl of Dewsberry.

Yes, she was well aware that had been her father's dream. Noble descendants. She understood now. There was an honor in setting up future generations. She also believed with all her heart that her father would reconcile with her. It would be a good moment. He would see what a good countess she was and be contrite for the rift between them. In turn, she would be gracious and understanding.

That was how a countess behaved.

Many of the country party's houseguests would

be leaving later that day, but first they planned to celebrate the wedding. Cassandra was thankful Willa was still here. She burst into Cassandra's room ready to make the day special.

"You will be the most beautiful bride anywhere," Willa declared. "What are you wearing?"

Cassandra showed her the white gauze dress with gold and green ribbon rosettes that she'd originally intended for one of the dowager's more formal dinners.

"It is perfect. However, it does need a pressing. Betty," she said to her maid, who had carried a vase of freshly cut roses into the room, "please take care of the dress."

"Yes, Miss Willa." The maid placed the roses on the bedside table and left the room to do her mistress's bidding.

"I ordered a bath sent up," Willa informed Cassandra. "Your stepmother isn't here and I believe I should fill her role."

"What are the roses for?" Cassandra asked.

"Every bride needs flowers in her hair. The dowager's garden is glorious with them. We will hold them in place with your mother's diamond pins. I assume you will wear the pearls?"

Tears welled in Cassandra's eyes. She nodded.

Willa was immediately concerned. "Are you all right?"

"Yes, I'm wonderful. Why do you ask?"

"I've never seen you cry before."

Cassandra dabbed the heel of her hand against another tear. "I'm not crying because I'm sad but because of what you are doing. You are making me feel very special."

"It is nothing but friendship," Willa assured her. She gave Cassandra a quick hug. "So, the pearls?"

"Yes, of course. They were my mother's favorites. I have nothing to represent my father."

"I pray the man stews in his own bile. I can't believe he behaved the way he did. There is nothing wrong with Dewsberry. I watched you last night over dinner, and I think the two of you make a handsome couple. I also believe he rather likes you."

"He likes my money." Cassandra moved to the washstand to collect a bar of fine milled soap. It was scented with lavender.

"Possibly," Willa agreed. "Still, I thought him very attentive."

He's like his father, secretive and conniving—

Cassandra shut her father's cruel words from her mind. That didn't mean she was all trusting. "It is merely a marriage of convenience," Cassandra said offhandedly, but in truth, it meant the beginning of a new life for her.

A knock sounded on the door. Her bath had arrived. Stalwart servants filled a hip tub. While Cassandra bathed behind a screen, Willa created a nosegay for her to carry to the church.

Betty returned with the dress pressed and helped Cassandra dress and style her hair. The maid loosely curled it, catching each curl in place with a rose and diamond-tipped pin.

By the time the hour came to go to the chapel, Cassandra felt a true bride. As she went out of her bedroom, she touched her mother's pearls and believed she felt her presence.

Outside, the May sky was a clear blue with only a fluffy lamb of a cloud or two. The Camberly family chapel was a short walk from the house. The stone building was nestled under aging firs. Headstones were in the yard around it. Some were quite ancient. The newest was the dowager's husband, Camberly's grandfather.

Inside, the chapel felt very close with its low ceiling. It could seat maybe eight people. Soren was already there, along with a local rector. The duke and his grandmother were also present. He smiled in greeting at Cassandra but then his gaze wandered to Willa. Cassandra silently vowed she would do what she must to keep the amoral Camberly from her dear friend.

Soren approached. He was attired in his formal clothes. Someone had seen to trimming his hair and yet it still looked a bit wild. She found she didn't mind. Indeed, she rather liked him the way he was.

"You are beautiful." He spoke without preamble as if he could not contain the words and didn't care who heard them.

Heat rushed to her cheeks. In that moment, she felt appreciated and treasured. He acted as if he wanted to marry not the heiress or the woman he was saving from disgrace, but *her*. As if he *valued* her.

The rector broke the spell. "Are we all gathered, my lord?" he asked Soren. Someone had said he was a cousin of the duke's who had the living here.

"Are you ready, Miss Holwell?" Soren said, as aware as she that soon she would no longer have that name.

"I am, my lord."

Soren nodded to the rector. "Then let us begin."

He sounded confident, and yet did she detect a hint of nervousness? That must mean this marriage was important to him.

Cassandra realized she wanted that to be true.

The ceremony began. The rector's voice reminded her of her father's sonorous tones. Unbidden, her sire's warning once again tried to echo in her brain. *He is like his father, secretive*—She shut it out.

Instead, she focused on her future. Her gaze met his gray eyes that now appeared open and honest. He was her childhood friend.

He was also the man who self-assuredly pledged his troth to her, and then he placed a plain gold band on her finger that was solid and real.

The ceremony was over. The rector introduced them as man and wife. As Lord and Lady Dewsberry.

Soren gave her hand a squeeze. She had been so caught in a swirl of emotions, she hadn't realized he was holding it.

The dowager was the first to wish them happy. Willa gave her a hug and then turned and made a pretty speech to Soren about how fortunate he was to marry one of her dearest friends.

Cassandra noted that Camberly watched Willa, a bit of interest in his eye, and yet he made no untoward move.

Soren tucked her hand in his arm as they led the procession up to the house where the other guests waited for the wedding breakfast. "Let me tell you again that you look lovely," he said.

Cassandra smiled. She was too tall for lovely. Everyone told her that, and yet his words sounded honest. They touched something deep inside where she hid everything she hoped was true and knew wasn't.

A great cheer went up when they walked into the dining room. The dowager insisted she and Soren sit in the center of the table side by side, and they were toasted repeatedly. The food was plentiful, the punch, wine, and ale more so.

Cassandra drank. One must have a sip when one is being feted. However, she wanted her wits about her when Soren took her upstairs. She was more than a touch anxious.

She did have a notion of what to expect in the bedroom.

However, seeing Camberly with Letty Bainhurst had been shocking. It hadn't been poetic at all. In fact, it had been far too intimate. It had also been completely counter to what she'd thought would happen.

The toasts grew rowdier and more suggestive. The niceties grew thinner and Cassandra became uncomfortable. When she'd attended weddings, they had been for family or very close friends. They were discreet, enjoyable affairs.

Here she was with the crème of London Society and she found them crude when they over-imbibed. And unhappy.

No wonder they hopped into different beds. The drinking, the laughter, all of it masked what people truly felt. Lord Bainhurst was flirting with the lady to his right. His wife was once again exchanging glances with Camberly. If there was a happy marriage in the room, Cassandra was hard pressed to find it.

Lord Drucker, one of Lord Bainhurst's friends, stood and lifted his glass. "Here's to having enough money to buy a husband."

The comment was met with mocking laughter and "Hear, hears" mingled with cruel twitters.

Cassandra was shocked. A knot of unease formed in her belly. She looked to Willa, who appeared equally stunned and offended. She shook her head as if saying to Cassandra she didn't know how to gracefully accept such boorish behavior, either.

The person who didn't seem upset was Soren. Not an ounce of tension. He drank to the toast.

And then he stood to make his own.

Everyone quieted down expectantly. The man who had made his jibe wore a sheep's grin across a face flush with drink.

Cassandra could not look at him. She felt shame. She was glad now her father was not here. The glow went off the day.

Soren raised his glass. "I first set eyes on my lady over a decade ago—Aye," he said, noting the piqued interest of the women in the room, "this is a romantic tale."

Romantic? Cassandra frowned at her lap.

"She and I met at the harvest day festival. It

was held at the church. At one time, all would have come to Pentreath Castle, my family home. However, the bad blood between her family and mine had destroyed that celebration two generations earlier. We were warned as children to avoid each other."

That was true. Cassandra raised her eyes to him. He was stood tall and proud. He could hold his own with any gentleman in this esteemed company.

"A York would walk on the other side of the road if he saw a Holwell coming. A Holwell would spit in a York's direction." He had the interest now of everyone in the room.

"So I was raised to look down upon the Holwells . . . and then at this festival—one my family was attending reluctantly because, after all, it should have been ours—" He paused and looked directly at Lord Drucker. "We may not have money but we have more than our share of pride." Heads nodded. And why not? For many noble houses, their vices made money a priority.

"Well, we prideful Yorks were at the festival along with every man, woman, and child for twenty miles around. There was a band of fiddles and drums, two great steers turning on a spit, and more gossip and conversation than anyone could hope for in a year. I was happy to see my friends. I was home on holiday and would soon be sent back to school. And we had a high time of it. You know, the sort only boys can have when the grown-ups are not watching them closely. A group of us stole some meat pies off a table before it was time to eat. We went running off, and it was then that a girl arrived whom I'd never met before. Oh, please, let me assure you, as a lad of thirteen, I noticed but rarely paid attention to the fairer sex—"

"Something you changed years later," Camberly shouted out with good humor, and the audience laughed.

"I have been a bit of a hound," Soren agreed easily. "But this day, the lass who caught my eye was not just anyone. She was my family's enemy. For the rest of that day, I circled and circled her, working up the courage to talk to her. In the end, she spoke first."

He looked at Cassandra; his gaze could be construed as a look of love. And everyone was listening now. Even she almost believed what he was saying. *Almost.* She knew different. After all, she'd been there.

Soren continued his "tale." "She told me she didn't know why her father warned her against me. She said I didn't look like such a bad sort."

"I wonder what she'll say after tonight?" Lord Drucker quipped. He was rewarded with a few chuckles, but the women in the room shushed him. They were caught up in the story.

"I told her I didn't want to be her enemy, and I didn't. She had curls like spun gold that fell all the way to her waist. Her eyes were bluer than any I'd ever seen before. My nan had told me stories of piskies, which are mischievous Cornish fairies who roam the hills, and she looked like one of them come to life. She also held a book in her hand. She was reading while the rest of us were looking for trouble."

The book part was true.

His talk of piskies was pure nonsense. Piskies were actually tiny, naughty old men. But no one in this room knew that. Instead, they were picturing her as a glowing little thing with wings.

"I spent the afternoon at her feet," Soren declared. "By the end of the day, we vowed to each other that we would not be enemies. That the feud our parents enjoyed was not ours."

Another piece of truth.

"Nor, in all the ensuing years, has there ever been a woman who has captured my imagination so completely."

His words formed themselves in the air over everyone's heads. In that moment, he had elevated her from a bride of convenience to a lover of significance.

She could feel opinions changing all around

her. Lady Bainhurst had raised a hand to her heart as if deeply touched. Willa appeared positively smitten. Even the men had been tamed.

The only one not pleased was Cassandra—because it wasn't true, save a smidgeon. He'd made it all up. Easily.

"To my bride," Soren declared, raising his glass. The company rose to their feet, albeit some unsteadily. They raised their glasses. "May we have a long and happy life together," Soren said to her. He drained the glass.

She did not touch hers.

The dowager leaned toward her, her eyes misty. "I did not realize this was a love match. That he has pined for you all these years. I've not heard anything so romantic." Lady Melrose nodded her agreement.

Cassandra had never heard anything so manipulative. Her temper began to build.

Yes, she understood Soren might think he was doing it for her because Lord Drucker was a bore and a fool.

But her father had warned her—and she was wary of conniving men.

She came to her feet, reacting to the sudden churning of emotions she could not explain. Why, she almost preferred everyone snicker at her than fixate on her with melting eyes because they wanted to believe Soren's fibs.

Her intent was to leave the room with her dignity intact. Cassandra never lied, and she was stunned at how easily he did.

His arm came around her waist and held her in place as if he had anticipated her actions.

"Kiss her," someone, possibly Camberly since he was well within his cups, called. The words were picked up by others.

"Keep smiling," Soren warned under his breath.

She turned to him. "I don't—" she started, ready to tell him that she didn't smile on command— but he kissed her before she could finish. Her lips had pursed on the word "don't" and he'd pounced on them.

By the roar of approval, the kiss must have looked loverly but it wasn't.

She was spitting furious with him. He'd just made up nonsense about them in front of everyone with complete disregard of the truth. Her father had always chided her to be honest. It was a virtue he favored.

Cassandra tried to pull away. Soren's arm around her wouldn't let her escape without a scene. She tried to protest; he took full advantage with his mouth.

Really, the man was insufferable. It was just as it had been on the dueling field. He kissed; she found herself kissed.

And then, *they* were kissing.

It became hard to reason, let alone to hold an angry thought. He had a hand on her back now, right between her shoulder blades. He bent over her, his lips following hers, and she found herself pressing up, not wishing to break contact.

Did they have an audience? She could no longer tell because all the awareness of her being was centered on this kiss—and then his arm around her waist moved down the backs of her thighs and she felt herself being lifted into the air with an ease she would not have thought possible.

The kiss broke with her surprise. She was in Soren's arms. He was holding her. Men didn't hold her. She was too tall, and yet here she was.

"That is enough," he announced to the gathered company. "My bride and I wish to be alone." With those words, he swept her out of the room ignoring the randy shouts calling them back or giving advice.

He carried her. He did so easily, as if her weight was of no consequence to him.

But this was unsettling to her. She wanted to be on her own feet. "You can put me down now."

"Not yet. They are watching."

And they were. Heads popped out from the dining room doorway. Camberly even came out into the hall as Soren brought her to the front stairs.

"I am too heavy," Cassandra whispered, embarrassed.

"Are you afraid I'll drop you?" he said.

"Of course I am. This is silly," she said.

"Really?" He started up the stairs but pretended to move his arms as if he would let her go. Instinctively, Cassandra threw her arms around his neck. Now, he had a better hold.

"That's better," he cooed.

The general company was now at the foot of the stairs. Soren turned on the landing with her. "Wave."

"No."

"Spitfire," he chided before kissing the angry pout on her lips, and continued his climb. At the top of the stairs, she thought he would put her down. When he didn't, she glared at him, ready to tell him let go of her, but he spoke first.

"Don't say it. Not one word." He looked pointedly at a few maids and valets who were waiting for their masters and had come out of the rooms to see what was going on.

She kept quiet. Servants were the worst tattlers, and though she had some very direct words for Soren, she did not want them repeated.

Soren walked to a room at the end of the hall. A valet, noting that his arms were full, said with a knowing grin, "Allow me, my lord."

"Thank you," Soren said, while Cassandra wished she had a scarf to put over her head and hide her embarrassment. The crude comments from downstairs reminded her that everyone anticipated what they would be doing in this room, including the valet who had just opened the door.

The door closed behind him. This was the "special" room but it wasn't much larger than the other bedrooms at Mayfield. Granted, the appointments were nicer. The bed itself was an ornately carved canopied bed of dark wood. The bed curtains and drapes were in a soft gold and there was a carpet on the floor. A well-worn one.

Soren moved to the bed. He opened his arms and let Cassandra drop.

Free at last, and without an audience, she hit the mattress and reached for a pillow. She rolled onto her knees, raised it in the air, and walloped him.

"Hey," Soren complained.

"It was all rot. Everything you said downstairs. Every bit of it." She hit him with the pillow again. He didn't have a place to run.

"It got you upstairs, didn't it? Isn't that what you wanted?"

She held the pillow, her arm poised to throw it at him. "Wanted?"

"They were into their cups," Soren said, combing the hair her pillow had mussed from his forehead. "I wanted to shut them up and take you out of there. And look," he announced like a magician who had something to show, "here we are, away from them. Isn't that what you desired?"

It was. She'd been very uncomfortable. Still . . . "You didn't have to feed them lies."

"I fed them what they wanted to hear. Besides, most of it was the truth."

Cassandra almost laughed. "In what way? Yes, we met at the Harvest Home but I remember you stealing pies—"

"I mentioned that—"

"—*after* I'd been instructed to keep an eye on them. You got me in trouble. Mrs. Morwath had said I failed as pie guard and had dismissed me. That was the reason I'd gone off to hide with a book." Mrs. Morwath was the rector's wife, and a more intimidating woman did not exist.

"Nor," she continued, "was my hair curling down my back. I always wore my hair up. Yesterday morning and the other night were the first times you've ever seen it down and even then, I had it in a braid." She sat back on her heels, holding the pillow in front of her.

"But I have a good imagination." Soren plopped onto the bed, making the mattress shift beneath her. "And your eyes are blue."

"Not bluer than blue."

"Did I say that?" He came up on his knees, close to her.

She did not dignify his challenge. Instead, she grumbled, "They are downstairs with all sorts of romantic notions."

"They don't have to be wrong." He leaned close to her as he spoke and lightly pressed his lips to her neck just below her ear.

His breath on her skin made her start. She snapped her head around. "What are you doing?" she said. Their faces were mere inches from each other.

"Seducing you," he answered. His voice was mesmerizing. "We are going to be very good together, Cass." He reached for the pillow she'd been holding in front of her.

"You don't know that," she whispered.

"I'm willing to find out. Aren't you?"

Chapter 10

Cassandra was an innocent. For all of her book knowledge, Soren knew she understood very little about men and women.

Then again, he had no doubt she had attempted to glean all she could from between the lines of her favorite poets. She'd always been eager to learn, and he longed to be her tutor.

He placed his hand on the pillow, anxious to remove it from between them. She caught his arm at the wrist. The movement brought them even closer together. Her breasts barely brushed his chest and yet heat shot through him.

She searched his eyes. "Can I trust you?"

"With your life. I'll always protect you, Cass."

"But will you be honest with me? Honesty was not stated in the vows. I believe it should have been. It is important."

"Why would I not be?"

"Did you not hear yourself downstairs?"

And yet, she was a politician's daughter. Everyone knew her father embellished stories. He did what was expedient.

But it wasn't MP Holwell who made the request. It was the woman he longed to please.

"I vow my honesty," he answered.

She released his wrist.

He dropped the pillow over the side of the bed and put his hands to better use.

His lips found hers.

Without a hint of maidenly modesty, Cass's mouth kissed him without an ounce of reserve. She was acting on instinct. Her kiss was raw emotion. He adored it.

He cupped the side of her face, to guide her. She responded. He eased her enthusiasm and deepened the kiss while he leaned her back upon the bed.

Cass's arm went around his neck. Her breasts arched toward him.

Did she know what she was doing to him? He'd thought he'd be the teacher. Instead, she was the one doing the schooling. If this was what reading poetry could do to a woman, well, every man should buy his wife a book. Perhaps even ten.

He ran his hand down over her hip, exploring, testing. Her legs were well-formed and shapely. Her hip had the sweetest curve that rolled into a perfect waist.

This was his wife.

And he was past ready to see all of her.

He eased onto his back carrying her with him. Roses, diamond pins, and golden hair fell around them. Her breasts rested against his chest. Sweet, sweet Cass. She smelled of violets and woman, a scent that had teased him all afternoon. He began unlacing the back of her gown.

Their kiss broke. "What are you doing?" she asked. Her lips were already swollen with the force of his desire. Her eyes seemed to be deep pools of blue, like the sea under a turbulent sky.

"Undressing you."

"That is what I hoped," she answered. She went back to kissing.

She had to know how aroused he was. She moved as if aware of his erection. He took her leg and gently brought it to his hip so that he could fit against her better. The movement lifted her skirts even higher. He coaxed her sleeves down over her shoulders, but he was having difficulty. The truth was, her kisses and his hardness were making it challenging for him to think.

She sensed the problem. "Here, let me help." She slid off him so that she could stand by the bed. First, she removed the famed strand of pearls and set them on the bedside table. Then, grabbing her skirts, she pulled her dress up over her head.

A low growl of satisfaction caught in his throat. She wore a lawn chemise that barely covered full, round breasts, and a petticoat of the same sheer fabric. The shadow of her legs in silk stockings was the stuff of men's dreams.

"Am I too bold?" she asked. She held her dress in front of her, bringing to his attention the fact that he stared. No, he did more than stare. He was bloody drooling. "Aren't we both supposed to be naked for this?"

Soren scrambled out of the bed. "Yes, *yes*," he agreed. He began pulling on his neck cloth. His fingers had stopped working properly or the knot had been too tight. He yanked it hard.

Of course, the real problem was that she had folded and set aside her dress on a chair and was now untying her petticoats. He could barely think coherently as he watched her slip the ribbons free.

She noticed his lack of movement. "Is something the matter?"

"No, nothing," he assured her. He still hadn't undone the knot. "Carry on."

"Oh, no." She held her petticoats in place. "You need to do your share."

"I do," he agreed, fiddling again with the knot, but then he noticed the creamy expanses of breasts against her chemise. Damn it all.

He'd never manage to undress.

"Let me help." She pushed his fumbling hands aside.

Her hair smelled like flowers warmed by the sun. Her body heat teased him as she tried to undo the mess he'd made of his knot.

He put his arm around her waist. His hand rested on her hip. She felt good in his arms. Her petticoat ribbons were loose. He could easily free her of the garment.

"You did yourself no favors," she said, working on the damage.

His response was to kiss her hair, her forehead. She put her mouth up for him to kiss, and so he did. She surprised him with her openness, her playfulness.

She won the knot and pulled his neck cloth from around his neck. Pressing her body against his intimately, she whispered, "This is it, isn't it?" She pushed his jacket down over his shoulders.

"Yes, it is," he assured her. He pulled his shirt over his head and then picked her up again and set her on the bed. Her loosened petticoat fell to the ground. Her lower half was naked save for her stockings. She pressed her legs together in modesty. Her breasts pushed against the chemise.

It was all he could do to unbutton his too full

breeches, especially with her intently watching his every movement.

He kicked off one shoe and then another. He took his time lowering his breeches and enjoyed the way her eyes widened.

Oh yes, this would be fun.

Cassandra scooted back on the bed and pulled her chemise over her head. Her skin seemed to glow in the room's late afternoon light. Her breasts were full and perfectly formed. Her waist and hips were a study in grace.

And, she still wore her silk stockings. She was bringing him to his knees.

"You are a beauty, Cass."

Doubt came to her eye. "Is that something you are just saying—?"

"No, I mean every word. And I assure you, I will be a good husband to you."

She nodded, but her gaze drifted to his proud arousal. "It is different than I had imagined."

"Hopefully in a good way?"

"I don't know."

He laughed, delighted. She was candor and innocence and completely herself. Had he thought to go slow?

That idea was gone. His Cass was full of anticipation. Their mating would be good. He threw himself on the bed beside her and drew her to his side. He stretched his body against hers and kissed her ear. Her answer was a soft gasp of pleasure, and then she kissed his ear.

She did it well.

Soren was down to business now. His wife was a perfect student. Whatever he did that she liked, she copied on him.

He bit her lower lip; she nipped at his. He nibbled her neck; she nibbled him.

But what he really wanted were her breasts. They were round and pink and responsive to his touch. How many hours, even when they'd been young, had he spent trying to imagine them? And here they were. His fantasies had not done them justice.

He now gave them proper attention.

Cass breathed his name in surprise at the sensation of his mouth upon her. Her fingers buried themselves in his hair as if to hold him to her. He paid her close attention. First one, then the other . . . even as he let his hand dip lower.

The heat of her was a beacon. He moved to her core, rested a moment for her to relax, and then he slid one finger inside, testing her.

She'd tensed. Her hands went still.

He found her ear. "Easy."

Cass swallowed and then turned to him, their lips inches from each other. "Will there be pain?"

"Not if I can help it. And if there is, it will be only an instant." At least, that was what he'd heard—and hoped. He stroked her. Her legs opened as if of their own accord. "I won't hurt you. I'll never hurt you."

"I believe you."

He lifted himself up over her to settle against her heat. "Help me, Cass." He slid his hand under her buttocks to curve her toward him. He knew exactly where he must be to make it easiest on her. He wanted to do this right.

But his wife was not one to wait. She moved against him. Her arms tightened around him, her movements a touch frantic, as if she distracted herself. She kissed his hair, the side of his eye, the middle of his forehead—and he did what must be done.

In one fluid movement, he entered her. He did not pull back but thrust deep. The thin barrier was nothing against the force of his need, and he easily claimed her.

She inhaled as if there was a bit of pain. He held himself still, waiting for her to signal whether he could go on.

Dear God, she was so tight, he prayed he wouldn't embarrass himself. His primal urge was to drive on, to take what he wanted. He employed every bit of control he had—

"Is that it? Are we done?"

Her questions broke his concentration.

Soren looked down at her. She had the most puzzled expression on her face. "How are you?" he countered. "Have I hurt you?"

"There was a needle's prick of uncomfortableness." She ran her hand along his shoulder as if admiring the play of muscles that were doing everything in their power to hold him back from pillaging her. Her lashes lifted up to him. "But if this is all there is, why do poets go on about it?"

Soren laughed. He couldn't help himself.

A smile came to her lips. "I felt that. You laughed and I felt it all the way through." Her brows came together. "We aren't done, are we?"

"We are just starting," he promised. He began moving to show her what he meant.

"That is very *nice*," she managed as if it was a complete understatement. "*Very* nice."

And then she took him to new places by raising her hips herself. He went deeper, and now Soren knew he had no control over himself. If she'd cried stop, he didn't know what he could have done.

Nothing had ever felt as good as being inside his wife. She'd been made for him. Her summer scent. Her passion. She met him thrust for thrust and kiss for kiss.

Her hold tightened. She cried his name as if lost and he was the only one who could find her.

He understood. She was coming close. He was almost past reason himself but he knew she needed his guidance.

"Let it go, Cass. Trust me. Let it happen—"

Her muscles constricted with such force he called her name.

Her release came in waves. She surprised him with the power of it. He could no longer let her be. He pushed forward, burying himself to the hilt, her arms and legs around him. He gathered her as if he could take her inside himself and found his own blessed completion.

The blinding force of it felt as if he touched eternity, and he lost himself in her.

Had he ever experienced this before?

Not with such magnitude. It was as if he and Cass had joined souls.

Her face was buried in his neck. He'd keep her there forever . . . and then he felt tears.

They confused him. He'd not harmed her. Or had he?

He also knew he was incapable of consoling her at this moment. He couldn't even move.

Ever so slowly, life came back into focus.

Cool air on his heated skin roused him to awareness. Then it was her skin, her scent, her warmth . . .

Soren shifted his weight. She grasped him

tighter, both arms around his neck, holding him as if she was hiding. "Cass, are you crying?"

She shook her head. She was lying.

"Did I hurt you?"

Another shake of the head.

He rolled onto his back, carrying her with him. Taking care, he lifted her chin so that he could look into her eyes. She tried to avoid him but he shushed her not to argue.

She let him see. The tears had not stopped. Her eyes shimmered with them. A shudder went through her as if she was trying to control herself.

Wrapping his arms around her, he begged, "What is it? What have I done to you? Was the pain that great?"

Her belly against his, her breasts on his chest, she looked down at him and said, "That was the most wonderful experience of my life. No one had warned me. My friend Leonie acted as if it was nothing. But it is something. *Truly something.*"

Relief released the tension inside him along with an accompanying swell of pride. "It was, wasn't it?"

"It was better than I imagined the 'passion flower of ecstasy' could ever be."

"The *what*?"

"The 'passion flower of ecstasy' was in a poem

I once heard to describe what happens between a man and a woman. I now understand why everyone wants to make love, why they go in search of it. Was it special for you as well?"

He brushed a stray lock of her hair away from her face. "Aye. Very special. A passion flower *full* of ecstasy."

She laughed. Her laughter had its own music, and it gave Soren great pleasure. This was the way a marriage should be between a man and his wife. There should be laughter and excellent sex.

Soren reached for the edge of the counterpane beneath them and pulled as much as he could over their nakedness. Their bodies were warm together but he wanted to protect her from the night air. In doing so, he gathered the diamond-tipped pins and roses strewn over the sheets. He set them on the table and snuggled her close.

"Can it be better?" she wondered, her breath against his neck.

He grinned. Was there ever a man so fortunate? He liked her ambition, especially in this area. "Yes," he assured her. "That was just our first try. If we practice enough, who knows how good we will become. There is a whole garden of ecstasy to discover."

She curled into him, rubbing her legs against his. Her stockings had been kicked off in their lovemaking. He ran his toes over hers, enjoying the feeling of her bare feet. "I'd like to become very, very good. How often should we practice?" Her hand slid lower down his abdomen.

He stirred. Of course he did. What man could resist her?

Still, he had to think of what was best for his wife. He caught her wandering hand before she could stray too far. "I've worked you out enough for the first night. I don't want you to be sore on the morrow."

Her nose scrunched adorably at the idea. "I can be sore down there?"

She had so much to learn. He could not wait to teach her.

Reluctantly, he eased out from under her body and climbed out of the bed.

"Where are you going?" She moved as if to follow him.

"Rest right there. I'll be right back." His movements had shifted the counterpane. He tossed his share over her. "I need to take care of you."

"You can take care of me right here." She pouted, patting the mattress beside her. "I can see you want to."

He did. This part of his anatomy had always had a mind of its own. "Cass, you've grown bold."

"I'm receiving lessons in bold. But you aren't paying attention."

"Oh, I am paying attention, as you noticed. It

is hard to be a man. I couldn't fake it even if I wished. However, *you* come first." He walked to the washstand. The water was cool but it would do. He poured it into a basin.

"I like looking at you naked," she announced, sounding almost defiant. And then she added, a touch shyly, "I liked it the other night as well."

"Then I will never wear clothes for you." He returned to the bed holding the basin of water and a linen cloth.

"Promise?"

Her coy response delighted him. "I promise, but I do think I will have some difficulty when I attend Parliament. They have a strict idea of how a lord should dress." He knelt by the bed on her side, setting the basin on the mattress.

"Pity," she said.

"Yes," he agreed, and in the next beat, the two of them were grinning like fools at each other.

Her hand reached out to lace her fingers with his. "I'm glad I married you."

"Because of what I can do for you on a bed?" He was only half teasing. Cass's openness touched him. In a world swimming in chicanery, she had survived fresh and unsullied. Even with who her father was.

"I would have been miserable," she continued, "living as an unmarried relation with Helen and her daughters. I've always hated their pity."

"Why would they pity you?"

"I don't know." Her easiness gave way to the sort of deep reflection he knew of her. "Sometimes I was jealous of them because they knew their mother and I had lost mine. I often believed they resented my inheritance. They would always refer to me as 'the heiress' in a tone of voice that was not flattering. A portion of my inheritance was given to them for dowries. I did not mind, but still they were rather cold. This will sound odd, but I used to sense that I was surrounded by secrets. Did you ever feel that way?"

"No, I knew all the secrets. My grandfather lost money, my father lost money, I'm trying not to lose money. It is all right there."

That wasn't truly the complete truth. He did need to tell her about his son and his first marriage, but now was not the time.

Her expressive eyes became solemn. "Am I putting too much faith in a kiss? You must tell me, Soren. I don't have very much experience, especially in these matters."

He raised her hand to his lips and kissed the backs of her fingers. His gaze holding hers, he said, "Trust our kisses. They never lie."

Her smile was as if the heavens had opened and blessed them—and he knew she would make everything wrong in his life, right again.

"Why did you bring the water over?"

"For you." He pushed back the counterpane. He gently began wiping the signs of their love-making, of her virginity from her thighs.

She tried to close her legs, squirming away from him, even as she reached for the cloth. "I can do that."

He waved her away. "This is no chore. I'm here to take care of you. As time goes by, we'll know each other's bodies better than we do our own."

Or at least that was his intention. It had not happened with his first marriage. When Mary left him, he'd felt as if he'd never known her at all.

But this time it would be different. He and Cass shared a common heritage. And he'd do all he could to keep her happy. He'd been too young and anxious to make his fortune in his first mar-riage to realize that his wife must come first.

Cass held still.

His task finished, he folded the cloth and carried it and the washbasin back to the stand and then returned to bed. He pulled the covers down so they could both slip under the sheets. She nestled up to him. It was a good moment. He decided now was the time to tell her about Logan.

However, before he could speak, she said, "The other night when I saw Letty Bainhurst and the duke in the reading room, they weren't doing what we just did."

"They weren't?"

"No, the duke was down around her knees."

That comment caught his interest.

She leaned on one arm to look at him. "He was beneath her skirts. Whatever he was doing, she liked very much." There was more than a hint of suggestion in her voice.

Ah, Camberly. "And you are curious as to what was happening?" Soren suggested.

"There are things I wonder about." She lay back down, her head on his pillow. "When I have questions, I can usually reason things out from what I've read in books."

"Such as 'the passion flower of ecstasy'?"

Her smile was quick. "I wasn't exactly certain what that meant. I know now."

"And here I was thinking I should read more poetry."

Her eyes took on a delicious sparkle in the room's thin light. "I will not argue that point with you, husband." She said the title as if she liked the taste of it in her mouth. "But, Soren, what *was* he doing?"

The blood rushed through him. "Around her knees, eh?"

She nodded.

"I could write a poem for you . . . or I could show you."

She didn't wait a beat. "Show me, please."

And show her he did. He spent the rest of the afternoon showing her and most of the night. Later, they would talk.

Right now was for pleasure.

Chapter 11

*A*t last, the world began to make sense to Cassandra. The connection she felt with Soren was intense. He'd opened her to a whole new appreciation of her being. For the first time in her life, she felt valued, adored . . . beautiful.

In the wee hours of the morning, she woke to find her back against his chest, her buttocks cozied up to him. He slept with a protective arm around her, creating an intimate haven.

So, this was marriage.

Moonlight streamed in from a window and fell across the bed. She rolled over to study her husband in a way she never would when he was awake.

The stubble of his beard shadowed his jaw. She could trace with her finger the bump in his nose. However, she did not see these as flaws. She liked him exactly the way he was.

He had said she would come to know his body

better than her own, and she already believed that to be true. His spicy masculinity, his heat seemed imprinted upon her forever.

She was his wife, and she was pleased.

No one had shown her the dignity and compassion he had. Her father never had. He thought such actions weak.

But Soren believed in kindness and it ennobled him to Cassandra. Nor did he chastise her when she asked for what she wanted or told him what she preferred. He acted as if he appreciated her speaking up.

"My father is wrong about you," she told his sleeping form. "He said I shouldn't trust you but I do, Soren. I trust you always to do the right thing. And you can trust me. I'll always stand by your side. I promise you that."

She burrowed into him and slept deeply. She woke the next morning to her husband making love to her. She has rolled back over on her side. His hands covered her breasts.

He knew she'd woken. "Shhh," he warned against her ear. "My love is asleep."

His love. Such wonderful words.

"Oh, no, she is not," Cassandra countered, and began moving to give him everything he needed. When they were done, she flung her arms around him and said, "I pray we wake this way every morning." And he laughingly promised her it could be done.

However, eventually, they had to join the world outside the bedroom. Soren was determined to return to London immediately to confront her father. If she'd had her way, they would avoid any meeting, but she knew he was right.

Cassandra chose an ivory day gown with a sprigged pattern, her pearls, and good walking shoes for the trip. She'd learned to be prepared for anything when she traveled.

Downstairs, they found more guests were leaving that morning. London was only three hours by coach.

Lord Bainhurst, who now proclaimed himself their matchmaker, offered to give them a ride to the city in his vehicle. Soren said yes—because they truly had no other way of traveling and this would save them from hiring a conveyance. Of course, that meant Cassandra would have to spend more time in Letty Bainhurst's company. Caught up in her new understanding of the intimacy of marriage, Cassandra was puzzled that the woman would cuckold her husband.

Camberly was on hand as they were preparing to leave. Cassandra noted the lingering looks the duke was sending to his lover. However, to Cassandra's surprise, Letty was decidedly cold.

When Cassandra had a chance for a private word with Soren, she said, "Apparently His Grace and Lady Bainhurst are no longer friends."

"Good," Soren said. "She is a man-eater. His grandmother and I both wanted him free of her."

"But he looks so sad."

He turned her to face him. "Do I need to call him out?" He sounded teasing, and yet was there an undertone of jealousy?

Cassandra had never believed herself capable of inspiring any such strong emotion. She laughed and gave him a quick kiss on the end of his nose, without regard to whoever was watching. "My eyes see no other man save the handsome one in front of me."

"Ah, the newlywed," Lord Bainhurst's bored voice chimed in. He'd overheard her declaration. "In a year's time, you will be like my lady and myself."

Cassandra prayed his words would never come true. She wanted to feel the way she did now toward Soren every day of her life. She liked how he rested his hand on the small of her back to guide her. She adored leaning toward him, knowing if she should fall, he was right there. It felt good to be treated as if she mattered. Perhaps if Lord Bainhurst was more attentive to his wife—?

But she did not voice her opinion. Why should she give him advice he would not heed?

Once they were comfortably seated in the coach, Lady Bainhurst asked, "Where will the two of you live in London?"

It all depended on her money.

Cassandra deferred to Soren. He was more adept at fielding money questions than she was. And besides wasn't that what good wives did? They let their husbands speak for them? After the night they'd shared, she believed she could tame her natural inclination to speak up.

"We haven't discussed the matter yet," he said. "If you will let us off at the Pulteney, we'll stay there until we reach a decision." He referred to a well-known hotel. "Of course, soon, I will need to return to Cornwall."

"But we will live in London?" Cassandra quickly pressed.

"We will need a London address," he assured her.

"I'll stay in London," Cassandra told him, "whenever you visit Cornwall."

"If you wish," was his answer.

She did wish. She smiled, certain that when it came to husbands, she had the very best one. They had just had a discussion and had reached a reasonable solution. The skeptical lift of Lady Bainhurst's eyebrow didn't bother Cassandra at all. Her Ladyship should look to her own affairs instead of judging theirs. She slid her gloved hand into the crook of Soren's arm.

The coach arrived in town in the early afternoon. Cassandra had never stayed in a fine hotel. There had been no need to do so. She'd rarely been in a country inn. It was rather exciting to walk into the Pulteney's reception on her husband's arm.

Had the gossip preceded them that they had married? Did people stop and stare? She didn't know. There had not yet been an announcement posted in the papers. Soren would do that on the morrow, once they settled the issue of her fortune.

Besides, she was too busy taking in this new experience, and Helen wasn't there to hiss at her to "school" her eyes.

She held back a few steps while Soren approached the desk to register.

"Lord Dewsberry?" the clerk repeated when he saw Soren write his name in the book.

"I am."

The man appeared flummoxed for a moment. He pulled the registration book toward himself as if he feared Soren would run out the door with it. Another officious gentleman noticed the action and hurried to confer with the clerk.

Something was wrong.

Usually when she went into a business establishment, clerks and owners bowed and scrapped in front of her. She'd never experienced this wary restraint.

Then she overheard the manager say the words, "Holwell Heiress" and the clerk's attitude changed.

Now came the bowing and scraping to Soren. A key was given to him with a flourish, and the manager himself offered to escort them to their room. A porter was called to carry their meager luggage.

Her husband was very quiet as they followed the manager. The man was most solicitous as he showed them the appointments of the room while the porter set down their luggage. Soren pressed a coin in each hand and they could not bow low enough.

However, once the hotel staff had left, he said, "I believe I will call on your father now."

He'd said he had intended on seeing her father once they reached London, but something in his voice gave her pause. She removed her bonnet and set it on the table. He'd not moved from his post by the door, his hat in his hand. She began pulling off her gloves. "Is our financial situation truly dire?"

Soren did not lie to her. "Worse than. I just gave the last coins in my pocket to those two so they won't go downstairs and announce they were right about me in the first place."

"Has it always been like this?" She'd not thought people would openly question whether one had money, although it was a common topic among the upper classes. She realized the staff of a hotel such as this would be very aware of their clientele's importance.

"You don't need to worry about it." He reached for the door. "I will return shortly."

"No, wait. I'm going with you." Here was her opportunity to prove herself to him in front of her father.

Soren had been more than generous to her. He'd been her protector at the dowager's house party. After the way they had been last night, she could already be carrying his child. In fact, she could be in love with him—

The thought came to her out of the air. *She could be in love . . .*

Funny how she'd not considered love in relation to Soren until this moment, but here it was, swirling around her.

Of course, she could love him.

Without her being aware, he'd come to embody every romantic notion she'd had about men. And he'd always been there. It had all started in their childhood when he had insisted the others include her.

That seemed like a factual and rather humdrum definition of love. Poets, she now realized, wrote about their carnal natures. The passion flower of ecstasy and all of that. She'd certainly experienced every bit of it with Soren, and hoped to do so again this night.

And, yes, he was entirely too human. The state of his affairs embarrassed him. However, she had faith in him . . . because she loved him.

"We will find our way through any difficulties," she said aloud. "Whatever I have is yours, and Father will understand how right this marriage is once he sees us together."

"Cass, this will be a difficult interview. Your father is very angry."

Cass. His Cass. The nickname now sang through her.

"My father is always angry at the Yorks. It is part of who he believes he is. Truly, Soren, he is not a bad man. But he is a fighter. He needs something to push against, and right now, that is more me than it is you. He's angry that I did not obey him. He feels I betrayed him."

"All the more reason for you to stay here."

"I'm not a coward. And if I avoid him, we will never reconcile. No, I must go. I also have some things to collect at the house. All I have to wear is what is in my valise. I need my books and clothing." And the rest of her jewelry. She had a set of sapphires that matched her garnets in size. They were truly beautiful and very precious. "Where will I have it all sent?"

"I suppose to Pentreath."

"I'm not going there," she reminded him.

"Eventually you will. It is our family seat."

"You told me we would live in London."

He looked at her as if she was a child.

"Do you not remember?" she prodded.

"Yes."

Cassandra reached for her gloves and began pulling them on. "Then I don't want my things sent to Cornwall."

"Except right now, we don't have a house in London."

"We will purchase one."

He picked up her hat and offered it to her, a sign he agreed she would accompany him. "If we can," he said. "It would be nice." He set his hat on his head.

"When we were in the coach, you didn't offer any objections."

"I'm not about to discuss anything of this nature in front of others. Especially Bainhurst. And to be honest, Cassandra, I know you are to inherit your mother's fortune at marriage, but I don't know how much that is."

"Forty thousand pounds."

Soren appeared to choke. "Forty thousand pounds?" he repeated as if uncertain he'd heard correctly. "Forty?"

"Are you displeased?"

"I'm overjoyed," he said. "That is an *incredible* fortune. You are certain of the amount?"

"Of course, I am." In fact, she was a bit annoyed at the question. "When I was sixteen, my grandfather's solicitor, Mr. Calder, called upon me and Father. He insisted on telling me the terms of my grandfather's will. The money that would have gone to my mother is to come to me when I marry. In fact, my father had not yet given me my mother's jewelry, like these pearls, and Mr. Calder insisted he do so in his presence because those should have been mine outright."

Soren took a moment to digest this information, his brow concerned. "Had your grandfather recently passed?"

"Oh, no, he'd been dead for a few years. He died when I was fourteen."

"Who had charge of the money?"

"My father."

"Has he kept your money separate?"

Cassandra frowned. "From what?"

"From his."

"I don't know. Why do you ask?"

"Something mentioned at Mayfield."

"There was talk of *my* money at the dowager's party?" She didn't how she felt about that. "Who would be so crass?"

Instead of answering, he said, "Do you think your father would *spend* your money?"

"Of course. He spent it on me and my needs. When my stepsisters married, he told me he used some of the money for their dowries."

"Were you all right with that?"

"Yes, Soren. Why would I not be? He gave them five thousand pounds apiece."

"Five thousand?" he repeated as if dumbstruck by the number.

"He called it my wedding gift to them."

"A generous wedding gift is fifty pounds."

She tried not to bristle at the implied criticism. Should she have questioned the amount? It had not seemed to matter back then. "They needed it. They are older than I am . . . and their prospects were not good." They had actually been terrible. Her stepsisters did not have good manners. In fact, calling them surly was not unkind.

"I imagine once it was put out they had dowries of five thousand pounds their prospects improved."

That had been true. Cassandra had never thought of it that way before. Still . . .

"I have plenty of money. Thirty thousand pounds is a goodly sum. My father has even invested a portion of my inheritance. He's told me that several times."

"What sort of investments?"

She did not like the way his brow furrowed as if there might be a problem. "Good ones," she answered, although she actually didn't know any of the details. Soren's questions were making her uncomfortable. "There will be enough for us to live on. Even to purchase a London home." After all, everyone knew she was an heiress.

"Come," she said, heading for the door. "Let us call on Father and he can explain everything to you."

"Very well." Soren opened the door. "I should warn you, we will be walking."

So that was it. He wished they could take a hack. She smiled her reassurance. "Soren, everything will soon be better. We may walk to Papa's house but we'll ride back to the hotel. Besides, I have good walking shoes." She raised an ankle to show him the kid leather pair she'd put on that morning. "They are the finest ever made. And you had best become used to those words, because from now on, my lord, you are a wealthy man." She sailed out the door.

HER FATHER HAD purchased the London house when Cassandra was fifteen. Until that time, they had lived in rented establishments.

The house was in Mayfair and had been owned by a marquis who had sold it to go off on an excursion to Greece. Cassandra had enjoyed living there. Her father had purchased new furnishings and it was the very height of fashion and comfort.

However, Cassandra had never stood on her doorstep as a guest before.

"Be prepared for anything," Soren warned.

"I am." She hoped.

Soren lifted the knocker.

The family butler, and one of only two man-servants since male retainers were taxed and females weren't, opened the door. "Miss Cassandra," Bevil said as if happy to see her. He was a slight man with an elegant air that her father greatly admired.

"Bevil, we are here to see Papa. This is my husband, the Earl of Dewsberry. Announce us."

The butler's attitude changed. His shoulders squared as if he was remembering himself. "We'd heard you married a York. But I did not want to believe it. A *York*, Miss Cassandra—?"

"She is Lady Dewsberry," Soren announced in a voice that brooked no contradictions. Nor did he wait for Bevil to invite them in. He plowed forward into the marbled front hall, and the butler stepped back. Cassandra followed in his wake because she wasn't about to be left behind.

"I wish to see MP Holwell," Soren said.

Cassandra half expected Bevil to tell them, "He is not at home." Instead, he answered, "The master has asked me to escort you to him. Lady Dewsberry"—he spoke as if the name was distasteful on his tongue—"I have been instructed to inform you that you are not welcome during this meeting."

"Not welcome? To see my father?" Cassandra didn't know what to make of that statement. She looked to Soren.

"It is probably for the best. I told you this might be a difficult interview."

That was true.

"This way." Bevil did not use Soren's title. He was rude. He would not have behaved in this manner when she had lived here.

Then again, a York would never have darkened their doorstep.

Soren made no issue of the matter and so Cassandra kept quiet. She watched as Bevil led him down the hall toward her father's study. After a moment, worry urged her to follow a few steps. She heard her father's surly greeting when his door was opened, and then it was shut.

Bevil did not return to the front hall.

Left alone in the hall, Cassandra looked around. The house seemed different to her, as if she had not lived in it for years. She realized that it was no longer a part of her, which was puzzling. How could she lose an attachment to the familiar in such a short amount of time? Perhaps because her loyalties had shifted? The marriage bed had bonded her to Soren. Even now, she wished she stood beside him. She needed the comfort of his person and his perspective.

There were no other servants wandering about at this time of the day. The downstairs maids would be in the kitchen helping Cook. The other manservant was the driver, and he only came to the house when required.

Cassandra started up the stairs. She didn't know how long the discussion over her inheritance would take but she had intended to collect a few things from her room, and so she should. She would also make arrangements with her maid, Abby, for packing some things for the Pulteney and the rest for storage until she and Soren purchased their home in Town.

The upstairs hallway was quiet. "Abby?" There was no answer. Cassandra wasn't about to search out Helen. At this hour of the day, her stepmother was usually at the shops.

She went to her room and opened the door. Her bedroom was decorated in apricot and periwinkle blue. The colors appeared girlish to her now. Again, she was conscious of having crossed some invisible threshold.

When she first walked into the room, everything seemed fine. Her wardrobe was closed and her bed made. The room was as tidy as ever—except the top of her dressing table was bare. No perfume bottles or ribbons or brushes. No books on the bedside table. Cassandra always had a stack of books there and even a pile on the floor. All was gone.

A bad premonition took hold of her. She moved to the wardrobe and opened the door. It was empty inside. Her beautiful gowns and dresses, her smallclothes, her shawls, and her shoes had vanished.

"My lady?"

Cassandra looked to the door. Abby stood there, her face so pale her freckles stood out in stark contrast. She quickly closed the door behind her as if not wanting anyone to know of Cassandra's presence. "My lady, I am so happy to see you." She spoke in a whisper.

"Where are my clothes?"

"The master had me pack them all up to sell. He ordered that everything should be taken."

"Even my hair ribbons?"

"He was a madman when he returned from the country. He tore everything out of your wardrobe and he was checking all of the drawers. He pulled them all out. Mrs. Holwell was shouting at him about everything being your fault. He kept saying he was ruined. What did he mean, my lady? It was frightening."

None of this made sense to Cassandra. "Ruined?"

"He wanted to know where your jewels were. I didn't tell him. I didn't. He shook me so hard, my neck hurt but I didn't tell."

Cassandra went cold inside. "Did he find the sapphires?" She touched the pearls around her neck.

"I don't know, my lady. He ordered me from the room, and only he and Mrs. Holwell remained. I could hear them breaking things as they searched. That is why your inkstand and little things are missing. They were all broken. The master and mistress didn't say anything to me when they left your room."

"But you didn't check?" Abby knew where the sapphires were kept.

"I'm afraid to do so. I don't want to know too much, but everything appeared to be left alone."

Cassandra nodded with understanding. "This must be Helen's fault," she said. She loved her father. She trusted him . . . but she'd always been wary of Helen. Her stepmother had been upset when Mr. Calder had forced her to give the jewelry to Cassandra.

Another memory from the day the solicitor had called came back to Cassandra. He had questioned whether all the pieces were accounted for. He'd asked about emeralds.

She'd been so overwhelmed and pleased with receiving the pearls, she'd not cared if Helen had kept the emeralds. The pearls were what was precious to Cassandra. When she had been a child, she'd sat on her mother's lap and stroked the pearls, fascinated by their creamy color and smooth surface.

Cassandra now walked over to her nightstand table. It had a false top held by a hinge. She removed the candlestick. The candle had never been lit, a sign it had been recently replaced.

Cassandra lifted the lid. Like her valise, the inside was lined in black velvet. She'd liked looking at the jewelry against rich material.

The sapphires were not there now.

Cassandra let the lid slam shut. She moved purposefully to the door. She must speak to Soren, to warn him.

"I did not tell him, my lady. I promise I didn't." Abby was openly crying now.

"It is not your fault." Indeed, it didn't make any difference whether she believed her maid's story or not. The jewels were gone.

Soren's earlier concerns now became hers.

Just as she opened the door, she heard Soren shout her name. She rushed for the stairs. He was at the foot of them, his hat already in his hand. *"It's gone,"* he said. "Your father stole your money."

"What?" She was confused. She started down the stairs. Her father stood off to one side, the set of his jaw mutinous, his body rigid. There were deep shadows under his eyes, and his clothes looked as if he'd slept in them. Bevil had returned to his post by the door.

Soberly, Soren said, "You have no inheritance, Cass. He spent it all. There is nothing left."

She paused halfway down the stairs. "Nothing? That can't be true. Papa—?"

At that moment, there was a pounding on the door.

Her father jumped to life. "Those are your creditors, Dewsberry," he said. "I sent for them. They want the money you owe them or they want Pentreath. Let them in, Bevil."

The butler obeyed.

Chapter 12

$\mathcal{N}o$." Cassandra charged down the stairs as if she could stop the door from opening but Soren blocked her way by catching her in his arms and gently setting her back on the step.

"Stay out of this, Cass. It will be all right—"

Before he could say more, three men marched through the door. One had the distinct look of a bailiff, including the silver badge of his office pinned to his plain wool jacket. The other two appeared prosperous. They did not remove their hats.

The bailiff looked around. "Lord Dewsberry?"

Her father pointed a finger. "There he is. That is your man."

Soren calmly said, "I am who you seek." To the other gentlemen, he said, "Hello, Brock, Lloyd." He did not introduce them to Cassandra.

They ducked their heads in a semblance of a

bow. "My lord," one of them said. "We didn't want to do this, but your note is past due."

"Huggett could extend it," Soren answered.

The one Cassandra believed was Mr. Brock agreed, "He could; however, he will not. He says you knew the terms. He has already been patient long enough. The bailiff has a letter from the court. Once you have signed it, your estate will transfer into his hands."

Soren was going to lose Pentreath Castle.

And he said she had no money. There was no inheritance. Cassandra was having trouble grasping what all this would mean. "Soren, what is happening?"

"These lads work for one Jeremiah Huggett. He is the man I owe. Where is the paper I am to sign?"

The bailiff was carrying a leather portfolio. He removed some papers. "Mr. Holwell, may we trouble you for a pen and ink?"

"Actually," her father said, "I wish you would take your business someplace else."

"We'll be done in a thrice, sir, once we have pen and ink," the bailiff countered.

"Bevil, fetch it." The butler left.

"No, wait," Cassandra said. "This is not right." She was horrified that her father was orchestrating Soren's demise. He knew what Pentreath

Castle meant to the Yorks. Why, it was as if he'd laid a trap for Soren.

Well, two could play those games.

She charged down the stairs. "Bailiff?" The man nodded. "I'm Lady Dewsberry and I want this man arrested." She pointed at her father. "And taken before a magistrate."

"On what charge, my lady?" the bailiff asked.

"He stole my inheritance." That was what Soren had said and she believed him.

That raised eyebrows. "You stole from Lady Dewsberry?" the bailiff asked.

At first, her father did not appear inclined to answer and then words burst out of him. But he didn't speak to the bailiff, he spoke to her.

"Your inheritance was spent on that ridiculous library of books you were so proud of and on the dresses you wore on your back. You tossed a fortune away just on shoes and hair things. Then there was the silliness of your 'literary salons.' Of course there is *nothing* left."

Her father had been drinking. The stench of brandy mingled with desperation.

"I had a fortune to spend," she countered. "At least thirty thousand pounds and you are saying it is all gone? I think not."

"Then you would be thinking wrong," her father snapped back.

"*What* did you do with my inheritance?" she repeated.

"It costs money to live in London," he said as if pointing out the obvious.

"But Mr. Calder said you received a handsome dowry when you married Mother. You were supposed to be just the guardian of my money."

"That man knew *nothing*."

"He knew enough to make you give Mother's jewelry to me." She approached her father. "The cost of gowns and my books would not approach thirty thousand pounds, especially if invested wisely. Where is the money, Father? Did it pay for this house? Your last two coaches? Even then, there should have been a fortune left over. Instead," she said, pointing a finger upstairs, "you have taken the sapphires and my belongings and done *what* with them?"

"I sold them."

She couldn't believe it. "You act as if you are destitute—" A new thought struck her. "*Are* you?"

It made sense. Lately, he had been grumbling about money. Then there was his quickness to toddle her off into spinsterhood.

Her mind worked furiously. "You've done your best to see that I *don't* marry these past two years and more, haven't you?" Could he truly be that deceitful? "You have turned down offers because you said you wanted a title . . . but what if you just didn't want anyone to learn that you'd spent my fortune? Especially if it had been supporting you—?"

"Birdie, I was going to earn it all back. I needed time."

"Earn it back? Are you a gambler?"

Fire came to his eyes. He did not like that charge. Then he would have been like one of the Yorks that he'd always railed against.

In fact, she realized, his insistence on his sense-less feud with the Yorks might not have been about pride at all. Perhaps it had been guilt?

"I'm not a gambler. I invested it. I tried to do my best but luck wasn't with me. I had *damned* luck. And now, everyone has their hand out. In-cluding you and Helen's daughters. Can you be-lieve they are asking for money after the dowry I handsomely settled on them—"

"*I* handsomely paid for their dowries," she said. "You told me to do it, and I'm not sorry. I would not begrudge my family."

On her words, the arrogance vanished from his demeanor, to be replaced with wheedling. He took a step close to her. "Then you have to under-stand, Cassandra, how hard it was to have control over all that money. It was a temptation. It gave me the chance to be important, and I planned to replace it all. Once I'd had a bit of success, I'd have given it back to you. But I was *rooked*. Several times." His hands curled into fists. "There are *liars* out there."

"What would you have done if Camberly had offered for me? You said that is what you wanted."

Her father's answer was a sharp bark of laughter. "He wouldn't have married *you*, Cassandra. He has his pick of anyone in London. I was not worried but his interest did open some doors for me."

Soren came up behind her as if worried by how erratic her father was beginning to sound. He started to say something but she reached back and squeezed his arm, silently asking him for a moment. Something was bubbling beneath the surface of her father's ranting. She would have it all out in the open.

"Why didn't you just tell me the truth about the money, Papa?"

"Because you didn't need to know. Besides, what would people think of me once they learned what I'd done?"

She understood. He was a proud man. She started to tell him as much, but he talked right over her.

"Your grandfather Bingham never gave me any respect. He thought I wasn't good enough for his daughter. That is why he wrote the will to favor you. But the money *should* have been *mine*. A wife's money goes to her husband. And yet he hired lawyers who knew the tricks and he made a fool of me. He's lucky I married his daughter. Most men wouldn't want another's leavings, especially when she's carrying his bastard. But I gave you my name and I've treated you well. I've kept the secret."

Now the world was not so certain. Or generous. Breathing became difficult.

She had trouble accepting the words that had come out of her father's mouth. They didn't make sense. Was he saying he wasn't her true father?

Soren placed strong, protective hands upon her shoulders, steadying her. "I believe that is enough, Holwell."

Her father sneered in response. He looked to Mr. Brock and Mr. Lloyd and the bailiff, raising a hand as if to present Soren and Cassandra to them. "Can you believe this? Even after Penelope died on me, I did what was right. And look what it has earned for me? A faithless daughter who hops into the bed of my enemy."

Soren lunged forward. Cassandra dug in her heels, to hold him back. She spoke, wanting, needing clarification. "You are not my father?"

The words said aloud answered many questions. In truth, they were not alike in looks, height, or temperament. And she'd never been able to please him, no matter how hard she tried . . .

MP Holwell lifted his chin in defiance. "I raised you, didn't I?"

He had. He'd also kept her at an arm's distance. He'd preferred her stepsisters over herself, and she'd never understood why. She'd thought the failing was hers. The only time he'd been happy with her was when her status as an heiress allowed them to attend the routs and parties of the titled and important. Otherwise, his abrasive personality would have shut him out.

"Is *any* of the money left?" she asked.

He started to answer and then closed his mouth as if he was a sullen clam.

"All my life I've been praised for my good sense and intellect," she said. "I don't feel clever now. Why didn't you tell me the truth, especially after my grandfather died? Why did you go on pretending?"

"You have my name. That is the truth."

"But you lied about any feeling for me."

"Of course I have some feeling for you."

"Do you? You were actually relieved I ruined myself at the Duchess of Camberly's, weren't you? You and Helen were anxious to ship me off and keep me unmarried because then no one would question where the money had gone."

"Well, the knowledge is out now."

More accurate words had never been spoken.

Cassandra looked around the hall at their audience—Bevil stood with pen and ink and a dumbfounded expression on his face. Mr. Brock and Mr. Lloyd appeared to have been fascinated by the unfolding of the story. The bailiff looked as if he wished he could just leave.

And then there was her husband, who had thought this marriage would save his family home.

"Cass? Are you all right?" Soren spoke close to her ear.

She looked back at him and wanted to burst into tears, but she wouldn't. She had to be strong. The sympathy she saw in his eyes was not good for her resolve.

Indeed, her knees felt wobbly as a complete understanding of what her father's faithless actions would mean to her. She had no money. She had no father. Everything she had thought about herself was a lie.

"You took my mother's sapphires." Her voice was quiet, but inside she had a strong desire to scream.

"What sapphires?" he said, looking right at her. He didn't even hide the fact he was lying to her.

Her fingers curled into talons. She could claw the smug smile off his face.

Soren's hold on her tightened as if he could read her mind. "He is not worth it."

"I'm not," MP Holwell agreed. "And you have other matters to worry over, such as where you and your penniless husband will live."

"I must insist these papers are signed, my lady," the bailiff said. He sounded regretful. "The court has ordered that His Lordship's estate be signed over to Mr. Huggett."

"Happy marriage, Cassandra," MP Holwell said. "Enjoy the bed you've made for yourself *as a York*." He turned and started back to his study, his step wobbly. "Throw them all out, Bevil."

To his credit, the butler did not move. He appeared as stricken as Cassandra with the news. "I'm sorry, my lady. I did not know."

"How could you?" she answered. Her gaze dropped to the gray marble floor. Her mind still struggled to make sense of everything.

Soren turned her around to face him. "We'll manage," he promised. "We will. Huggett isn't a bad sort. He only wants his money. The day may come when I can purchase Pentreath back from him. Believe in me, Cassandra. We'll come back from this." He moved to take the ink and pen from Bevil. "I will sign the documents here." He indicated a side table in the hall.

However, something he said struck her. Mr.

Huggett didn't want the castle. He wanted money. He wanted payment—

"Wait," Cassandra said. "Will Mr. Huggett accept payment for the debt?"

"That is what he wants, my lady," Mr. Brock answered.

"Then give him these." Cassandra lifted the Bingham pearls from around her neck.

"No, Cass—"

"*Yes*, my lord." She offered them to her husband. The pearls weighed heavy in her hand. Certainly they could cover whatever debt he owed. They were known for their perfection. "Pay the debt with them, please."

He didn't move. "They are yours. They are your mother's legacy to you."

"Do you have another way of paying *our* debt?" she asked.

Of course he didn't. His silence was the answer.

"The man who claimed to be my father has wasted everything that was mine on his vanity and pride. At least I know that by giving you these, you will secure the future for our children. Save our *son's* birthright, Soren. Do what must be done."

Her words did not reassure him. He appeared stricken, as if he'd failed her in ways that she could not fathom. He did not move toward her, and she thought she understood. There would be a cost to his pride. He had nothing to offer in return, except he had already given her so much. He had been here when she needed him.

Now, she wanted to be a buttress in his life as well.

Mr. Lloyd spoke up, "My lord? Do you wish to discuss this with Mr. Huggett? He might be very interested in the exchange. Those pearls are quite extraordinary. They could clear the debt and then some."

Still, Soren did not move.

"For *our* son," Cassandra urged. "So that he has something to inherit."

At last, he nodded, as if forcing himself to face what must be done. "I should see my wife to the Pulteney before I speak to Huggett."

"I can make my own way, Soren," Cassandra said. They still didn't have a coin for a hack. "Take care of this matter. Let's be done with it."

"I'll go with her, my lord," Abby said from the stairs behind her.

Cassandra smiled up at the maid, thankful for her loyalty. "See, all is well. Right and proper," she assured Soren. "You call on Mr. Huggett and I'll be waiting for you at the hotel. Don't let Holwell win."

It was her last words that moved him. She could see the change. He went from being conflicted to willing to fight with all he had. He kissed her. It was a hasty kiss, one performed in front of others, but it was also a promise.

"I will make this up to you, my lady."

The wedding vows that she had repeated without any actual understanding echoed in her head. "All I have is yours, my lord."

He nodded, and then faced Brock and Lloyd. "Let us see Huggett."

Cassandra watched them go out the door before standing one last moment in the house that had been her home. She looked to the butler. "Why, Bevil, you appear ashamed of yourself, as you should."

The servant's response was to duck his head and move down the hall toward the back of the house. He was still carrying the tray with ink and pen.

"Are you ready, Abby?"

"Yes, my lady. Let me fetch my bonnet."

In a few minutes, the two of them were out the door. It was late afternoon. Once they left the pleasant surroundings of Mayfair, the streets grew busier. Cassandra remembered walking this way with Soren, except she had a different attitude now.

She wasn't an heiress. She didn't know quite how she felt about that. The idea of being poor hadn't completely set in yet. That she was no longer apart from others because of money might not be such a bad thing.

Her father wasn't her father.

That was a thornier issue.

So, who was the man who had sired her? What sort of character did he have, and was he still alive? Her thoughts went to her mother who had carried a secret that was now the mystery of Cassandra's life. She reached up reflexively to touch the beloved pearls, and dropped her hand to her side when she was met with empty space.

She considered Soren and her deepening feelings for him. Had her mother felt the same way toward her lover? Had Cassandra received her passionate nature? And how could such a wealthy young woman be able to have what must have been a forbidden assignation?

Cassandra had been well chaperoned since she had first been sent out into Society. The Bingham Heiress would have been far more valuable than the Holwell Heiress—so why hadn't her grandfather been more vigilant?

"If he had, I wouldn't be here."

Cassandra didn't realize she had spoken aloud until Abby said, "I beg your pardon, my lady?"

"I was thinking."

Abby nodded. This was not the first time Cassandra had become lost in her own thoughts.

She looked to the maid. "Losing the sapphires is sad, but I will miss the books."

"I knew you would, my lady."

They had reached the Pulteney. Cassandra was exhausted. Today had been one of highs and terrible lows. Her legs hurt from the unaccustomed exercise, and yet it had helped her frantic thoughts to walk.

At this time of the day, the Pulteney was extremely busy. Cassandra faced the maid. "I had thought to ask if you'd like to be in my employ. I would still like to do so, although I'm uncertain of our circumstances. Perhaps once my lord and I are settled, we can discuss the matter?"

Abby blushed and bobbed a curtsey. "Thank you, my lady. I understand. I've seen difficult times myself."

Difficult times. Cassandra had never known one second when she had to fend for herself. She'd read about hardships and had heard lectures in church concerning them. She'd always assumed that she'd have the moral character to face them . . . but she hadn't truly thought she would ever do so.

"With the state my father—"

Cassandra stopped. "My father," didn't sound right. She tried again, "With the state your employer is in, I doubt he will welcome you back after you walked out the door with me."

"I know that Mr. Holwell will not keep me

in his employ," Abby assured her. "I knew that when he took your dresses away to sell. Don't worry about me. My aunt works for the Duchess of Bedford and there is a position in that household. I hadn't accepted it because I have enjoyed working for you."

"The Duchess of Bedford is a step up, no?"

"Yes, my lady. Well, you would have been a step up and I would have been honored to serve you. However, I need to see to myself."

"I'm not criticizing you at all, Abby. I believe you are quite wise. You can find your way home?"

"Yes, my lady, I walk this city daily. Be careful." Abby bobbed another curtsey and took her leave, and Cassandra found herself on the street alone.

It was a strange feeling.

She made her way to the reception. The clerk remembered her and bowed and scraped as he handed the key to her. Considering his reaction to the Dewsberry title when they first arrived, she wondered how he would act if he knew she was broke. She would soon find out. Bad news had a nasty way of making itself known.

Going up the stairs, Cassandra's mind puzzled over this twist to her life. It would have been nice to have had more dresses and definitely the smallclothes. However, her life of social obligations was about to end. What did people do who didn't have money?

She unlocked the door to the room and let herself inside. She crossed to her valise and removed the clothing and shoes. She treated them with respect. This was all she owned. Three day dresses, two gowns, the accoutrements she had needed to wear with each, and her nightclothes. Her sensible pair of walking shoes was currently rubbing a blister on her right heel because she'd never walked in them as much as she had today. She also possessed two pairs of the softest kid slippers ever made.

She took off the shoes and slipped her feet into a pair of the slippers. Immediately her feet felt better.

Once the valise was empty, she lifted the false bottom and picked up the garnet necklace and bracelet and her diamond hairpins. Why had she not thought to take the sapphires to Mayfield with her?

She held the jewels in her hands. These, too, she would give to Soren. She assumed they would be sold and she didn't mind. They didn't hold the sentimental value of the pearls.

She put the jewels back in the velvet-lined compartment and replaced the false bottom. She spent a few moments hanging her clothes. She must take good care of them now. She was also probably going to be her own maid. She knew little of pressing dresses and laundry. She hoped she wasn't going to have to learn about those things.

After she was done, she sat and wondered what else she could do. Evening was falling. She was tired and hungry. She had no idea how to find a meal for herself and no money to pay for one.

It would be nice to have a book. She had taught herself to read when she was the precocious age of four. She'd always sensed that books were important. Her first book had been her nurse's Bible. Nurse had been one for telling stories, and Cassandra's curiosity had wanted to know where the stories had come from. She now tried to keep fears at bay by thinking of those stories of faith and resiliency.

At some point, she dozed in the chair. A knock on the door woke her with a start. The room was dark.

"Cass?" Soren's voice said from the other side. "Let me in."

She'd never known such relief as having him return. She moved hesitantly toward the door, found the handle, turned the key, and opened it.

Light from the hallway sconces made her blink as she stepped into Soren's reassuring arms.

"Come down here and light the candles," he called to a porter sitting at the top of the stairs.

"Yes, my lord," the man said, and hurried into the room to do Soren's bidding. "I'm sorry, my lord, I didn't know anyone was in here."

Once the porter had left, she explained to

Soren. "His chair was empty when I came to the room. I didn't know to ask him to light the room and then I fell asleep."

He smiled, the expression tight. She could not tell if he was happy or not. "What did Mr. Huggett say?"

"My debt is paid. I own Pentreath."

"That is good?" She was asking because he didn't seem pleased. Instead, he paced the room as if dissatisfied.

He stopped, reminding her of nothing less than a caged lion sensing the air. "Yes. Good."

Her stomach knotted. She did not like his mood. It made her uncomfortable. Another first. She'd rarely worried about others' moods before, save her father's. Such is the life of the humbled.

"I will make this up to you, Cass."

He was standing no more than five feet from her, and yet she sensed there was a chasm between them.

"It is of no import," she lied.

"That is not true. Those pearls were valuable. Huggett knew a jeweler who recognized them. They are rather infamous."

She nodded. "I said they were known."

"I—" he started and then stopped. He pushed himself to go on. "I'm embarrassed."

She crossed the chasm, sliding her arms around his waist. This was good. This is what she'd been wanting. He held her tight. Holwell had been wrong about him, about them.

He drew away so that he could reach into his pocket. "The jeweler allowed me to save one of the pearls for you once I explained how important they were to you." He pulled out a single perfect pearl strung on a piece of black ribbon.

She touched the pearl. It was warm from his body heat. "Thank you." It looked lonely.

"Let me put it on you," he said. She turned, and he tied a knot where she wanted it.

Soren surveyed his handiwork. The single pearl rested on her breastbone. She could pull the ribbon over her head.

"Someday, I'll buy you a chain of gold for it. I promise. I will not let you down, Cass. I will make the most of your sacrifice. The money from the sale of the rest of the strand paid the debt on Pentreath with enough left to carry us through the year. Most of the servants have gone without wages. I'll be able to pay them and, if we are frugal, we will overcome this setback." He took her by the arms. "We'll build Pentreath up until it is the envy of all our neighbors and a proper home for an earl and his countess."

She smiled, her earlier gloom lifted by his confident determination . . . until understanding dawned about what he was *really* saying. "We are leaving London?"

Chapter 13

Soren was tired. He was trying to be optimistic and he didn't understand her question. It should be obvious to her they didn't have the money to live in London.

Carefully, he answered, "Cornwall is where our future lies, Cass. We will come back to London—well, actually, *I* will probably return by myself at first. I do have my obligation to the Lords, but even letting the smallest room available, I won't be able to afford to stay long, not with our financial circumstances. However, it won't be forever," he hurried to promise. "I know how to economize. Now that Pentreath is secure, we'll build a new life for ourselves. And of course, we'll take trips to the city from time to time." But it would not be in the near future. He knew that.

She took a step back, her brow worried. "I don't know."

What the devil did that mean? "Know? What do you wish to know?"

"I don't like the country."

He didn't like the stubborn note in her voice.

Soren kept his tone calm. He didn't wish to work her into a lather over nothing. "We are the earl and countess and belong at Pentreath. We are Cornish. It is our home."

"But I didn't feel comfortable when I lived in Cornwall." She took steadying breath. "They thought I was odd."

"Cass, no one in Cornwall thinks ill of you."

"I didn't say they thought ill of me. What I said was they thought me different from them. You knew that even when we were children. I am an outsider there. The happiest day of my life was moving to London. There is always something interesting to do and I have met women who are the same as me."

"Same as you?"

"Yes, women who think."

"Women think in Cornwall." *Keep your temper, Soren,* he warned himself. He had fought the wolf from the door. Now, he needed to make decisions that were in their best interest—and she argued?

"Yes, the women think," she agreed. "But not about anything interesting."

" 'Interesting,' " he repeated. "What does that

mean? Is it 'interesting' to realize we can't afford to live in London?

Her chin lifted. "I just don't believe you are taking my concerns seriously. Or that you are not listening to me."

Now, here was something he had heard before. Hadn't that been Mary's complaint against him— that he hadn't understood? He'd believed Mary's accusation had been because he was white and she a native . . . but that wasn't the case here. What if Mary had been trying to tell him that she had needed something more of him?

What if he *was* being too dismissive?

That was an uncomfortable thought.

However, the clear fact was, they didn't have the money to live in a city like London and re-build Pentreath. "Cassandra, life is about making good choices. If I could let you live in London, I would. But we don't have the money. Perhaps, *you* could be the one to make country life interesting. As my lady, you'll have the power to create the community you wish around Pentreath and you might find it very satisfying. I admit, I actually prefer the country. It is more relaxed so my thinking seems clearer."

"To the point of boredom," she countered. "There are no museums or plays. I don't like sport. I'm a timid rider. The only activities a gentlewoman can perform are church and good works. But the true problem remains, they *don't* like me there. You know how set in their ways they are. They don't admire clever women and I'm not pretty enough for them to accept me on looks."

Here was a charge he could sink his teeth into. "I don't know who told you that you are not attractive, but they are wrong. You are lovely, Cass, and beautiful to me. I am proud of your bright mind. I pray we have children with your intelligence."

"Says the man who owns the castle I just saved."

It wasn't just the denial of his words that set him back, it was the vehemence in her response.

He held up a warning hand. "Whoa. I'm trying to understand your feelings."

"You can't. Everyone likes you."

"They like you, too."

"That is a lie and we both know it."

CASSANDRA HATED ARGUING with him. He thought she was being ridiculous. He believed *he* was making the best decision.

But it wasn't one she wanted. Every fiber of her being rebelled against it. She had to make him understand. Not only was he her husband, he was now the only family she had.

"Soren, when I'm in the country, I feel as if I've been buried alive."

"Did you feel that way at Camberly's?"

"At the house party? Three hours from London? You know it isn't the same."

"Cass, you are—"

"*Cassandra.*" The word exploded out of her.

Her best intentions—to let him call her whatever he liked as long as he was happy—were suddenly a denial of herself. Her hands had balled into fists. "I prefer to be called Cassandra. I've said this before. You ignore me."

She waited, ready for him to belittle her desires.

A tense silence settled between them.

He spoke. "I must return to Pentreath."

"I will stay here."

"You can't. There is not enough money. But the most important reason for you coming with me is that you are my wife."

"Then why don't you want to please me? Why would you want me to be so *unhappy*?"

"Why must you be *coddled*?"

That charge upset her. "Coddled?" She warned him back with a raised hand. "I've just saved you from ruin and I don't receive a say concerning my future?"

"No," he answered. "I want you with me and I must return to Cornwall. I must return to my son."

That was not an answer she could have anticipated.

The world seemed to reel a moment in her mind

and when it righted itself, she looked to him, believing she'd misunderstood. "Son?"

"I was married before."

That news shocked her even more. She moved away from him. There was a chair by the desk next to the window. She sat, folding her hands in her lap, and leaned back against the hard wood. It was solid, unlike anything she was feeling right now.

Soren had a son. He'd been married. "Why didn't anyone tell me these things? Why didn't you?"

"Cassandra," he said, her name both a plea and an impatient demand for her to be sensible.

But she wasn't feeling particularly sensible at the moment. "You had time. I danced with you—"

"You actually were trying to do everything in your power not to dance with me," he reminded her.

She conceded the point. "But you could have mentioned a son."

"I did. I told you yesterday morning I wanted to save Pentreath for him."

She frowned. "I don't remember you saying anything of the sort."

"It was on the dueling field."

Cassandra shook her head.

"Well, there was quite a bit happening at the time. You can't be blamed for not fully understanding what I meant."

He had not followed her across the room but stayed his ground. That was good. She needed the distance from him to think. He had a son. A child by another woman. "This is a great deal to ponder on top of the other revelations of the day. Everything I believed about you is now suspect, just as everything I had once thought about myself, including who my father was, has turned out to have no more substance than mist."

"I'm not mist, Cassandra." He'd used her full name without any "witticisms" to it. "And I believe we can work together to build something of substance."

She didn't know if she agreed with him.

Now, he crossed the floor to her and took a seat in the chair on the other side of the desk. "She was a local from Upper Canada." He spoke as if she had asked the question.

She hadn't. She was incapable of managing clear thought.

"The marriage turned out to be unhappy."

She didn't look at him. Cassandra couldn't. Her thoughts were in turmoil. *Dear Lord, she was married to Soren, and she knew nothing about him. She knew nothing about herself—*

"There was a massacre. Mary was killed in it."

His statement startled Cassandra out of her dark daze. "Massacred?" Did he jest? No, his expression was too solemn. "What happened?" She had to ask.

"It was before the war. Shortly, that is. Things happen. People take matters in their own hands on the frontier."

"Who killed her?"

"It is not known. She was Lenape and it—"

"Wait, Lenape?"

He leaned an arm on the desk. "The Lenape are a tribe. Mary was native."

"Oh." Cassandra had no other response. She hadn't pictured Soren with a wife, let alone one who wasn't of his class.

When she didn't say more, he continued. "Mary's clan was not warlike."

"And they were massacred?" Cassandra vaguely remembered reading of such things happening. She'd not imagined it as anything that would impact her life . . . but it had been part of Soren's. He'd killed men. He'd fought. He'd known a world that was alien to her.

"Yes. By another tribe. I know nothing beyond that."

"You weren't there?"

He sat back. A wealth of pain and regret shone in his eyes, bringing home to Cassandra that they discussed a woman who had obviously been important to her husband.

"I wasn't there," he said. "She'd left me. She wasn't happy living in my world."

"Why not?" Cassandra asked with a surge of loyalty.

"I supposed she felt much like you do on the subject of living in Cornwall."

Cassandra experienced a jab of guilt. "I don't know that I would leave you over the decision."

He shrugged. "We each make our choices." His offhandedness worried her. That was not the sort of person Soren was. It meant his wife's leaving had impacted him deeply.

"Did anyone say anything when you courted a native woman?" she wondered.

"Native women and soldiers being together was common," Soren said. "Mary was an interpreter at the fort. She was well respected." Then gently he added, "They said something when I married her. That is the reason I left the military."

He'd given up his commission for his wife. He wanted Cassandra to move to Cornwall, but he had forfeited his career for this Mary. "Your parents couldn't have known about the marriage."

"They didn't. I saw no reason to tell them. I was living my life my way."

"But now you are back."

He didn't say anything.

A jealousy that Cassandra had not thought herself capable of feeling welled up inside her. "Did you love her?"

Love. Once again that word had popped up in her head.

He didn't flinch in answering. "At one time. I did very much so."

That was not what Cassandra had wanted to hear. "You must have been devastated when she was murdered."

The sorrow deepened on his face. "The marriage wasn't good, Cassandra. We were at odds. I learned that it was possible for two people to fall out of love and for reasons that could have been predicted. She left me to return to her people."

"Why would she do that?"

"First, the Lenape are a matriarchal tribe that is broken into clans. The husband lives with the wife's clan. Considering her work at the fort, I thought she had accepted white society. Once we married, well, it was all different. She wished to return to what was familiar and made sense to her. I had no desire to play Lenape brave."

"So, you let her leave with your son?"

"I didn't know about my child. She kept that from me. Maybe she didn't realize she was pregnant when she left. Or perhaps she was done with me. Thinking back, I realize now she was very lonely. I wasn't around. I had to earn money for us since I'd given up the military. I was setting up my businesses. I was busy and very involved in other things. To be honest, I expected her to see to her own needs. One day I came home and she was gone."

"Did you look for her?"

There was a beat of silence. "I knew where she was."

"But did you go to her? Did you talk to her?"

"Cassandra, she'd made up her mind, but, yes, I did go. She refused to see me. Her clan supported her. I was angry when I left. And I didn't hear of her again until after she died. Her brother delivered Logan to me. He was almost four years old and had no idea who I was."

"And you'd known nothing of his existence until then?" Soren was so resourceful, it was hard for her to believe he'd been completely unaware.

His gray eyes met hers. "I knew nothing until then. Mary wanted him raised in her culture and she knew rightly that I would be set against it. I would want him safe with me. And to be honest—"

"Ah, there is that word, 'honest.'"

He ignored her. "—in those days, I wouldn't have known what I'd do with a baby or have the time to care for him. Did I love her? Aye, at one time. I gave her all I had. But love can't thrive when two people become set against each other. In fact, I'm fortunate that her brother brought Logan to me. As I said, the Lenape are matriarchal and the other women in the clan could have decided to raise him. But there was no one left after the attack, and he knew where he was going would be dangerous. It was really only by chance that I learned of Logan's existence or that he was given to me."

"How did that meeting go?"

"Miserable. Logan had lost his mother, his grand-mother, his aunts. And he found himself with me."

"What did you think when you met him?"

Soren's expression changed. His eyes softened and there was a gleam of pride. "He's quick. Smart. And strong and healthy. The moment I lifted him into my arms, I felt a connection with him that was stronger than any bond I've known." He looked as if he couldn't believe how fortunate he was and once again, Cassandra felt the pangs of envy.

"I'd never intended to return to England," Soren confessed. "I liked Canada and I didn't like my father so much. Or Cornwall."

"I can empathize with the feeling."

He nodded acknowledgment "However, holding Logan changed everything for me. I found I wanted Pentreath for him. Over there, I watched fathers mentor their sons. They helped them become good men and that is what I want to do for Logan. He deserves his birthright, but I also want him to be worthy of it."

"So, you'd always meant to return to Pentreath after we married because your son is there."

Soren sat back. Somberly he admitted, "I hoped we could work out something that would meet both of our needs. Back when we thought there would be money," he added.

"And you don't think you were being a bit deceptive with me?" she wondered. "You knew I didn't hear you speak of a son yesterday."

"I did."

She drew a deep breath. "Then when were you going to tell me all of this so that I clearly understood?"

"When we had a moment together."

"We had many moments together last night," she pointed out.

A muscle tightened in his jaw. "We were preoccupied," he answered.

He was right.

And Cassandra didn't know how she would have reacted to all of this information if she'd learned it earlier. Would she have refused to marry him? This was not how she'd expected her life to be. Having *had* a stepmother, she had never thought to *be* one.

"Logan is my heir, Cassandra." His voice was firm. "I will not set him aside for anyone. Mary and I had a Christian marriage."

"She was Christian?"

"Yes."

That information surprised her.

"I will love and value our children," he continued, "but it is my hope, indeed, my deepest desire, that you will accept and nurture Logan."

"And how does he feel about all of this? Won't he wish to return to Canada?"

"Perhaps. Someday maybe and I will help him when he does. However, my concern is right now. Logan has had a great deal of upheaval in his life. While I'm here, he has been in my mother's charge. Pentreath is not Logan's first choice, either. Perhaps the two of you will have something in common."

He extended his hand across the desk. "We can make this marriage work, Cassandra. In spite of everything that has happened today, I ask you to believe in me. I also know I must return to Cornwall. Will you come with me?"

She looked at his hand.

"I doubt Logan wants a stepmother," she murmured.

"It will not be a problem. Logan is accustomed to listening to many women. It was part of his culture."

A new thought struck her. "Does he speak English?"

"Absolutely. I told you he was a smart one. His English is as good as ours."

"And he is how old?"

"Five, I think. There aren't good records."

"He must have a day that is known as his birth date?"

"The Lenape don't think of time as you and I. Age is also not that important." He lifted his hand, showing her it was still being offered to her.

She knew she had little choice. She had nothing. She didn't even know who she was any longer.

And what about Society? Was there anything for her in London? Once the gossip started about her father spending her inheritance, Soren would be a laughingstock. He'd married the heiress who wasn't.

Humbling, so humbling . . .

"I'm afraid, Soren."

"Of what, Cassandra?"

Of losing myself completely, she wanted to answer, but she didn't. Instead, she said, "I had dreams. I was going to set up an important salon and discuss great ideas."

"You may do that at Pentreath."

"A literary salon in Cornwall?"

"Why not? We could use great ideas. This will be a new life for both of us. We are both feeling our way."

"This is not what I expected my marriage to be," she confessed.

"Life rarely meets our expectations. But sometimes, when we are lucky, we discover things are better than we could have imagined."

Her thoughts went to last night, to being in his arms. He was right. She could never have envisioned that pleasure. Not even poetry did it justice.

She placed her hand in his. He lifted it to his lips and kissed her fingers. "Thank you. It is all out now. No secrets between us. I want you to know that."

Cassandra nodded. Did she believe him? She wasn't sure. Today had proven to her how little she knew of human nature. She'd been so naïve.

However, her acceptance was enough for Soren. He stood. "Come, the hour is late and I'm hungry."

At his suggestion, her stomach growled, although she could have claimed she was too tense to eat. Soren laughed and led her to the door. They put on their gloves and hats, she picked up a paisley shawl, and they left the room.

It was good to move and to be out in the fresh air, such as it was in London. Cassandra didn't say much. Soren didn't notice. He was in good spirits and happy to talk for both of them. He spoke freely about his son now.

They took their dinner at an inn several streets over from their hotel. "We are practicing economies," Cassandra repeated to herself as if it was a novelty.

It was.

They ate shepherd's pie and shared a pitcher of good local ale. By the end of the first mug, she relaxed and found her voice.

"I'm angry that MP Holwell—I refuse to call him Father—spent all the money and there is nothing I can do."

"We can call on my lawyer on the morrow before we leave London. He might know of some recourse."

"We'll leave tomorrow?" The idea wasn't as alarming as it had been. The ale had helped. She tapped her mug with a finger, signaling she was ready for more. With a dubious lift of his brow, he filled her glass halfway from a pitcher on the table.

She smiled her satisfaction and looked around the room. They were the only couple in the dining room. Everyone else was either single or in a larger party. There were also several families. The mothers appeared tired, while the children were full of movement. She tried to judge the age of the children, gauging where Logan would be.

"Logan," she repeated, testing the name.

Soren smiled. "I believe we should start brewing ale at Pentreath."

"Don't," she said, lifting her mug. "I don't drink it." Or she hadn't before, but obviously she'd started.

His smile became a laugh, but she didn't feel he was laughing at her. He seemed content. He reached across the table and touched her often. Her acceptance of his, no, *their* circumstances had pleased him.

Then again, he didn't know what was going on in her head. Because if he did, he might not be so satisfied.

She had no mooring, she realized. The truth of her life was a question mark.

All she had was what she could experience in this moment, and although she smiled at Soren, she was conscious of a kernel of anger deep inside. He'd loved another woman.

She was second best and she was aware that he'd never used the word "love" with her.

Her son, when he was born, would not be her husband's heir.

The thought caused her to down her ale. She would have asked for another, except Soren stood. "Come, wife," he ordered playfully. "I'm tired and ready for my bed—and for you."

That didn't seem such a terrible idea.

He tucked her hand in the crook of his arm and they went back to the hotel. She was glad he held her steady. She had to concentrate to walk.

Cassandra was amazed to discover that she could be so quietly furious with him, and yet want him to make love with her.

He hadn't been playing when he'd made his comment in the inn. He started pulling at her laces in the back of her dress practically before they'd entered the door of their room.

They didn't speak. They undressed. She was naked for all save the singular pearl around her neck.

He moved her toward the bed. She stopped him, grabbing his wrists. He let her hold him. His head lowered. He kissed her skin in the tenderest of places. He whispered words to her, calling her "golden" and "bold" but he did not try to break her hold.

That didn't mean he didn't touch her in other ways. She could feel his erection between them. He pressed it toward her.

Had she thought to control him? Why did she hold back? And then she understood—she wished he understood how hard it was for her to lose so much. His plans had not been her plans.

His lips brushed her ear. "If it could be any other way," he whispered.

He knew.

She wasn't certain if his knowledge reassured her or made her angrier.

His knee came between her legs and he eased her onto the bed. He found her lips.

This kiss was not like their others. It was emotional, raw, needy.

She wrapped her legs around his hips, bringing her to him and yet she wanted to push him away as well. She stretched out her arms, letting him lie upon her.

He found his way to her. He didn't need his hands because she was more than ready. He went deep, deeper than he had the night before.

Their kiss changed. His tongue thrust with hers. It was as if she could swallow him whole. She groaned, the sound primitive and passionate.

In answer, he rolled onto his back, taking her with him. The kiss broke in surprise as she realized where she was. She sat on top, her knees a vise keeping him in place.

And she still held his wrist.

He looked up at her. His eyes were dark with desire. "Have me, Cass. Do as you wish."

She didn't understand what he meant until he moved, lifting his hips.

This was good. Very good.

The ale in her blood heated with lust. She was angry, and yet passion poured out of her. She released her hold on his wrists.

This was their marriage—and here, on this bed, she was his equal. She'd not have it any other way. Her hips matched his pace and then she set her own. She demanded. The pearl around her neck swung with her movements.

And he was wild as well.

He held her hips, encouraging her to take. She liked him beneath her. Liked feeling she had power. Her arms rose into the air as if she was a goddess praising the universe, and she sank deeper down on him. It was good, good, *good—*

Her muscles tightened with a will of their own. Her body exploded with sensation. She *was* a goddess. She *did* own the universe.

And Soren was her mate. For good or for bad, he was hers.

He called her name. She was so lost in the moment of her coming, she heard it as if from a great distance, and then he flipped her over onto the bed. He spread her legs, lifting them in his arms and thrust deep and hard. Once, twice, and on the third, he let go.

She felt the rush of heat and the surge of his life force, and they were one.

He held her legs around his waist as if wanting her to hold him there. She obeyed. She had no will of her own. She had turned to stars and dust. She, who had known all power, was now without defenses. She nuzzled his ear and curled his hair around her fingers.

And she was still angry.

But she would go to Cornwall.

He moved first, rolling off her and gathering

her close, her buttocks against his hips. As was his way, he covered their nakedness with the bed-clothes.

She crumpled the feather pillow under her head, letting him hold her in his arms. The room smelled of them. She was wet between her legs. *Her* son might already be within her.

"I'll make it up to you, Cassandra." Were his words a promise or a plea?

He pressed a kiss on her shoulder. His whiskers scratched. She liked the feeling of his chest against her back.

Cass. His Cass, she wanted to whisper. Instead, she said, "I wonder who my father is."

He shifted, bringing himself closer as if he could protect her. "There might be someone who knows in Cornwall. Who remembers from that time."

"But what if it is something I don't want to know?" She stared at the wall on the other side of the room. "Some lies have been good to me."

"Until the truth interferes."

She stirred to look over her shoulder at him. He watched her carefully. "Would I be happier to know that perhaps a great lord was my father? Or a groomsman? Or a traveling tinker?"

"Will it matter to your life right now?" He lifted a lock of her hair and smoothed it back.

"Nothing matters right now," she confessed. "Except this." She could feel he was aroused again.

He kissed her neck before whispering, "Another go?"

Of course.

Desire was a good foil for anger.

Her body was tender from the intensity of their last time. Consequently, she experienced even his slightest movement more keenly than ever, almost to the point of needle-sharp pain, and still her blood sang with the joy of being a part of him.

It was quick, forceful, and satisfying.

When they were done, she was finally exhausted. The anger might return on the morrow, but for now, she finally knew peace. It had been his gift to her.

At last she understood women like her stepmother who followed her husband around as if he was all-important in her life. She could even sympathize with Dame Hester, who had such an old husband.

Was Letty Bainhurst right to cuckold her lord?

Cassandra didn't know. However, she could appreciate lovers in any situation.

She moved so she could study her sleeping husband in the dark's shadows. She'd not told him about the garnets, nor would she.

The pearl he'd given her was still on its ribbon cord around her neck. She caught the gem in her hand. Its luster shone in the moonlight.

The truth, she realized, was whatever one could make others believe.

It was time she discovered her own.

Chapter 14

The next morning, Soren roused her by whipping the covers off the bed. Cold air hit her skin. She reached for the counterpane, not ready to leave the bed's warmth.

She was usually an early riser but yesterday had been a day of too much emotion. She curled into a ball, her pillow scrunched in her arms, and tried to continue sleeping.

He wouldn't let her. He bounced on the bed beside her. "Come along, love, the day is marching on."

Love?

She opened one sleep-crusted eye in surprise. He was fully clothed, boots, jacket, and all. He even wore a dashingly knotted neck cloth.

He didn't gaze at her how she'd imagined a lover would. This was not a moment of soul-wrenching fervor. No, he looked at her as if he was impatient for her to start moving, albeit with a smile on his face.

"I'm ready to eat," he prodded, playfully walking the line of her shoulder with two fingers. She reacted to the tickle. "Wake up, Cass-an-dra," he cooed. "The day is passing."

She doubted his words and kept her eyes closed tight. In her dreams, when she received a declaration of love—a meaningful one, she corrected—she had always imagined herself in a lovely gown with rosettes and lace. She'd look absolutely perfect when he declared himself to her.

Instead, she smelled of her own body and of him and sex. Her hair probably looked as if she had been in a windstorm. It didn't matter. She never appeared her best first thing in the morning, especially when she'd been sleeping hard.

He could not possibly find her attractive, and for that reason alone, it was best she stayed right where she was.

As if giving a lie to her thoughts, Soren whispered close to her ear, "You stay in that bed much longer looking as delectable as you are, you might be my breakfast."

That brought her awake. She sat up, holding the sheet to cover her breasts and pushed the mass of her hair back. Why, there were grainy bits of sleep in her lashes. "Delectable?"

His smile turned knowing. "Deliciously so."

"Soren, I look a fright."

He raised himself up and kissed her. Whatever protests she might have offered evaporated. They knew how to kiss very well now. Their practice had perfected it.

And then he broke the kiss off. "You could use some tooth powder," he murmured, the twinkle of jest in his eye.

Her response was to grab him by both ears and kiss him again. And he laughingly let her wrestle him to the bed, where their kisses began to take on heat.

"To the devil with breakfast," he whispered in her ear, his hand going to her breast.

Cassandra derived great pleasure for picking *that* moment to hop out of the other side of the bed. "I'm so sorry. I must use tooth powder," she said airily, going to the washbasin and picking out her brush. The tooth powder was already sitting there. She was happy that Soren was a man who valued cleanliness—

His hands cupped her breasts. His body pressed against her as he nibbled that spot just below her ear that always weakened her resolve. "Your teeth are fine."

She put the brush in her mouth and made a garbled sound.

His lips curled into a smile against her skin.

His hand dipped lower down her belly to more responsive places. "I don't need you to talk, Cass. I just need this." His fingers slid intimately between her thighs and she forgot about her teeth. She wiped her mouth with a linen towel.

He was unbuttoning his breeches. He bent her forward and entered her. Her legs went weak from the pleasure. His hand around her waist held her up or else she would have fallen to her knees.

Who would have imagined this? She could barely breathe. She tried to talk but all she could whisper was "Please, Soren, more."

And he gave her what she wanted. He always did.

The moment was heightened by glimpses of their reflections in the small looking glass over the basin. Her face was flushed. His was a study of concentration as if he offered all.

They both almost collapsed at the completion.

When she could find her voice, she admitted, "You've turned me wanton."

"I'm a blessed man." He sounded as if he'd been running a great distance.

Facing him, her hand went to his hard, flat belly, and she lightly rubbed the skin beneath his shirt. He kissed her forehead, her nose.

"We'll have differences, Cass. That is the way of things, but as long as I can reach for you and you reach for me, there is nothing we can't weather together."

She thought of the jewels she'd kept hidden, and the intrusion of his first wife.

Instantly, he sensed something was amiss. "Did I say something wrong?"

"No." She reached for her toothbrush to finish the task.

Soren didn't move away from her. He buttoned his breeches. "What is it? Go on. Speak your mind. As I said yesterday, I've told you the truth of all."

"Were you as honest with your first wife?"

He leaned against the wall. "No, I learned the importance of honesty from her. After she left, I realized that she had been turning her back on me for several months. I had thought it was the way of things between a man and a woman. I was busy. I traveled because I wanted my shipping company and trading post to be successful. Now, I realize that she was unhappy. Maybe even lonely. It wasn't her way to complain. She was a proud woman." He drew her close to him. "If I'm not doing what you need, tell me."

Did that request sound like the statement of a man who had merely married her for money? Or were those the words of one who had called her "love" before he'd taken her hard and fast? Even now, if he touched her, she'd fall into his arms again. Did that mean she "loved" him in return? Certainly the word had come up in her thoughts.

Cass didn't know the answers. She'd never seen passion between her father and Helen.

She'd read about it, as often as she could. There had been times when she'd stared at a sonnet or a poem trying to fully understand what was being said. She'd study the space between lines and wonder what was being left out.

Now she knew. She was also discovering that the knowledge of this mystery between the sexes didn't add clarity.

"You dress," he said. "I'll be in the dining room, unless you need me?"

She shook her head.

"Shall I order food for you?"

"Yes, that will be nice. What time is it?" She poured fresh water into the bowl.

"Around half past nine. I sent a note to Winslow Forrester, a solicitor who has done work for my family. I asked if he could see me at eleven." He ran an interested finger along the curve of her bare breast, as if he could not resist one last touch. Her skin tingled, hardening her nipple. With a regretful sigh, he drew his hand back and started for the door.

"Are we still traveling to Pentreath today?" she said.

"I would like to be on the road by early afternoon. That gives us five hours to reach the Rams Head, an inn I favor. Are you certain you don't need my services as your abigail?"

"I'd never be dressed," she answered.

He laughed his agreement. "I shouldn't overwork you." And then he did something that truly shocked her. He blew her a kiss. It was small gesture, a playful one, and yet it slipped past her guard.

Cassandra stared at the door after he had left. Why, a little over a week ago, she'd been wishing he would disappear.

And here was her confusion—she was still angry and she didn't believe it was with him. But he made an excellent target.

Perhaps she and Mary had much in common.

It had been unfair of Mary not to tell Soren he had a son, but Cassandra could see how anger might convince a woman to keep secrets. After all, Cassandra had the garnets.

Cassandra gave herself a quick but very thorough cleaning with the milled soap from her valise and a linen cloth. The scrubbing gave her a sense of some control. She dressed and tried to do something with her hair. She had never been good at styling it herself. She ended up knotting it at the nape of her neck and holding it with the diamond pins. She should purchase sensible hairpins, but not just yet. She put her things back in her valise. She still wore the pearl around her neck.

The time was closing upon ten when she presented herself in the dining room. Soren's nod of approval for her appearance was all she could have wished. He pulled her chair out for her. "You are lovely."

"Thank you," she murmured with a flush of shyness over the compliment. She looked around the room and realized that many eyes were focused on them. "Are you certain there isn't anything wrong, though? Everyone is staring."

"They are staring because you are tall and beautiful."

That brought a deeper blush to her cheeks.

Cass didn't know how to respond to flattery. She knew she had even features, but she'd never garnered any male attention for anything other than her money.

Of course, there had been that evening when Mr. Roger Edmonds, the poet, had kissed her, but he didn't count. He was an odd character. Whereas Soren, even as impoverished as he was, would have been many a debutante's first choice—especially once he smiled at them.

He had finished his breakfast but he waited for her to eat. A waiter placed a plate of sausage and toast in front of her. She was famished.

As she tucked in her food, Soren observed with

a wicked wink, "You have an appetite this morning, my lady."

"Pleasing you is hard work," she replied, a piece of sausage on her fork ready to pop into her mouth—

The clearing of a masculine throat prevented her from eating. The Duke of Camberly had approached their table and had overheard her comment.

Soren laughed and stood out of respect to his friend's title. Cassandra wished she could crawl under the table. She started to stand but the duke waved her to sit.

"Please remain in your chair, my lady, and finish your meal. And don't look so mortified. I envy my friend. I'm happy the marriage seems off to a good start."

"Please join us, Your Grace," Soren invited easily.

Cassandra had set down her fork and knife. First, it was always uncomfortable eating in front of someone who wasn't dining. Secondly, she caught herself comparing the two men. She wondered if God had brought the duke to their table as a test.

Yes, Camberly was extremely handsome. Almost physically perfect. She understood why at one time she'd been excited over the thought that he might have been interested in her.

However, now she believed he lacked the character Soren possessed.

Indeed, the duke didn't look as if he was feeling quite well. There were dark circles under his eyes, the sort that were caused by anxiousness.

"I can see that Lady Dewsberry won't eat in my presence," he said, taking a step away. "I didn't mean to disturb you."

"Please sit, Your Grace," she heard herself saying. "Have you eaten yet?" The words flowed out of her. Before she'd been too self-conscious around Camberly to say very much of anything. Their conversations together had been quite stilted as a consequence. However now, her concern for him set her at ease.

"That's very kind of you. But I can't intrude any longer."

"We are traveling to Pentreath today," Soren said. "If you have the opportunity, it would be an honor if you visited."

"I may." The duke shook Soren's offered hand but he did not let it go immediately. He looked from Soren to Cass and smiled, the expression sad. "I'm envious of your obvious *true* affection for each other."

On those words, he released Soren's hand and went striding toward the door.

Soren sat. He leaned toward Cassandra. "Do I have a reason to be jealous?"

She grinned. "Are you?" She bit into the sausage.

"A bit. You were once quite taken with his looks."

"You knew that?"

Soren's gray gaze met hers. "Sometimes, Cassandra, I believe I know everything about you."

"Not everything." It felt good to be able to say that, especially after the day she'd had yesterday. She picked up a piece of toast. "Although you do know what I like for breakfast."

"You are English. We are predictable." He rapped the table once and said, "Spill it, what were you thinking when you were talking to Camberly?"

"I was thinking he appeared quite downcast. Did you not notice?"

"No, I was too jealous."

That made Cassandra laugh and then she stopped, struck by a new thought. "If I had married the duke, do you believe Camberly would have stayed beside me once he learned MP Holwell had spent all my inheritance?"

"Matt is a good man. However, you are not dispelling my jealousy."

"I do not believe you have anything to be jealous over, my lord." MP Holwell had been right—Camberly would never have chosen her. Her statement made Soren smile. "However, I sense the duke is upset."

He reached for a piece of her toast. "And why do you think he is?"

"I believe he is not taking Letty Bainhurst's defection lightly."

His brows rose as if she might be right. "It is still a good thing she has ended it."

"I don't know. I've never had a broken heart."

"Camberly's supposed love life doesn't interest me. My focus is on you and Logan. Come, let us see what can be done about Holwell stealing your inheritance."

MR. FORRESTER WAS a thin man with a pleasant disposition. He treated Soren with respect and, of course, extended that courtesy to Cassandra. He apparently was working with Soren on properly entailing Pentreath Castle. Part of the pearl money would go to that endeavor.

After Soren laid out what he and Cassandra knew about her inheritance, Mr. Forrester gave the matter a moment's thought before saying, "You are quite right, my lord. There probably is little money left in Lady Dewsberry's inheritance. This is not a singular case. There are often dangers when a guardian has control of a minor's money. It is well known that MP Holwell spends prodigiously. I have heard rumors of disastrous investments he's made. I wondered why any sane man would throw about money in such reckless manner, and now we know. Perhaps he was attempting to recoup losses. I admit I have been jealous of that new coach he purchased."

"You mean, that *I* purchased," Cassandra said.

"Quite so."

"There is nothing I can do?" she pressed. "He stole my mother's sapphires from me."

"If the jewels had belonged to his late wife, then they would have gone to him."

"Except my grandfather's solicitor visited and clarified that in my mother's will the jewels had been meant for me. He made my stepmother hand them over to me."

Mr. Forrester leaned forward. "Do you have a copy of the will?"

Cassandra sat back uneasily. "No."

"Do you know your grandfather's solicitor's name?"

"Mr. Calder. I am told he is well respected."

"He was. I regret to say he passed away several years ago," Mr. Forrester said. "Do you have any documents that can support your claim?"

"I do not. My father had those. I'm certain he will not share whatever papers he has."

Mr. Forrester's face grew long. "Then it is your word against Holwell's, my lady, unless someone else knows he took them."

Helen knew, but she would not side with Cassandra. Ever.

The solicitor continued, "As for the money, he will claim he spent it, as a guardian should, on your welfare."

"Then may I claim his London house?"

"We may try . . . but again, do you have documents naming you as your grandfather's sole heir?"

"Everyone knows he left his fortune to me," Cassandra answered.

"But we don't have papers that say as much, do we? I'm not trying to beleaguer you, my lady. However, the courts will demand proof."

"If Mr. Calder is no longer with us, then it will be my word against MP Holwell's."

"Exactly. Including any discussion on *how much* money you were to inherit."

"Or whether or not I owned the sapphires."

Soren leaned toward her. "It is up to you. If you wish to go after him, I'll give it all I have."

But they didn't have much. Cassandra stood. "Thank you, Mr. Forrester. I appreciate your counsel." Soren followed her out of the office.

Outside on the walk, he placed his hand on her arm. "We do not need the money from the sapphires. Your pearls have given us enough. We will manage."

She shook her head. "The money never seemed real to me. But those jewels are all I truly had of my mother." She touched the pearl on its ribbon.

She thought of the garnets she kept hidden. "As time goes by, I grow further and further away from her. I used to remember her perfume, but now I can't recall it. Sometimes I can see her face, but it is hazy. And there are many things I wish I knew about her. Such as the story of my father. I wonder why he did not do what was honorable?"

She squared her shoulders. "Are we taking the mail to Cornwall? Or do we have the funds to travel privately?" She believed she was being very brave to put forth the idea of the mail. It was a horrible, crowded way to travel, but she'd do what she must.

"I thought we would go by chaise."

She couldn't hide her relief, and Soren laughed. While she prepared for them to leave at the hotel, he made arrangements for a vehicle. Within two hours, they were on the road.

And Cassandra regretfully said farewell to the city that had once been her every dream.

Chapter 15

One thing Soren had learned over his years was that chasing vengeance was an empty endeavor. There would come a time when Holwell would pay for his betrayal, but it would not be at Soren's expense.

He firmly believed the best action he and Cassandra could take was to pour their energy into something that had meaning, such as Pentreath. His vision was of the two of them and Logan living as a family.

He knew Cassandra had doubts. He'd had a moment's twinge when he'd brought the post chaise and driver to the hotel to collect her. She could have bolted, but she hadn't.

And he was pleased, because he was in love with his wife.

Deeply in love.

And it had little to do with their bed sport, although that made him very happy. Every man wanted a partner who matched him in passion.

However, Cass had always attracted him. The youthful infatuation he'd felt for her had given way to a strong admiration for her resilience. He knew how hard leaving London was for her. He'd felt the same when he'd left Canada.

She had stared out the window as they rode through London as if she would memorize all the sights and sounds.

Once they left the city, she'd lowered her head, resting it in her arms as if in deep grief.

"It will grow easier, Cassandra."

She nodded but didn't look at him. In time, she fell asleep in that pose. He reached over and gently pulled her to rest her head on his shoulder. His thought was to make her comfortable—

"Why did you marry your first wife?"

Ah, so she wasn't asleep. Soren shifted his weight so he could settle them both more comfortably in the close quarters of the post chaise's interior. The road was good here and the ride smooth for a hired vehicle. The afternoon sky had promised rain, but the clouds were beginning to clear.

He answered her question because he had vowed honesty. He wanted her trust. "I thought she was the most exotic woman I'd ever met."

Cass stirred. "Exotic?"

"Being an interpreter is man's work. She didn't hesitate to take her rightful place. I told you the Lenape were matriarchal."

"To the point they'd let their women roam freely?"

"Her father trusted our commander. We valued our native allies and knew our boundaries. Mary was treated with respect."

Her head returned to his shoulder. "I can't imagine having such freedom. Or purpose." Her voice was wistful.

Soren found her hand and laced their fingers together. "You will have freedom in Cornwall," he said, wanting to make his point. "You will be the lady of Pentreath. You may do as you wish."

"But what will there be to do?" She paused and then added, "Besides pleasing you?"

"Cassandra, there will be plenty. Were you raised on a pillow to be carried everywhere?"

"I was chaperoned and escorted and watched everywhere I went," she said in her defense. "My father insisted on approving who I saw and what I did . . . while he was stealing what had been rightfully mine. It was all a ruse."

"Then live a *real* life," Soren answered. "Find what gives you meaning."

"It is easy for you to say those words. You are male. You can do whatever you wish."

"That is nonsense. We all have restrictions. Mary had more liberty to make her own choices than I had as an officer. They told me I couldn't marry her. They were set against it. I made the decision to choose my own path."

"And now you are back in this world."

"By *my* choice. And for a strong reason." He leaned back in the seat. "This is not the journey I thought I wanted. However, good things have come to me."

"Such as?"

"You." He couldn't believe she had to ask. "I have you now."

And I love you, he could have added, but he didn't. She'd not believe him. Her heart was too busy mourning for what she believed she had lost. There was no room for him right now. A humbling truth. But she would rise above her disappointments, and when she did, he planned on being right beside her.

Cass was quiet for a long time. Her head rested on his chest, directly over his heart.

"I wish I did have a new dream," she said at last.

"You will, love. You will."

HE'D DONE IT again. Called her "love." Was it just an easy word for him?

Did he know how wary it made her feel? And how vulnerable? She knew he wanted her to trust him, but she didn't dare. After all, she was on the way to Cornwall.

Cassandra sat up. The time had come to quit moping. She looked out the window and took in the sight of the driver riding the lead horse. This would be her view for days.

Soren pulled a pack of cards from his jacket. "Do you wish to pass the time?"

"I'm not a good card player."

"Then let me teach you." He waved a hand for her to scoot over to her side of the seat so they could use the space between them for their cards.

Playing games turned out to be a good idea. It did shake Cassandra loose from thoughts that were dangerously full of self-pity. Both she and Soren knew it.

His mind was quick with math and numbers. He remembered the cards.

As for herself, she was hopeless at piquet. She rather enjoyed a form of faro that they designed for themselves, but she lost more than she won. They played with imaginary money, and she was soon deeply in debt to him.

"I'd rather be reading," she grumbled as she lost again.

"Is that how you usually travel?"

"Always with a book," she answered. "I had been looking for a book the night I ended up in your room." The incident seemed ages ago.

"Then I am blessed you like to read." He gathered the cards to shuffle.

She sat back in her corner of the vehicle. "If you keep speaking this way, Soren, there will be those who will think we are a love match."

Her words had been spoken lightly, but once they were in the air between them, they took on a deeper meaning.

Gray eyes met hers. His lips parted as if he was going to say something, and her breath caught, waiting, hoping . . .

He looked away, focusing his attention from her to the cards he deftly shuffled.

She could have cursed. She shouldn't have used those words. And yet, she believed Soren valued her for more than the money she was supposed to have brought to the marriage, and found herself yearning for words from him of what he truly thought of her. After all, in poetry, it was the gentleman who made the grand declarations. It seemed safer to her that way.

"I'm tired of cards," she murmured.

"Then I will tell you stories," he answered, and he did. He spoke about his adventures in Canada. Cassandra didn't know that she wanted to listen to him. She leaned against the door so that she could look out the window at the passing scenery. It would take them days to travel to Pentreath.

Against her initial desires, she found herself caught up in his narrative of native tribes and soldiers, of an untamed country, and of the foolhardy souls who were bent on seeking their fortune. Soren could tell a story. In fact, listening to him was better than reading.

And at some point, her sense of the world righted, just a little.

In this manner, they arrived at his favorite inn, the Rams Head.

Soren was greeted with a glad shout. The innkeeper, Mr. Piper, had seen service in Canada as well. He couldn't bow and scrape enough to Soren and Cassandra. His wife took them to a private room for their meal. It was a simple repast of roasted capon and barley and vegetables, but it was tasty.

The cider served was Mrs. Piper's pride and joy. "The recipe has been in my family since before my grandmother."

"Sit and have a drink with us," Soren invited.

"Oh, no, I can't, my lord," she said.

"Of course you can. Where's Piper? I've been boring my lady with stories all afternoon. It is time she heard from a true storyteller." Ignoring Mrs. Piper's protests, Soren went and fetched her husband herself. The portly innkeeper didn't have any hesitation at sitting and swapping stories with Soren, while his wife was so nervous, she barely touched her cider. However, she did look pleased to be in such company in spite of needing to excuse herself from time to time to the kitchen.

"You stay here," she said to her husband, as if sensing this was a good thing for him.

Cassandra was fascinated by the camaraderie between her husband and Mr. Piper. She couldn't imagine her father sitting with an innkeeper and his wife. He would have been too proud.

The stories they shared were different from the ones Soren had told her in the post chaise. As the evening progressed, and the cider was sipped, the two men talked of battles for new frontier. Occasionally, the story was left unfinished. She sensed they didn't feel it necessary to trouble her.

The table candles sent flickering shadows across the wall behind Soren. He was leaning in the chair, his long legs crossed, a smile on his face over something Mr. Piper had just said. He looked the picture of a country lord at ease, and she was suddenly glad he was away from that frontier. Away from war.

And that he had brought his son to a land of peace.

She slipped her hand in Soren's. He smiled at her before laughing over a quip from the innkeeper, and she found herself content.

The hour grew late. Mr. Piper stood. "I must

help Carrie. I've left too much of the burden on her this night. Thank you, my lord, my lady. You honor the Rams Head with your presence. Is there anything I may fetch for you?"

"We're fine, Piper. In fact, I believe we'll be happy to be taken to our room," Soren said.

"Come with me, my lord. I had the lad take your luggage up, and we have fresh hot water in the pitcher."

Soren helped Cassandra stand. Rising, she realized how tired she actually was.

Their bedroom was well-appointed. There was nothing fancy about it, but the sheets were clean and the bed ropes tight. There was a desk and chairs, and she thought it far more to her liking than the Pulteney.

They didn't waste time in seeking their bed. She thought she would fall asleep in a blink. Instead, she lay awake. Finally, she rolled toward him, wondering if he was asleep.

He wasn't. His eyes reflected the moonlight from the window. "I can't sleep, can you?" he asked.

"You've spoiled me," she confessed. His smile widened and he reached for her.

The mood of their coupling was different from the other times. She began to understand that this act between them could be a primitive need, or a reassuring ritual, or a way to communicate what couldn't be spoken.

Soren took great care this night with her. He savored her skin with his kisses. His touch was a caress. It was as if he wanted her to know he was sorry she was not completely happy with the choices they had been forced to make.

She blinked back tears because a part of her still resisted and always would. He kissed away those tears.

When they were done, she put her arms around his neck and rested her head against his chest. "It will be good," he whispered.

She nodded, and realized that whether it was or it wasn't, he was the only person in her life who cared what happened to her. Even if he didn't understand her . . . or so she thought.

The next morning, when Cassandra prepared to climb into the post chaise, already weary of travel before the day had begun, she discovered a book sitting on her seat.

Chapter 16

Soren had been waiting for her to go to the coach. He was ridiculously pleased with himself for what he'd done.

Also a bit uneasy. It was a book; however, the topic . . .

Cassandra, looking delightfully charming with her hair curled over one shoulder beneath her bonnet, picked up the book and held it as if she had been given a bar of gold. She read the title, and then her brow lifted in confusion. "*Practical Education*?"

Soren winced. "I know it isn't the most enticing subject. Someone left it at the inn. Piper doesn't read, and once I told him the title, he was happy enough with ten shillings for it." Books were expensive. Ten shillings was all Soren could reasonably afford. He'd been lucky. "You may not want it, either."

She opened the cover to the first page. "The

author is female. Maria Edgeworth. I've heard of her."

"Truly?"

"Yes . . . she writes silly popular novels. They are romances, I think."

"With a title like *Practical Education*?" He grinned. "If it is a romantic novel, what do you believe is being taught?" He let his voice take on heat so his intention was clear. "Hopefully something very 'practical.' " Their driver, who waited at the head of the horses, guffawed his agreement.

Cass playfully slapped his arm with the book. "Behave."

"Yes, dear," he said with false meekness. She gave him a teasing frown as she climbed inside the vehicle. She carried the book with her.

Soren nodded to the driver that they were ready to go. While the man mounted the lead horse, Soren took his seat and closed the door. With another wave, they were off.

Cass put her nose in the book. "I am not one for light novels," she said again.

Soren pointed out, "It says volume one. If it is a romance, it must be epic if there is more than one volume to it."

"Perhaps you should write *your* memoirs, my lord," she suggested, giving him half of her attention.

"That would be at least ten volumes," he assured her, and she laughed in a way she hadn't since she'd first discovered Holwell had spent her money.

"I don't know if my feelings should be hurt by your laughter, wife," he mock-complained.

Her answer was to kiss his cheek. She slipped her gloved hand in his. "I was thinking five volumes. Several of which haven't been written yet." She held up the book. "Thank you for this."

"You are most welcome."

She smiled, and then pulled her hand away and went back to her book. Soren wondered if giving her such a gift didn't make him his own worst enemy. It completely absorbed her attention.

However, she didn't shut him out. After a bit of reading, she said, "This is not a work of fiction. I've read books of ideas written by women before. Mary Wollstonecraft wrote a treatise remarking on the importance of educating women."

"That doesn't sound like an interesting book, either."

Her smile was quick. "Oh, but it was. I agreed with many of the ideas."

"I'm unsurprised."

Her smile widened. "Listen to this." She read the opening paragraphs. "Miss Edgeworth wrote this with her father, or at least the first part on proper toys. They are attempting to inform the reader about raising children." She looked up at him. "Does one need a book on such a topic? Isn't it a standard understanding?"

"I don't know if my tutors ever read a book about how to educate me. They should have," he assured her. "I think I still have bruises from the knocks around my head, and the blows never helped my learning."

"But does one need to have toys explained? It seems odd to me to offer such instruction."

"There had been times I've sought advice, especially when Logan first came to me. When we were on the ship, I'd need to redirect his attention to keep him out of trouble. He does have a will of his own." That was an understatement. His son had not settled into Pentreath comfortably, and Soren wasn't certain why. His fear was that, as his mother direly warned, his son would never become a part of English Society. Logan mourned for his mother and the life he'd known.

"The authors refer to their thoughts as the 'art of education,'" Cassandra said thoughtfully.

"The topic is too dry for me."

She didn't answer. She'd dived back into the book, ignoring Soren, but he didn't mind. He would have purchased her a dozen books if he could afford it. The downheartedness that had hovered around her yesterday had dissipated.

She was an active reader. Her brows knit or lifted as a thought struck her. She pursed her lips as if in disagreement, or twisted them when she found insight.

From time to time, she shared. Holding her finger on the page to keep her place, she said, "Miss Edgeworth believes children are remarkably perceptive and sensitive."

"I agree."

"I've never met a child who wanted anything but a sweet treat."

"They like that as well."

"I was told to stay in the nursery and to keep quiet. Miss Edgeworth writes as if children have a curiosity we should encourage."

There was a telling statement.

"Did you never rebel, Cassandra? Or throw a tantrum?"

"Why?"

Her response puzzled him. "Because you were a child and there is more to life than four walls and a book."

"Books were my life," she answered. "They were my friends."

And they had nurtured her vibrant spirit, keeping it alive. If he'd had MP Holwell in front of him, he would have tied the man into a knot and thrown him into an ocean.

For all of her wealth, Cassandra's life had been

remarkably sheltered. No wonder she'd been considered such an oddity in Cornwall, where there was fresh air and open fields and a more relaxed manner. London hadn't been the salvation she'd believed of it. She'd just experienced a bit more freedom there.

A question came to her eye. "Why are you staring at me?"

"I'm staring?"

"Yes, as if you are trying to unlock my mind."

Perceptive as usual.

Soren leaned against her. "I am," he admitted. "Talk to me about the books that kept your imagination alive in your childhood."

She blinked as if surprised. "Why would you want to know that?"

"Because they were important to you. I was never much of a reader but I did enjoy the Roman myths."

"I liked them as well."

"Which was your favorite?" he asked, and what followed was the first conversation between them where he felt she was completely herself. There wasn't anything she hadn't read, and his respect for her intellect grew. Especially when she said, "My own education is spotty. Father was not one for spending money on teaching women very much of anything that couldn't snare them a husband. I didn't mind dancing and learning

French, but the lessons on handwork? You'd best not lose a button, my lord, or you will find yourself lacking."

"That's unfortunate, my lady, because you are very hard on my buttons." He indicated his breeches.

She lifted a brow. "Am I, my lord?"

"Terribly hard. Fortunately, I can sew on a button."

Once again, his reward was her laughter. Sweet, musical, and still slightly rusty from disuse—and he could not resist her. He reached for his wife.

"Soren, the driver—"

"Cannot see us." His lips were almost upon hers.

"But he might hear us."

"Not if we are quiet." He kissed her then, and to his everlasting gratitude, she set the book aside to kiss him back properly.

Or perhaps she realized his buttons were fair close to popping and she wished to save him a bit of sewing.

THERE WAS ONLY one way overland into Cornwall, and that was crossing the Tamar.

For the past two days, Cassandra had found herself lulled into the routine of digesting Miss Edgeworth's very direct advice on children and their education, or, at least, one volume's worth, and having her husband all to herself, which was a gift.

Their conversation on books had opened her to him. He didn't act bored or dismissive of the topics that interested her.

It was as if he genuinely cared.

In turn, she allowed herself to share bits and pieces of her that she'd always kept to herself.

Of course, it helped that the rest of the world was at bay while they traveled. She could pretend the events of the past or the future had no bearing on her—not that they didn't discuss the future.

She discovered Soren could go on for hours with his talk of cattle and sheep and his plans to reclaim a soggy patch of marshland for grazing. The herds were not where he wanted them. He had planned on using her money to add to their number. "But they will grow on their own," he assured her. "They'll breed, and all I need is patience."

He was not afraid to dream big.

She envied him.

But his true passion was his son. The child was never far from his mind, but Soren seemed to tread lightly on the topic. She knew his hope was that she would be a good stepmother to Logan.

She wasn't certain she understood how, but

as time passed, and her respect for her husband increased, she knew she would try to be all he wanted from her.

However, passing this threshold into Cornwall warned her that the haven she and Soren had created during their travels was about to end.

She leaned against the window. As the horses pulled them over Greystone Bridge, the coach bounced as if the bumpy road was leading them into an entirely different world.

Many thought of Cornwall as miles of coast, but she was from the moors and the forests. "And to the moors I return," she said.

Soren had been dozing in spite of the bouncing of the coach. He roused himself. "I beg pardon?" He sat up.

She shook her head. "I was just thinking. How much farther do we have?"

He looked out the window. "We crossed the Tamar, have we?"

"Yes."

"Then three or four hours more, depending on the roads. Thank the Lord we've had good weather. Do you wish to take a stretch of the legs?"

She did. He called out for the driver to halt.

The ground beneath her feet didn't feel any different on this side of the river than it had on the other. Even the wind was the same, and yet her senses warned her of the difference. There was the hint of salt in the air and the always present possibility of piskies listening. "Cornwall. The ends of the earth."

"Or the beginning," Soren said with his usual optimism. They walked along the road while the driver watered the horses. "It depends on the perspective. By the way, I had a thought. What if I asked for you to write a poem to me?"

"It would be a shabby thing. I'm no poet."

"But that doesn't mean you couldn't write a book. Like Miss Edgeworth's."

"Are you trying to give me a purpose to my life, my lord?"

"I am," he said, proving once again that he was very attuned to her thoughts.

It was an interesting idea. "What would I write about?"

"Whatever you wished. She wrote on a topic as deadly dull as education and yet you seem to enjoy her thoughts on the matter."

"That is what I am saying, I don't truly have an interesting direction."

"One will come to you, Cassandra," he said.

A strong wind blew around them. The day was fair but it could always rain. Her hair threatened to become undone. She tucked in a stray lock of hair. "I will find it here? Out in the wilds of England?" She let her doubts be known.

"You can only start where you are." He put a challenge in his voice.

"It is easy for you, Soren. You are male."

He feigned concern. "Did no one tell Maria Edgeworth only males should write? Perhaps we should notify her. She must cease. And are there not a half-dozen women penning novels?"

"Not even that number. See what I mean? You challenge me to do something that is not easy."

"Ah, so, it is the easy life you wish?"

She released her breath in a huff. "You are impossible. Look, the driver is signaling we are ready to go." She spun on her heel and started back. He fell in step beside her. She braced herself for more of his "encouragement."

He wisely kept his counsel to himself.

However, once they were back on the road, she touched the book beside her on the seat as if just the cover could give her insight.

She'd never considered writing herself. Important people wrote books.

Furthermore, now was not the time to start. Who would want to read anything written in Cornwall? London was the center of the world, and yet, Miss Edgeworth wasn't from London. Neither were several other female writers.

Had it been Soren's purpose to make her question herself? If so, he had succeeded.

And, yes, it would be lovely to accomplish as important a task as writing something that could make people's hearts feel or their minds think.

She looked to her husband. He studied the view outside the window. "I've never seen Pentreath Castle," she admitted.

"Ever? It's a landmark."

"Not to a Holwell."

"Oh, yes, the dreaded feud." He shook his head as he did whenever he thought she'd been overly sheltered.

"That and because I haven't been back to Cornwall in years."

"Fortunately, little of it has changed," he assured her. "I was gone longer than you were and all was right as I'd left it. Especially Pentreath. Parts of it haven't changed since the days when it was the guardian of the moors against invaders from the east and the north. I believe you will be well pleased with the house."

"Do you think your mother will be pleased with our marriage?"

"I couldn't say."

When she was younger, Cassandra had often seen the Dowager Lady Dewsberry out and about, although they had never spoken. "I rarely saw you and your mother together. Are you close?"

"My mother is . . ." He paused, shrugged, and obviously changed his mind over what he'd been about to say. "Her family is from Hertfordshire. She doesn't like Cornwall, either. The two of you will have something in common."

She leaned against her corner. "Because we don't embrace whatever you wish us to?"

"Cass—" he started, but she cut him off.

"Soren, be fair."

"About?"

She made an impatient noise. "You are a survivor. You do whatever must be done whether it was going to Canada, giving up your commission, or marrying for money."

"What does this happen to do with my mother?"

"It means that you may not be able to understand a person's resistance to an idea."

"Such as being trundled off to Cornwall?"

"Yes, exactly."

He held up a hand. "Let me first say, you and my mother are worlds apart."

"Or we may be more alike than you think."

"Don't even wish that in jest," he answered, and he was serious. "We don't stand on ceremony in Pentreath. Perhaps that is what Mother misses. Perhaps if she felt she was more important—?" He broke off with a shake of his head. "Who knows."

"You aren't painting an endearing portrait of her," Cassandra observed.

"I can't. She has spent her life waiting for a golden coach pulled by four snowy white horses to come driving up. Life has not been what she wished."

There was a warning in there for Cassandra. She sensed it.

And then he said, "My father had a mistress."

His statement caught her attention.

"Had you known?" he asked. When she shook her head, he said, "Then I had best tell you because everyone pretends it is a secret, even though it is common knowledge around Pentreath and beyond. Deborah Fowey is still in the area. She is married to the wainwright. However, before that, she and Father had three children. My half brother is in the military and my two half sisters are happily married."

"When you say common knowledge, does that mean your mother knows?"

"If she doesn't she is a fool, and Arabella York is no fool."

Of course, Cassandra knew that men kept mistresses. But this was the first time she'd ever thought in terms of herself. What if Soren took a mistress?

"I'll not tolerate any of that," she informed him. "I won't."

"I'm not my father, Cassandra." He reached for her hand on the seat. "I also don't want you to become my mother."

"What exactly does that mean?"

He gave her hand a squeeze. "I'll let you form your own opinions."

THE POST CHAISE turned down the hardened dirt drive to Pentreath Castle. After a half mile or so, a portion of the stone castle wall loomed over the road. The gaping hole that had once been the entry gate was wide enough for a host of elephants to pass through. Their vehicle easily made its way.

Soren's whole manner had changed once they had turned on the drive. He sat forward as if urging the horses faster. He smiled at her, the expression quick and expectant.

"You are ready to see your son?" she hazarded.

"Absolutely. I'm past ready."

A jolt of panic gripped her. "Soren? Do you think Logan will like me?"

"Of course."

"Why are you always so certain of things? What if I am not a good stepmother?" What if she felt nothing for the child? Or worse, considered him a rival for Soren's affections, the way she'd always believed Helen considered her?

He leaned back in the seat and took her hand. "All I ask is that you are kind to him. The rest will all evolve naturally. Besides, you learned how not to be a stepmother from the one you had."

He was right. His blunt assessment startled a laugh out of her and eased some of the worry. It would all be fine, she told herself, trying to adopt some of her husband's confidence. She donned her bonnet, preparing.

And now, as they drove under the stone arch, she saw the house—and she was pleased.

Pentreath was every bit as fine as Mayfield, the duke's estate. Perhaps even finer. Surrounded by woods, it was pure grace itself, with even lines and simple but stylish cornices. Made of Portland stone, like all elegant houses in the area, Pentreath boasted no fewer than twelve chimneys. Cassandra couldn't even imagine how many bedrooms that meant.

Her family home of Lantern Fields was a mere farmhouse in comparison.

Dogs barked to herald their arrival. A pack of white and brown hounds came running from the back of the house. The bravest came out to greet their vehicle. The others hung back and sounded a warning that visitors approached.

The front door opened and a servant came out

on the step. He called for others to join them. Servants flowed out of the house.

Cassandra looked to her husband. "This is grand."

He grinned. "Do you think you might like it here?"

"Let us see." She was actually anxious to have a look inside.

The post chaise had barely rolled to a stop before Soren opened the door and jumped to the ground. He offered a hand to Cassandra. That was when she noticed there were no welcoming smiles on the servants' faces. They grouped together as if preparing themselves for something terrible to happen.

Her first thought was that they were judging her for being a Holwell. They must have heard about the marriage. They disapproved. Everything she'd been taught about the Yorks was true.

Soren, too, noticed the solemn faces. "Something is not right," he warned.

A tall, older servant moved forward to greet them.

"Elliot, what is wrong?" Soren demanded.

"Young master Logan—" Elliot started.

"What has happened? Is he all right?" Soren looked around. "Where is he?"

Before Elliot could reply, a cool voice spoke

from the doorway. It was Soren's mother, dressed in black trimmed with a purple band of ribbon under the bodice. "He's gone," she announced. "Disappeared."

She did not sound displeased.

Chapter 17

"What do you mean he disappeared?" Soren countered, moving toward his mother. The servants scuttled to move out of his way."

Arabella, Lady Dewsberry, had not changed much over the years since Cassandra had last seen her except now she wore black. The woman had been much admired for her even looks and the crystal gray eyes she had given to her son. Her hair had gone silver and she might have put on a stone's weight but she was still attractive.

This was the first time Cassandra had ever heard her speak. She was surprised there wasn't more warmth in her voice toward her son and only child.

Then again, Soren had little warmth for her. In all the conversations Cassandra had shared with Soren over the course of the trip, they had rarely talked of parents. She'd thought he was being considerate of her raw feelings on the topic. Now she realized he might have his own burdens to bear.

"I mean, he left," Arabella said. "One moment he was here and in the next, he couldn't be found. Is that not right, Elliot?"

The servant hung his head. "It is right, my lord. The lads have been out searching for him."

"How long has he been gone?" Soren asked the man.

"Three days, my lord."

Soren swore fluently. "Who is in charge of the search?" He didn't look to his mother for answers. Those he expected from Elliot.

"Toby and the stable lads. Rhys Butler and his sons were with them yesterday and the day before. Mr. Morwath organized the men from the parish and they have been covering the western area."

"In the marsh?" Soren sounded beside himself.

"They haven't found a sign of him. He's probably not gone that far. We haven't given up, my lord. Toby won't come in until the late hours of the night. His brother has to drag him in."

Soren took hold of Elliot's shoulder. "Thank you. I know you are all doing everything you can. I need a horse."

"Rolland, fetch one," Elliot said to a tow-haired stable lad.

The lad went running.

"Do you know where Toby is searching?" Soren asked.

"By the miller's pond."

Soren nodded and took a step as if to go off in the direction of the stables, but then stopped. "The dogs are here." As if knowing he spoke of them, the hounds milling about came to attention, their tails wagging.

"Toby used them for the past two days. They did not pick up a scent so he's left them here. He said they were becoming more trouble than help. It doesn't seem possible that they'd not find any trace of a wee lad," Elliot said.

"A wee lad who is a *heathen*," Arabella answered. "Tell them, my lord. Reassure them. Your son was raised in the woods. It is his natural habitat."

Cassandra never wanted Soren to have cause to look at her the way he did his mother in that moment. She was surprised the woman could stand the force of that single glare. It would have cut her in two.

But when he spoke, his voice was controlled. "My son does know his way through the woods. It will be what saves him." He turned and took steps through the crowd to a path leading around the house but then stopped. He looked to Cassandra as if just remembering she was there.

"I'm sorry," he said. "I must go."

"Yes, you must," she said. "Don't worry about me. Find Logan."

He nodded, distracted, but then said, "Mother, help my wife settle in, or is that too much to expect of you, either?"

Her answer was a thin smile.

"I'll be fine," Cassandra informed. "You go."

Soren set off running toward the stables.

Elliot looked to the servants. "Here now, back to our work. Susan, come with me and let us properly greet our lady."

A young maid with fresh good looks and chestnut hair tucked neatly away under her mobcap followed in his wake as he approached Cassandra. He bowed. "My lady, it is unfortunate that we have not been able to greet you properly. I'm Elliot, my lord's butler. I've served his family for two generations. I'm proud to be of service to you."

"Thank you, Elliot," Cassandra said. "This news upon my lord's return is very upsetting. He was most anxious to see his son." It certainly had rattled her.

"Aye, my lady, we've been distraught."

Arabella hadn't been.

In fact, she was no longer at the doorway. Apparently, she saw no reason to welcome Cassandra.

"You will see to the driver?" Cassandra asked Elliot. She didn't have any money.

Before the butler could answer, the driver said, "Don't worry yourself, my lady. The horses and I need a rest before we return. I'll settle with Lord Dewsberry after he finds his child."

"Thank you." To the butler, she said, "You'll ensure the driver is treated well. Now, please, show me into the house and then do what you can for my lord."

It was the right sentiment. Elliot gave a nod as if he thought she was a game one. Cassandra recalled now how everyone had an opinion in Cornwall, from the fishwife to the highest lord, and approval was always good. "This is Susan," he said. "She'll be your maid and see you settled in as our lord requested."

Susan bobbed a curtsey. She shook a little as she did it, as if she feared doing it right. "My lady."

"Thank you, Susan." Cassandra kept her voice low and warm. "You have served a lady before?"

"No, my lady."

"It is of little import. We will do fine," Cassandra assured her, and was rewarded with a shy smile that was quickly schooled away as if she'd been warned about proper manners.

Another servant approached. By the keys hanging from a cord tied to the waist of her brown day dress with its high neckline, she had to be the housekeeper. Elliot introduced them. "This is Mrs. Branwell."

Mrs. Branwell's curtsey was more relaxed. "My lady. Welcome to Pentreath. If there is anything you wish to know about the house, I am at your service."

"Thank you. I'm well aware that we arrived at a critical time. I, too, wish to find my lord's son. Go on, Elliot, do what you must to help the search. Mrs. Branwell, Susan, show me to my rooms. I would appreciate a tour of the house, but let us wait for that until things are settled."

"Yes, my lady," Mrs. Branwell said. She was a good and officious housekeeper. Did they come in any other form? "Please, follow me. Susan, you as well."

"I will have a lad bring your luggage to you, my lady," Elliot said.

Before she followed Mrs. Branwell, Cassandra said, "One moment." She reached into the post chaise for the Maria Edgeworth book. She'd lost one book in a coach and she didn't wish to lose another.

They entered the house. Two of the hounds started to follow but stopped at the door. "They won't come in, my lady," Mrs. Branwell said. "Unless Lord Dewsberry allows them in."

"Does he do that?"

"Lord Dewsberry is fond of dogs." There was a beat and then she said, "His mother is not."

Cassandra could have guessed that answer.

The floor of the main hall was stone with a leaping stag carved into it. The stag of the Yorks. Cassandra had always heard of it but had not thought to see it.

The walls were a deep red with white wainscoting that needed a coat of paint. A display of polearms with different hatchet heads and long, sometimes carved poles lined the walls. It was an impressive entrance.

Arabella was not there, either. Cassandra had thought perhaps she might be, to frown her displeasure some more, if nothing else.

The stairs leading to the first floor were through a set of doors at the left of the hall. "There is a second stairway exactly like this on the other side of the main hall," Mrs. Branwell informed her as they climbed.

"Very good," Cassandra murmured. The honey-eyed, slightly resin scent of beeswax was in the air. No dog hair lingered in the corners. Mrs. Branwell ran a tight staff.

Their footsteps echoed on the hardwood floors. Or at least, Cassandra and Susan's did. Mrs. Branwell seemed to float.

At Mayfield, it had been obvious by the rectangle discolorations of the paint that pictures had been removed, presumably to be sold off. Cassandra remembered thinking that Camberly should have seen to a good coat of paint.

In Pentreath's halls, there were no discolorations because if pictures had been removed, it had been some time ago. However, paint would do wonders. The walls were a dirty, aged yellow. But the place was clean and Cassandra said as much, complimenting the housekeeper.

"Thank you, my lady. Lady Dewsberry is quite strict." Mrs. Branwell stopped at the last door before the end of the hall. "This is the countess's suite. Susan, fetch fresh cloths and water." The maid hurried to do her bidding, taking the back stairs. Mrs. Branwell opened the door.

The countess's suite had a canopied bed with burgundy drapes and coverlet. The walls were a shade of blue that was not to Cassandra's taste at all. The furniture was nice, but heavy. Thinking of their financial state, she knew she'd make do—although she would encourage Soren to invest in buckets and buckets of paint when they could afford it.

Mrs. Branwell crossed the room and opened another door. "This is my lord's set of rooms."

How convenient.

The furniture in his room was as heavy and dark as hers. Burgundy again was the color of choice for bed clothing although the walls had been painted a creamy ivory. His room was also twice the size of hers, with a lord's-sized hearth and a cozy chair before it. There was a writing desk by the window. Both rooms had large wardrobes.

"Susan will return shortly. Is there anything else I can do for you, my lady, before supper? Would you like some refreshment?"

Cassandra thought of Soren out searching for his son. She could not sip sherry as if nothing was wrong. "No, I'm fine. I need a moment to take it all in."

"The meal will be served at half past five." Mrs. Branwell acted serene and as if there weren't scores of men scouring the countryside for a lost boy. Cassandra found her attitude disquieting.

"Now, with your permission, may I leave, my lady?"

Cassandra nodded that she could leave, but then stopped her. "Please tell me, was Logan upset before he left? Had something happened?" Mrs. Edgeworth's observations about the tender nature of children were fresh in her mind.

"If I may be candid?"

"Please do."

"He is a wild boy, my lady. Almost like a wolf's cub, he is. You can't make him do what he doesn't want to do."

Cassandra protested, "He's but a small lad."

"He is the most remarkably stubborn child I have ever met. Now, if you will excuse me, my lady, I've said more than my share of words."

"I do not mind plain speaking, Mrs. Branwell. Thank you." Cassandra wondered how many of her strong feelings were shared by the staff.

The housekeeper left. Susan appeared with a pitcher of water and freshly laundered linen towels. The lad with Cassandra's valise was with her. He also had Soren's, which he put in the other bedroom.

"Do you wish me to unpack for you, my lady?" Susan asked.

"Yes, please."

It did not take long to hang the dresses and line up the shoes. While Susan was busy, Cassandra carried the valise over to the small dressing table by the window. During the journey, Soren had managed to find simple hairpins for her. She set these out with her brush. She took the tooth powder and milled soap to the washstand.

"Is there anything else, my lady?"

"No, that is enough, thank you." Cassandra waited for the door to close before lifting the valise's false bottom. The garnet necklace and bracelet were there. She replaced the bottom and set the valise in the wardrobe. She didn't know where this house kept luggage, but she wanted the valise close to her until she found another suitable hiding space for her jewelry.

Did she feel any pangs of dishonesty? Yes, especially with Soren out searching for his son. She didn't know why she hadn't told him about the garnets yet. It wasn't that she had a distrust of him, not any longer.

However, the description of Logan as a wolf cub and Arabella's lack of concern over his disappearance were not reassuring. Soren's impression of his son was far different, and she wondered who was right. She didn't know what she would do if Logan could not be found or harm had come to him. Soren would blame himself. She knew it.

Years ago, she'd heard of a family who had lost a child. They never found him until one day his body was discovered in a nearby lake. He had been trapped under some low-hanging bushes.

The thought was disturbing. Cassandra didn't want that to happen to Logan.

However, the truth—ah, there was that word again—the truth was that a five-year-old boy was a complication to the life she thought she would have. And now that he was missing, well, she felt callous and stingy for her earlier selfish thoughts.

They made her a bit like Arabella, and she didn't like that image at all.

Miss Edgeworth's book was making her do some thinking, not only about children in general, but also about her own childhood. She'd not been a wolf cub, but there had been many a servant who would not have had something flattering to say if she'd been missing. It went without saying her stepmother and stepsisters had resented—

Cassandra sensed rather than saw a movement in her husband's room.

But she had not heard the door open. And if Soren had returned, he would have said something.

She waited. All was quiet. Footsteps sounded in the hall. Perhaps a servant had run an errand in her husband's room and she'd not been paying attention?

Cassandra walked over to the bed and picked up Miss Edgeworth's book.

Stepping through the door between the two bedrooms, she again sensed she was not alone. That she was being watched. Carefully, she scanned the room, and it was then she noticed the wardrobe door was cracked open. It had not been that way when she'd looked in the room not more than thirty minutes earlier.

She walked over to it and, placing her book under her arm, opened the door.

Soren's wardrobe held a few of his things. He

did not own much. This did not surprise her. The space smelled of bay leaf and the orange spice of his shaving soap. She ran her hand over a jacket of bottle green superfine. She hoped he returned soon, and with Logan—and then, from the corner of her eye, she once again spied movement.

A shadow had shifted in a place where there should have been only stillness.

Was it her imagination or did someone else breathe in this room? Was there another heart beating?

The dogs started barking outside. Cassandra walked to the window. From this vantage point, she overlooked a small garden and a corner of the stables. There was a pond, and apparently two of the dogs had gotten into a fight over who knew what. A stable lad shouted at them. The post driver was there as well. She was pleased he was being taken care of—

Again, her inner sense noticed a movement.

This time, Cassandra did not doubt herself. The movement had come from the massive four-poster.

She crept closer. Her instincts were not wrong. Someone was under the bed. It could be a dog, but then its behavior was uncharacteristic.

When she was a few feet away, she dropped to her knees and peered under the bed frame just in time to catch sight of a small bare foot disappearing behind the back of the headboard.

Could Logan be here? In this room, waiting for his father?

Cassandra rose up on her knees, ready to call for help, when a black-haired child dressed only in breeches took two bounding steps across the mattress toward her. With a loud war cry, he leaped in the air to attack her.

Chapter 18

Cassandra surprised herself with how quickly she could roll out of the way.

Her foe landed on his feet with the grace of a cat. He raised scrawny arms, his hands in fists. She came up on her knees, holding the book for protection. He was still shorter than she, but he was wildly ferocious. He shouted gibberish for a second and then switched to English. "*Where* is my father? *Where is he?*"

This was Logan. The wolf cub. Her husband's child.

Her stepson.

His face was contorted in rage. He behaved as if he expected to fight for his very life, and he blamed her.

He moved as if to strike and, with all favorable consideration of Miss Edgeworth's admonishments on the sensitive nature of the children aside, Cassandra put the book to good use. She thumped him smartly on the head with it.

She'd not used much force but it made a nice whacking sound.

Logan blinked, his scowl deepened. He looked like a miniature Soren except with dark eyes and black hair. Still, he had his father's jaw, and she recognized the shape of the lips. Soren could never have denied his son.

He opened his mouth, prepared to give a shout, and she said, "Stop this nonsense or I will give you another thump." In truth, her heart was beating madly. He had given her quite a start.

Before another move could be made, Soren's door opened. Arabella was there. "Ah, you found him." There was no surprise in her voice.

Logan immediately backed away, moving toward Cassandra.

His change from brave attack to uncertainty gave her pause.

She looked up at his grandmother. Arabella's face was a mask of disdain—whether for Cassandra or Logan or both of them, she did not know.

Cassandra rose to her feet, wanting to regain her dignity. Footsteps ran down the hall toward them. Elliot appeared in the doorway. He stopped when he saw Arabella and then glanced in the room at Cassandra. It took him a moment to notice Logan. Her terrible attacker had moved even closer to Cassandra, as if hiding himself in her skirts. The wolf cub had become a distrustful child.

After seeing the look on Arabella's face, Cassandra didn't know if she didn't agree with him.

"My lady, you found him," Elliot spoke with genuine relief.

"Rather, he found me. Send word to my lord that his son is safe."

"I will, my lady. We have a signal of two shots with a musket." He left. There were other voices in the hall. The servants were sharing the information among themselves.

Arabella took a step back so that all would notice her presence. The questioning voices went silent.

"Well," she said, turning back to Cassandra, "that was a nice entertainment. I shall see you at dinner. Do you wish me to close the door?"

She had no questions for Logan? No concern?

Two musket shots sounded. Elliot had not wasted time. Their echo reverberated in the air. She prayed Soren wasn't far.

"You knew he was here all along," Cassandra said.

"Did I?" Such false innocence.

"You did," Cassandra answered stoutly. "Did you bring him food? Let him know you cared?"

Logan was all legs and arms. He could use a few good meals.

"Are you questioning me?"

Cassandra had heard the silky tone before. She'd heard it from the lady patronesses at Almack's and from the mothers of other debutantes. It was the tone people used when they wanted to let her know she was not good enough.

Well, they were wrong.

And she was Logan's stepmother.

"I most certainly am questioning you," Cassandra returned coolly in a tone that would have made any of those patronesses proud. "Did you not see how worried my *husband* was at learning of his child's disappearance? How could you have not have said something?"

"The boy appears unscathed. Any worry on my part would have been misplaced." She walked away.

"Well—" Cassandra started, flummoxed by the woman's cavalier attitude. She turned to Logan, and discovered him gone. She whirled around the room and then heard the door to the hallway quietly shut on her side of the suite. She ran through Soren's door out into the hall, but the wolf cub had once again vanished.

How could he have moved so quickly? Then again, Arabella was not there, either. It was as if Pentreath had swallowed them whole.

She held up the book. The title mocked her. "Who is receiving the education, Miss Edgeworth?" she muttered.

At that moment, she heard the dogs barking and Soren's voice. He had returned. She quickly dropped the book in her room and went to meet her husband to tell him the story of finding Logan.

The house was big. It took her several minutes to make her way downstairs and out into the great hall. The front door was open and Elliot was standing there. She hurried to the door. Soren was dismounting a good-sized chestnut. He was hatless and his hair windblown. He'd not been gone that long but it seemed as if he'd been put through an eternity. One of the men riding with him took the reins of his horse.

He looked to Elliot. "He's been found—?"

Before he could say another word, a blur raced past Cassandra and out the door, straight for Soren. Logan was still barefoot; however, he'd made an attempt to dress by putting on a shirt and jacket. He leaped at his father with the same athleticism he'd used to attack her, except this time, he wanted his father's arms.

Soren caught him. He hugged him as if he'd never let him go. Logan's skinny arms and legs were just as tightly holding his father. His dark head buried itself in the crook of Soren's neck.

Cassandra was touched by the unconstrained show of affection.

Her father had never welcomed her in that way. There had been a time, long ago, when she'd wanted to run to him, so thankful he had returned from wherever he was. She'd not liked being left behind with the servants . . . and none of them had referred to her as a wild thing.

Soren spoke to Logan softly in that language the boy had used upstairs. Cassandra assumed it was his native tongue.

The words buoyed the child, who lifted his head. He'd been crying. He was a proud lad and she could only imagine what it took to break him. She empathized with him all the more.

Soren saw her and smiled, the expression both relieved and proud. He carried his son to her, stopping to ask Elliot, "Where did you find him?"

"Your lady found him, my lord."

"Truly?" Soren moved on to Cassandra. "You found him?"

She smiled, conscious that they had a growing audience. As word spread, hunters from wherever they had been came racing up. Some were on horseback. Some ran. Servants poked their head out from doorways, interested in what was going on. Even Mrs. Branwell stood to one side.

The one person who wasn't there was Arabella.

She could feel Logan's watchful gaze upon her. The set of his mouth was far too solemn for such a young boy, and she thought about how she'd felt when her mother had died.

The world had not been her friend.

"Is there someplace more private for introductions?" Cassandra suggested.

"Ah, yes, quite right," Soren agreed, finally noticing how much attention surrounded them. He told Elliot, "Have Cook prepare a tray. We will be in the library."

A library? Cassandra practically danced as he led her down the hall to a good-sized wood-paneled room. Windows as big as doorways overlooked at back portico with a balustrade, and graceful stairs led down into the garden.

But there wasn't a book. Just as it had been at Mayfield, there were bookshelves, but no books. Her heart fell.

Ledgers were stacked on a huge desk in the middle of the room. This was obviously where Soren managed the daily affairs of Pentreath. There were also several groupings of old but comfortable-looking chairs. They would be excellent places to enjoy a cozy read, if there had been a book to enjoy.

He carried Logan over to a table and chairs located close to the desk. "My lady," he said, using his free hand to pull out a chair for Cassandra.

"A gentleman always sees to the niceties, Logan," he instructed his son. He could have used both hands. Logan was not about to let go.

She sat. Soren took the chair next to her and stretched out his legs. At last, Logan released his grip but kept his head against his father's chest as if listening to his heart.

"Where was he?" Soren asked quietly.

"In your bedroom. He'd been there the whole time."

"Ah, waiting for me, eh?"

Logan didn't answer. He viewed Cassandra gravely.

"When did you send the letter to your mother announcing our marriage?" Cassandra asked.

"I had it sent out the afternoon we agreed to marry."

"And he has been missing for three days?" she said.

"Which would have been around when the letter arrived." Soren looked to his son. "Is that what it was?"

Logan didn't answer. Instead, he turned from Cassandra and grew very interested in the knot in Soren's neck cloth. A maid appeared with a tray of sandwiches, whisky for Soren, and cold spring water for Cassandra and Logan.

"Beg pardon, my lady, but shall I fetch some sherry?"

"No, this is fine," Cassandra said. She set about serving the sandwiches as the maid poured the water.

"I'll take a water as well," Soren said. Cassandra had noticed that he only imbibed in spirits on occasion. She still had much to learn about this man that she married.

The maid left. Cassandra set the plates out. Soren sat up but Logan did not make a move. He'd hooked his skinny bare legs around his father's thigh as if he was on a horse.

"Where are your stockings, Logan?" Soren asked.

Large dark eyes glanced up to him, but he did not answer.

"I thought we talked," Soren continued. "Proper young men wear shoes here. They wear shoes in Canada as well."

"I don't like those shoes." Logan spoke clearly.

"You are not used to them. If you wear them, they will fit your feet."

"They are stiff."

"They are new."

Soren glanced at Cassandra as if asking if she was taking this all in. He then said the words she sensed both she and Logan were dreading. "My son, I want you to meet your new—"

Whether he was going to say "stepmother" or "mother," Cassandra knew neither would be acceptable.

Logan's determined little chin lifted. He spoke in his native tongue.

Soren's expression was carefully neutral. "In English, my son."

Logan was not afraid to comply. "I had only one mother."

"And I imagine she was a very good one," Cassandra agreed with him.

The child drew his brows together in suspicion but he gave one curt nod. Logan was not one to waste words.

"So, if it is all right with you," she said, "perhaps you should consider me a friend."

"A friend?" Soren made a face. "What is he going to call you? Friend?"

She thought of the child who had clung to her skirts. "If he chooses. I like the name Friend." She pushed his plate and sandwich toward him. "I'm not certain I like the flavor of the cheese on this sandwich. Please let me know what you think, Logan." He had to be hungry. Whatever he could purloin from around the foodstuffs in the house would not be enough for a growing child's appetite.

Still he sat.

"Does my offer of being your friend sound good to you, Logan?" she asked, wanting him to respond to her.

He looked to Soren. "Is she your friend?"

"She is my wife," Soren answered gently.

"My mother was your wife."

"Yes, and your mother has left us." Soren's tone was infinitely patient, the way a father's should be.

"Is she the wealthy woman?" Logan asked.

Cassandra doubted anyone had said as much to him. Well, perhaps Arabella. But he was a clever youngster. He probably heard everything that happened in the house.

"Your friend is my wife," Soren answered in a firm tone.

The look on Logan's face let her know it would be some time before *he* considered her a friend.

She took bite of her sandwich. "I hope I have an appetite for dinner." She tried to sound cheery in the silence between father and son.

"Cassandra, I believe Logan and I need a moment."

She didn't question the request but swiftly rose. Soren and his son came to their feet out of respect. Logan stood on his own, but his hand slipped into his father's. The child was a strange mix of fierce independence and needy insecurity, an insecurity she understood too well.

She excused herself, and lacking anywhere else to go after leaving the library, she took a turn on the back portico. The days were growing warmer. The flower beds desperately needed tending. It didn't look as if anyone had paid attention to them for years. Here was a project she could take on. Soren encouraged her to find a passion. Many a lady enjoyed gardening, although she didn't believe she would.

From this vantage point, she could hear voices from the library. Logan had turned very talkative. As she reentered the house and passed the library door, she caught sight of Soren and his son. Logan sat in his own chair, stuffing sandwiches in his mouth as if he hadn't eaten in months while chatting happily. Soren seemed to be hanging on his son's every word. As she watched, he lightly touched the back of his son's head as if offering a benediction.

It was the gentlest gesture Cassandra had ever seen a man perform—

"He dotes on the child." Arabella's disapproving voice startled her. Cassandra had been so caught up in her thoughts, she had not heard her approach. The older woman stood in the doorway of an adjacent room.

Cassandra walked over to her mother-in-law, not wanting Arabella's words to carry into the library. "They have not seen each other for some time."

"I have little patience with coddling," Arabella said. She looked Cassandra up and down, obviously unimpressed. "You know why he went after you, don't you? He wanted your money. And your land. It is the only way a York would ever marry a Holwell." Her gaze went past Cassandra to the library. "His father married me for my money and my life has been miserable ever since."

For the briefest of seconds, her directness unnerved Cassandra. Arabella was going to be unpleasantly surprised when she learned how little money Soren's marriage had brought to Pentreath. Or, and this was a new thought, that Cassandra wasn't truly a Holwell and therefore, *wouldn't* inherit Lantern Fields. Who knew who she was? And in this moment, for the first time, she found herself glad of it.

Never again would she have to feel an invisible wall around her because of her father and his prejudices. Soren had been right, there was a measure of freedom in the acceptance of this new truth.

However, Cassandra decided it was not her place to enlighten Arabella.

In a moment's clarity, she realized she did not want to be aloof or distrusting like either Arabella or Helen. These were women who had nothing but their place in Society to give them authority.

She wanted more. And Soren had been right, she wouldn't have been happy resting on a title.

Even when she'd dreamed of being a duchess, it was because then she could pursue her enjoyment of poetry and ideas . . . and Soren's suggestion of her writing came to her mind. What avid reader such as herself had not imagined writing a book?

It still didn't seem the most appealing thing she could do with her time and energy—but she now, with the acquaintance of Arabella, understood why Soren urged her to discover what she *was* passionate about.

"I shall see you at dinner," Cassandra said, excusing herself and wanting to put distance between herself and this woman, who was one of many she'd met who had no life.

She went up to her room. She had no difficulty finding it.

Cassandra pulled the valise from her wardrobe, removed the false bottom, and took out the garnets. The stones were bloodred and the gold around them heavy. She seldom wore them. The pearls had been her favorite, and she was discovering the one pearl was enough for her.

Now she considered her true motive for keeping them hidden from Soren. Yes, her mother's memory was involved, but so was her fear to trust, to act in good faith.

She went to search out her husband.

Chapter 19

$\mathcal{I}$t had been a long day. Watching his son eat as if he hadn't had food in days, Soren struggled to keep his anger in check.

Toby, the head of Logan's search party, had mentioned that life had not been good for the child over the month Soren had been gone. With a few quiet questions, Soren had learned that the nurse he'd hired, a grandmotherly Mrs. Williams with family in the area, had refused to lock Logan in his room on a daily basis and had been let go.

"Who asked her to lock him up?" Soren had asked.

He knew the answer even before Toby said, "Lady Dewsberry. She feels the boy is in need of discipline."

"Has my son misbehaved?"

He saw that Toby did not wish to answer that question. "Go on," Soren prodded. "Your loyalty means you give me the truth."

"Your father never asked for that."

"I'm not my father." How many times had Soren reminded himself of that fact? The answer: Every time he'd attempted to overcome the host of almost insurmountable problems surrounding Pentreath.

And he'd vowed to never stop doing what he must.

Except Toby almost broke him when he'd told him of the war of wills between his mother and his son. Arabella had shown no kindness. She ignored that Logan was caught between two worlds. One had been the open freedom of not only his tribe but even the life Soren had lived around his shipping company and businesses.

And then there was this world, the one filled with his mother's resentments and disappointments.

Her true grievance was with Soren. No, actually with his father, but Soren was starting to believe she was having difficulty telling the two of them apart.

Her weapon of choice apparently was his son.

He couldn't imagine locking Logan in a nursery room and keeping him there like a pet. Apparently, Mrs. Williams had objected and had been given the sack.

"That kept the rest of us quiet," Toby had said. There was a pause, a test, Soren sensed, and then the man added, " 'Course some think him an odd child."

Now there was a truth.

Logan had the blood of chiefs running through his veins. He'd not come willingly to Cornwall, especially with a father he barely knew.

He resisted this new life, just as Cassandra resisted.

In truth, there were times Soren didn't wish to be here, either.

Why *was* he burdening those who mattered to him with it?

He touched his son's hair. It was need of cleaning. The boy had been neglected, and it tore at Soren's soul.

"I'm sorry," Soren said. "I did not abandon you. I told you I would return."

"I waited." He'd even staked out Soren's room.

"You are a good and clever lad. Don't let anyone tell you differently."

Logan's answer was to dive into Soren's arms. Soren tightened his hold, wanting to be a solid presence his son could trust. He owed this to him. He owed this to Mary.

The first time Logan had reached for him had been during a storm on their ship crossing. Soren cherished each time his son looked to him to be a father.

His mother interrupted them. "Dinner will be

in half an hour. Since your son has eaten, there is no need to send a tray to the nursery. I shall tell Mrs. Branwell."

She started to walk away but Soren called her back. "Mother, I would have us talk."

"Perhaps later."

"Now, Mother." From the moment he'd returned, Soren had treated his mother as a woman in grief. He'd been solicitous. But he was no fool. She might wear black with a touch of purple, but she was not displeased her husband was dead.

Her smile was cool. "I'm not a pup you can order about." She would have walked off except for Soren's next words.

"You will move into the dowager cottage. I shall tell Mrs. Branwell to make the arrangements."

He had his mother's attention now. She came charging up to him. "I will not move. This is *my* house."

"No, Mother, it is mine. However unfair you believe it to be, I make the rules here. I paid the price to save Pentreath."

"I knew you would not be happy with your marriage—"

"Well, you are wrong." He stood, using his full height to lord over her. Logan slid from his chair to stand next to him. "I chose Cassandra Holwell. I love her." The truth of his words seemed to ring in the air around him. "I want her to be happy here." He placed his hand on his son's shoulder. "Logan is my heir—"

"He is not fully English. He's—"

"A member of a proud tribe. His mother was one of the bravest women I knew. My son will be the next lord of this house and I expect all to respect him."

There was a long beat of silence. His mother stood as if trying to swallow her words. She failed. "I will not accept him. Not completely. But I shall do what I can."

"And you will do it from the dowager's cottage."

Her face contorted into fury but Soren was having none of it. "You had your chance to prove your mettle. I left my son with you and you did not see to his welfare."

"I knew where he was. He was safe."

"Don't think me a fool. And if you do anything in the future to harm my son or my wife, I will move you even further away."

She shook with anger. Soren remembered battles between his parents when she'd behaved just this way. When he'd been Logan's age, her temper had frightened him. He squeezed his son's shoulders, urging him to be strong.

Of course, he needn't worry. Logan had faced worse dangers than an old woman's tantrum.

"I will not be down for dinner," his mother announced. She turned, and only then did they all see Cassandra standing by the door, her hands by her side, her eyes wide.

His mother walked up to her. "You'd best have a care. My son has no allegiance to anyone but that wolf child of his."

"I'll take my chances," Cassandra said, and Soren's heart swelled with pride.

"Fool." His mother left.

Cassandra blinked as if shocked.

"She must always have the last word," Soren said.

Her response was a very direct question. "Do you really love me?" She walked up to him.

So she'd overheard. The game was over. He was exposed.

He looked into her eyes and confessed, "With all my heart."

"And why?"

He had to laugh, Cassandra always expected an explanation. "Because you aren't afraid to speak your mind. Because you *think*. You are a survivor, my love, and I admire strong women. And I must also say, I love you because at one time, I thought you the prettiest girl in Cornwall and I still believe so today."

"Soren, I'm not—"

He cut her off. "Why do you deny what I'm saying? It is the truth, Cass, *my* truth. And I apologize for my lack of poetry. I just like the way you look."

I JUST LIKE the way you look.

The compliment went straight to her heart. If he thought her pretty, who was she to point out her failings?

"I know I am not what you wanted—" he started, but she stopped the flow of his words with her fingers on his lips.

"I've never said that," she answered.

"You didn't have to, Cassandra. I knew."

"Then you knew *wrong*."

He went very still. "I don't know if I believe what I'm hearing," he said. "Tell me again."

"If you don't know how deeply I care for you by the way I hold you in my arms, well, words won't convince you."

"I adore being in your arms but I have this wife who assures me words are important. Say them, Cassandra. I pray you return my affections."

He loved her.

He'd spoken the words.

She held up the fist she'd kept hidden in her skirts to reveal the heavy gold jewelry. The bloodred stones caught the light. "I've kept these from you."

"What are they?"

"These are my mother's garnets. I've had them hidden from you."

"Why? Did you think I would demand them?"

"Perhaps. Yes. I . . ." She paused. How to express her fear? "I wanted protection in case I might need money someday."

"To leave me?"

The direction of his thoughts shocked her, and yet, was that not what she'd been hedging against? Too late, she remembered that Mary had left him. Cassandra had been so selfish and caught up in her own worries, she'd not even thought of how he might consider her motives.

She now sought to reassure him. "I've lost so much, Soren. Everything in my life was unraveling, but these gave me some reassurance." She'd also checked their hiding space every chance she safely could, she realized. "But I'm not afraid any longer."

"You *never* had anything to fear."

"I knew that, but my life had been turned upside down. And then you gave me a book."

"It was not such a big thing."

"To me it was. It meant you accepted me. You understood."

"Cass, you've had many books before. Especially from your father."

"Hardly. Before we went to London, and I

learned I could borrow from a lending library or visit a bookseller, the only books I read were the ones I borrowed from the Vicar Morwath. He'd let me read whatever his children were reading, and then later, when I surpassed them, he shared from his personal library."

She pressed the necklace and bracelet toward him. "I want you to have these. Use them for Pentreath . . ." Her voice trailed off. The burn of tears stung her eyes. She blinked them back and forced herself to meet his gaze. "I'm sorry I didn't trust you. I was confused. I—"

His arms came around her, shutting off anything else she would have said. She snuffled her face in his jacket and he gathered her close. "Cass, Cass, Cass."

Yes, *his* Cass.

"The necklace is yours from your mother. Pass it on to our children or use it to do whatever you wish. Buy books if you want. We will be fine. You have already given enough."

"You aren't angry that I kept them from you? That I didn't trust you?"

Her tilted her chin to look at him. "Have I acted angry?"

She shook her head.

"That is because I have received the best part of the bargain, Cassandra. You. I love you."

"And I love you, Soren. Very much."

No bells rang. No birds sang. But it seemed to her as if in that moment, everything was absolutely right in the world.

They kissed, and it was one of the deepest, most fulfilling ones they had ever shared because it was the pledging of a new troth between them.

Soren broke the kiss.

"Logan?" she said to him expectantly. He nodded.

She leaned around her husband. His son had climbed onto a chair and sat with his back to them as if shutting them out.

She knelt in front of him. "I love your father. I love everything about him. Do you understand what that means? It means I love you as well. You don't have to love me in return, but let us be kind to each other. I want you to know that, like you, I lost my mother. I was sad and very angry. It seemed as if everyone wanted me to carry on. It was hard." An unbidden tear over the memories ran down her cheek. "I won't ask that of you."

To her surprise, Logan reached out and gently brushed it away. Her heart expanded at his soft touch.

"Thank you," she said quietly, and he nodded.

"Someday, your father and I will have a child together. However, I want you to know that you will always be *the* firstborn."

It would have been nice to end that with a

hug or some sign of acceptance. Instead, Logan watched her with eyes that had already seen too much in his young life. She would have to wait for him to come to her.

There was a footstep at the doorway. Elliot's voice said, "I'm sorry to interrupt, my lord, but Cook wondered if anyone would be coming to the table?"

"Oh, I believe we can eat more, don't you, Logan?" His son nodded. "We will be right there, Elliot."

The butler withdrew. Soren helped Cassandra to her feet. "That was well said," he said. "Thank you." He tapped his son lightly on the head. "Come, Logan. We must wash for dinner."

In that moment, Cassandra fell in love a little bit more. Did he understand how manly he was when he showed his son how to be a proper gentleman?

Logan rose from the chair and dutifully took his father's hand. But then he held out his other. "Come, friend," he said.

Friend. Just as she had suggested.

And someday, he might call her mother. Or think of her as one.

She prayed she would be worthy of the title. She took his hand.

Chapter 20

$\mathcal{I}$t had been a long time since Soren had sat at Pentreath's dining table and enjoyed a meal, if ever.

Certainly, he couldn't remember laughing. The unhappiness and dissatisfaction of the house's occupants—his mother's, his father's, even his own—had made the air in the room almost impossible to breathe. It had not been a happy house, or childhood, he realized.

He'd wanted something different for his son. Instinctively, he'd known he would need a wife who could help him reclaim all that had once been good at Pentreath—and he'd found her.

Yes, he'd gone after Cassandra because it would take her money to save Pentreath. However, he realized he'd also been searching for her quiet dignity and her grace. She would help guide Logan through Society because she had navigated those same treacherous waters herself and survived.

His wife appeared radiant as she sat at the table with Logan between them.

Their declarations of love, spoken from their hearts, seemed to have freed her. Or perhaps it was the unburdening of her secret. Hiding her jewels did not seem a bad action to Soren. He considered it rather wise.

That she'd felt guilt was to him a testimony to her character.

And he was well pleased with his choice of a wife.

She wore the garnets at the table along with the pearl on its ribbon. However, for his tastes, what he liked best was the way the candlelight reflected off the gold wedding band he had given her. He'd purchased it with money he could not afford to spend, and yet he had never made a better investment.

The servants did not act as if it was strange for his mother not to be present. Who knew what the attitude between his parents had been when he'd lived in Canada. He'd overheard whispers. Apparently, after he was sent to his uncle's, his father had spent most of his time living in the village with Deborah. No wonder his mother was bitter. And yet Soren could not let her bile spread to his small family.

Logan ate his weight in roast mutton, potatoes, peas, and carrots. It was as if he'd not eaten the plate of sandwiches earlier. Soren was pleased that he was using a fork. There had been a time when Logan had defiantly eaten with his hands. Or perhaps he was trying to impress Cassandra. Either way, this was a good sign.

That night, when Soren took his son to his bed in the nursery, Logan stopped him in the doorway. "I don't want to sleep here."

"But this is your room."

"I don't want this room. No lock," Logan insisted, and Soren understood what he'd meant. If he'd been held prisoner for weeks in a room, would he want go back into it? He thought not.

"One moment," he told his son. He went into the room, set the candle on the dresser, and then paused, looking around. The top of the furniture was dusty. Further inspection showed that the chamber pot had been emptied but not cleaned. He would have words with Mrs. Branwell. His son was right not to want to sleep here.

He picked up the mattress, bedclothes and all. He went out in the hall. "Let us go, sir."

"Where are we going?"

"To my room." He didn't have to repeat himself. Logan skipped ahead in happy agreement.

The two of them set up a pallet on Soren's floor in the space between the wall and the bed. "Here now, brush your teeth," Soren said. He brought a chair over to the washstand for Logan to stand on as he performed the task.

The door between his room and Cassandra's opened. She stood there in a nightdress and the green dressing robe she'd worn that fateful night. Her hair curled down around her shoulders, the way he liked it.

"You have company," she noticed.

"Hello, friend," Logan said, before spitting into the basin.

"You don't spit there," Soren warned. "You spit in this mug." He moved it closer to the basin.

"Why do I have to do this?" Logan complained. He held up the brush.

"To keep your teeth in your head," Soren admonished. He'd met a barber who swore teeth fell out because mouths were filthy. "And so you don't wake with the breath of a goat."

Logan laughed.

"What does he wear to bed?" Cass asked, looking around the room.

"The same thing I do."

"You're kidding. He will freeze."

"He hasn't yet." Soren looked at her. "Perhaps his nakedness might be why my mother locked the door?"

"You know her better than I."

"The nurse did make a comment. She said she would dress him for night and in the morning, he would be undressed."

"Again, like his father."

He grinned and walked over to her. There was a kiss and a second one. "I will see you later," he whispered.

She smiled. "I hope. Don't dress." She closed the door.

Having finished with his teeth, Logan jumped off the chair. He picked up Miss Edgeworth's book that was on the upholstered chair before the hearth and, with a busy air, walked to the connecting door and knocked.

Cass opened the door. "You forgot this, friend." Soren's son handed her the book.

She knelt to his eye level. "Thank you. Do you like books?"

His answer was a shake of his head. "His father's son," Soren said. "But then, I'm not certain how well he understands what they are."

Cassandra changed her question. "Do you like stories?"

"What kind of stories?" Logan asked.

"Stories about adventurers like you," she said, touching his nose. "Or about places you have yet to see. Even places you've already been."

"I like stories."

"I do, too." She stood. "Tomorrow, we'll share some stories. I will tell you one and then it will be your turn to tell me."

Logan liked the idea.

"Come now, to bed," Soren said. "We have work to do on the morrow." His son obeyed. He'd always listened to Soren, who had never understood why his mother had the issue she did with this child . . . save for her insistence Logan was not all English.

She refused to appreciate how strong and healthy he was. How white and straight his teeth were. Or admire his energy and ingenuity, two qualities Soren valued. Logan was going to do well in life. And if Lord Liverpool, who was rumored to have Indian blood, could rise to the highest offices in the land, then so could his son.

Soren went through the motions of preparing for bed himself. Logan watched quietly a moment, apparently content, before he slipped into sleep. His child was exhausted, as was Soren.

However, he'd become accustomed to having his wife beside him. As soon as he believed it was safe, he climbed out of his bed and made his way to Cassandra's.

He'd hoped she'd be waiting up for him.

Instead, she slept as if she was home at last. Even when Soren put his weight on the mattress, she did not stir.

The last days of the full moon that had followed them from London streamed through her window and outlined her body. She was naked, and he silently laughed.

She'd done it to tease him, and it would have worked, if she'd been awake.

He did not have the heart to disturb her. He lifted a lock of her hair and rubbed it between his fingers.

"Thank you, my love," he said. "And I promise you will never regret this marriage."

For the first time since he'd silently made this promise to himself, he knew it would come true.

THE FIRST RAY of dawn woke Cassandra. She was not ready to start the day. The bed had felt better than she could have imagined. She stretched as she turned over, and then saw her husband's body beside her. He wasn't under the sheets with her but had the counterpane over his most intimate parts.

He was very enticing in his relaxed state.

She wondered what would happen if she nibbled on his neck.

Rolling onto her belly, she carefully scooted her way toward him—

Soren rose up and leaped on her. He'd been lying in wait.

His hand over her mouth prevented her surprised cry. And then his lips on her mouth kept her busy.

He was already fully aroused. She should have noticed the change in the counterpane. It didn't matter. She now had what she wanted.

Their coupling was good, very good . . . *quietly* good. He turned her on her side to enter her, his thigh over her hip. She covered his hand with hers, holding him to her.

It was all so right, and just when she felt his release, when she, too, experienced that sharp shiver of completion, the door between their rooms started to open.

"Logan, wait," Soren ordered. He grabbed the counterpane to cover them.

To his credit, the child did stop.

"I will be right there." He gave Cassandra a hard buss. "We will have to think this through."

"I may have an idea."

"Will it mean you are in my bed?"

"That is where I wish to be."

"Then do it." Leaving her the sheet, he wrapped the heavy counterpane around him and walked out of the room.

"It would help if you wore nightclothes," she reminded his retreating figure. His answer was a grin.

But she did have an idea, and she had Miss Edgeworth to thank for it. She would turn her bedroom into Logan's room. Then she could share Soren's.

It didn't take much to make the change. Over breakfast she outlined her plan to Soren and Logan. "I need your help," she informed her stepson.

"We were going to tell stories," Logan answered.

She was pleased he remembered. "We can do it as we change the rooms." He liked that idea.

And, so, while Arabella was moved to a cottage by the house servants, four stable lads helped Logan and her set up what she was calling the "children's" room. Because, she told him, he was too old for a nursery. He agreed.

She used Miss Edgeworth's book as a guideline. The first advice was to have only furniture that, should it be spoiled, would not cause anyone grief. Cassandra had her bed moved to the nursery and the nursery's furniture in her room. She had Logan pick out toys that interested him. There were not many. So, she instructed one of the stable lads, following a suggestion in the book, to cut different shapes and sizes of wood into blocks.

Later, when the room was set up, she and Logan sat on the portico and sanded those blocks of wood so they would not give him splinters. He liked having work. He was also proud of what he'd done and showed his handiwork to his father.

That night, Cassandra slept in her husband's

bed and it was exactly as it should be, although she could not convince either of the men in her life to wear nightclothes.

THE NEXT DAY, she made it a point to call on Arabella. She had Cook prepare a basket of bread, jam, and cheese. "Do you wish to come with me?" she said to her men.

"She sent me a note letting me know she is highly displeased," Soren answered. "I shall give her more time."

"And you, Logan? Will you join me?"

He looked to his father. "It is your decision," Soren told him.

Logan considered the matter in his grave manner that was actually endearing in such a young child. "I will go with you, friend."

"Do you drive, Cassandra?" Soren asked her.

"It has been some time, but I imagine I could," she answered. She'd had no need to drive herself in the city.

"I drive," Logan announced.

"There, you are in good hands," Soren said.

Cassandra thought he was jesting, until one of the stable lads brought the cart around. Logan set his hat, a miniature version of his father's, at a rakish angle and picked up the reins.

He barely waited for Cassandra to take a seat before he flicked them and off they went.

She looked back at Soren, who was laughing. "You should see him ride that pony," he assured her.

It was lovely day for an outing, even though it was a bit overcast. Yesterday, they had told each other stories. Today, Cassandra shared her favorite poems she'd memorized with him. Logan liked the language of the poems, sometimes repeating the words.

Another advantage to having Logan drive was that he knew where he was going. He followed a wagon track through the wood, and on the other side was a house that Cassandra would be hard-pressed to call a cottage.

It might have been a home the first Dewsberry built for his family. It was Elizabethan in style with mullioned windows, a stone roof, and a brick walk. Rooms had been added on over the years. No wonder Soren didn't have money, she reflected. This was quite an estate to maintain.

One of the maids from the main house answered the door. Cassandra knew that Soren had assigned a number of them to see to his mother's comfort. "I shall see if she is in to you, my lady. Would you like to come in?"

Logan had stayed by the cart. "Are you coming in with me?" Cassandra asked.

"I will keep my pony company."

"Don't ruin your clothes," she said to him.

His look was one of complete surprise that she would even think of him doing such a thing. She went inside carrying her basket.

Of course, the house was in a bit of disarray. It would take time for Arabella to arrange the rooms the way she wanted them. The maid left her in a lovely sitting room overlooking the front lawn, where Logan had unhitched the pony. Cassandra watched him hop on the animal's back without the benefit of a saddle—

"What are you doing here?" Arabella demanded from the doorway.

Not the best welcome Cassandra had ever received, but what could one expect? "I brought you some treats."

"Give them to the girl."

Cassandra handed the basket to the maid, who appeared a tad befuddled over what she should do with it. "Take it to the kitchen, you stupid child," Arabella said.

The maid ducked her head and did as bid. Cassandra felt sorry for her.

"You don't need to pretend to care for me," Arabella announced.

"You are my lord's mother. Of course, we care what happens to you."

"But I have been put out of my home." She'd not taken one step into the room.

"I can understand how upsetting that is. However, Soren and I will not let anyone hurt Logan."

"It isn't right," Arabella said. She walked into the sitting room and saw Logan out the window. He was now trotting the pony in circles on the front lawn. "He isn't all English. He should not be Dewsberry's heir."

"By all that is right, he is English and he is the heir."

"I've never seen proof of a marriage. Have you?"

"I take my lord's word for it."

Arabella cut the air with a dismissive hand. "Then I am better off where I am."

Cassandra silently agreed they all were.

Her mother-in-law faced her. "You don't have to stay."

"No, but I wish to visit. If you have time."

"All I do have is time. Until death." She looked around the house. "I might as well be here as anywhere."

Cassandra adopted some of her husband's words of encouragement. "I'm sure there is something you can do. Why, you could garden," Cassandra suggested, too late remembering the mess of the gardens in Pentreath's back lawn.

"What does that do for me?"

"It feeds the spirit."

"My spirit was fed by being Lady Dewsberry.

Even when my husband shamed me with that harlot of his and his bastard children, the title gave me importance. Now that I'm widowed, I am nothing."

Cassandra could have felt compassion for her plight until Arabella added meanly, "But I rest in the pleasant assurance that someday you, too, will be supplanted."

"Is that what you think I'm doing? I'm not taking your place. I'm trying to find my own way."

"You are in Cornwall," Arabella haughtily informed her. "There is nothing for us here."

How many times had Cassandra said the same herself?

And yet, hearing her mother-in-law speak this way drove home the realization that, if she wasn't careful, this could be her fate.

Cassandra was not going to let that happen. She moved to the door. "Well, thank you for your counsel," she said. "I will take your advice to heart. If you need anything, please send word to the house. We want you comfortable."

Cassandra then marched out of the house, anxious to leave.

"Logan, let us go."

He hopped off the pony and quickly harnessed it. His clothes were a bit of shambles but he still wore shoes and socks. She counted that as a success.

She climbed into the cart.

"Are we going home, friend?"

"Yes, yes, home."

They rode in silence. In truth, Cassandra buzzed with frustration over Arabella. "I'm not going to end up like her," she informed Logan.

"No, friend."

"I've a good brain and sound mind."

"Yes, friend."

"I want to do something useful. I believe in ideas and knowledge."

"Like us telling our stories?"

He had impressed her yesterday. She'd shared her favorite myth about Icarus, who flew too close to the sun. Logan had immediately understood and told her a story of an Indian boy who boasted too loudly that he could throw a ball farther than anyone else. Then a new boy had appeared and challenged him. The boy was actually a rabbit who had changed to teach him the dangers of pride.

Soren had been right. His son had a quick mind and it needed to be put to work.

They had discussed the issue over their pillows that morning. A tutor would have to be hired. Soren didn't know if he wanted to send his son away; however, there was not a school in the village or anywhere close.

Cassandra, too, believed that sending Logan

away to school would not be the wisest course of action for him.

A thought now struck her. At first, she pushed it away, but it came right back.

Her dream had been to create a literary salon where important ideas were shared.

But what if, instead, she created a school? A school that used modern ideas like Miss Edgeworth's, such as educating both boys and girls?

What if the important ideas she was destined to share were not with adults who were already set in their ways, but with bright minds like Logan's? What if she put *Practical Education* to the test?

The idea took flight in her mind. Suddenly, Cassandra could not wait to return home.

She found Soren out in the sheep shed where he had been observing the shearing. The bleating of animals prevented him from hearing her excited explanation of her idea. He took her outside where they could talk.

"What are you trying to say?"

"I'm going build a school," she informed him.

"A school?"

"Yes, like the sort Miss Edgeworth and her father encourage. And I must find the second volume of their work," she said, making a mental note to herself. "Yes, that is what I shall do."

"How are you going to build a school? I'm not being critical, Cassandra, but practical."

"I have the garnets. I will sell them and buy books and whatever I need. Perhaps there is a building here at Pentreath we can use. Or a building in the village. I'd rather not use the old schoolroom upstairs. It is too small for what I envision."

"What *do* you envision?"

"A wonderful school. I don't care about the sex of the students but I am interested in their willingness to learn. I've thought of a good name for it. One that is positive and uplifting. The Dove School. What do you think?"

He was unimpressed.

She thought a moment more on it. "The Rising Dove School for Boys and Girls."

Soren winced as if the second name was worse. Then he said, "How about the Dewsberry School? Because this will be your concept, Cassandra. You will have the running of it."

"The Dewsberry School." She liked it. "Everyone in the area will know exactly where it was located."

"The name will also burnish the title," Soren observed. "We will go from a reputation of being gamesters and spendthrifts to gentlemen, gentlewomen, and scholars."

"Yes," she agreed with enthusiasm. "This is something *I* wish to do."

"Then do it, Cass. Do it with my blessing and make a gentleman out of that child." He nodded for her to look up. Logan had climbed to the top of the sheep shed. He'd shucked off his shoes and stockings and walked the roof line.

"He will be hard to tame," she predicted.

"I don't want him to lose his spirit, but I want him to succeed in the world. Therefore, he is your first pupil."

Her reply was to kiss him for being so generous and encouraging. "Now to make plans." She set off for the house at a brisk pace, but then stopped and looked back at him. "Oh, and your mother knows about your father's mistress. And, if you ever—" she started, pointing a finger for emphasis.

"*Never*," he swore crossing his heart. "You are woman enough for me, love. It is all I can do to keep up with you. Now, go create your school."

She threw him a kiss and hurried away.

Chapter 21

The Dewsberry School took over Cassandra's imagination and her life. It gave her a sense of purpose. She used Miss Edgeworth's thoughtful wisdom to prepare a philosophy for the school. She didn't care if she had twenty pupils or only Logan. What mattered was opening minds.

The next weeks were a blur of activity. Mrs. Branwell ran the house. Cassandra would meet with her most mornings to discuss menus and the like and then the two women would go about their day.

Over time, a growing respect for each other began to form.

Cassandra moved a desk into the library on the opposite end of the room from Soren's. They spent hours there, each busy with their own work. It was a good arrangement.

She even set up a small desk for Logan and she gave him assignments. He thought he was helping her create lessons for the school. She knew she was educating him.

He still called her "friend" on occasion. Lately, he'd taken to referring to her as "m'lady," a slurring of the "my lady" the servants and Soren used.

Once in a while he would call her Cass. "His Cass," just as Soren referred to her on occasion. Usually this was when he was nodding off to sleep. Stories had become their nightly ritual. First, she told him a story and then, eventually she began reading stories to him so that he would understand the usefulness of words and books.

There were few books around Pentreath but Cassandra had found a Bible and that was all she needed. She read about Jonah and the whale, and the earth swallowing the Israelites, and Daniel taming lions, and sometimes Logan would share stories his mother and aunts had taught him.

It was a special time of the day between them. She no longer feared being a stepmother because she did not consider herself one. She was his mother and he was her son, a relationship built from a growing bond of love and respect.

Soren sometimes joined them but he was usually keeping late hours balancing the estate books and scheming of ways to "rob Peter to pay Paul." She and Soren made sure they took care of each other's needs whether talking about their day or having a good romp.

Meanwhile, she was anxiously awaiting word from Mr. Huggett in London, who was tasked with selling her garnets for a fine price. Then she would buy books and fill Pentreath's library with them. The building for her school was still under consideration. They could build, or there was an abandoned granary on the estate close to the village that Soren thought might make a good school.

It was during this time of waiting that a letter arrived for her from Willa Reverly. Cassandra almost didn't have enough money to pay the franking. Yes, money was that tight, but she had to admit, money was meaning less and less to her.

However, Willa's news in the letter shocked her.

"What is it?" Soren said, seeing the change in her expression. They were in the library, each at their own desk.

"Willa says she is being married off to Camberly."

"Is she now?"

"This is terrible news."

"And why is that? Or did you want the points?" he teased.

She'd told him about their long-ago game. He'd thought it funny, and she remembered it as sad.

She had explained that back then, the game had been what they needed to make themselves go through Season after Season of meaningless routs and parties.

Cassandra scanned the letter. "She doesn't sound happy. She said the announcement has been made and then he disappeared." She looked up. "He did that one other time. He attended the Marquis of Devon's rout and then seemed to vanish."

"Yes, when he was enjoying Letty Bainhurst."

"You knew where he was?" she asked.

"Apparently, he owns a hunting lodge that is good for clandestine meetings."

She frowned. "I don't want Willa to marry a man who can't love her. She deserves better. In fact, we *all* deserve better."

"I love you," he said.

"I am so blessed." She frowned at the letter. "I'm thankful you are in my life or I could have been in a marriage like this."

"No, you would have been shuffled off to a miserable spinster's life. I saved you."

She laughed. "And I saved you from marrying a *true* heiress." She held up the letter. "You could have offered for Willa."

"And I would not be half as happy as I am now."

She had to run over and give him a kiss. "Well said," she whispered in his ear. "And this sort of marriage is what I want for Willa." She still held the letter. "If the duke was going to disappear, why did he go through the motions of making an offer to her?"

"I just hope his disappearance doesn't involve Letty again."

"That is two of us. Poor Willa. What shall she do?"

"Become a duchess. Camberly needs her money."

"But he may never be faithful."

"She will still be a duchess."

"That is not enough," Cassandra declared. "I'm going to write and tell her as much. But first, I need to call on the vicar."

"Mr. Morwath, why?"

"I asked him if he had books he could lend us for the school and he said he had several that his children no longer enjoyed. He has offered to donate some of them."

"Excellent." He was already returning to the task of listing the grain purchases. It would be nice when the day came that they could hire a steward to manage the details for him.

She kissed the top of his head and left the room to gather her bonnet and driving gloves.

It was a warm August day. The drive to the rectory would be enjoyable. Logan was out riding with Toby, but she had become rather handy with the reins and drove herself places in the pony cart.

An hour later, she reached the parish church. Mr. Morwath was in the back of the rectory cutting the limbs off an overeager hawthorn bush. He was a tall man with stooped shoulders. Every time Cassandra saw him, she always thought he appeared overwhelmed by life.

She could also commiserate with the difficulty of his gardening task. She'd had a time cleaning out the beds around Pentreath. She'd done it herself since there were no servants to spare for such a task, save for when Mrs. Branwell found a moment to help.

She parked the cart and tied up the pony.

The vicar came out to greet her. "How is everyone at Pentreath, my lady?" he asked. With a wave of his hand, he invited her into his home.

"Pentreath is fine. And how are your wife and children?"

"Mrs. Morwath is at market day in the village. She enjoys her time there since two of our daughters usually meet her and they have a time of it." He had several married children and a host of grandchildren. "And how is Lady Dewsberry? Did I hear that she is out of town?"

That was the good news. Arabella had been a glum presence until she had written to her brother in Hertfordshire inviting herself for a visit. Over the weeks since she had been moved to the dowager's cottage, both Cassandra and

Soren had made efforts to call on her several times a week. Each call was met with her stiff disapproval.

However, when her brother had said she could visit, and Soren agreed to hire a decent coach and provide pin money, her attitude had been what some might call happy. Soren swore he'd seen the inklings of a smile upon her face.

"I hope she returns a changed woman, my lady," Mr. Morwath said.

"I agree, Vicar."

He led her to the cramped space he used for his office. She remembered it well from her childhood. Books were piled everywhere. Just as she'd done as a child, she sank down to the floor so she could plunge into them.

Cassandra said, "My favorite part of the week was calling upon you and borrowing another book."

"Many of these are going to waste. Take what you like. None of my children became strong readers. Not like you."

"What of grandchildren?" she asked. "Won't you want these for them?"

"My hope is that they will attend your school."

She smiled. "Then that is my hope as well." As she went through the books, she shared with him the stories she and Logan told each other. "Even my lord is taken with our tales."

The stack of books beside her began to grow.

"I would like to hear Lord Logan tell a story sometime."

"We should invite you and Mrs. Morwath over for dinner. We have been so busy we haven't been able to entertain but the time will come." She looked at the pile she was building. "I admit I'm greedy. Many of these bring back memories of what was happening in my life when I read them."

"After your mother died, I always hoped they would give you some solace, my lady."

"They did." She smiled at him and opened a book of *Aesop's Fables*. "This was a favorite. And I'm taking so many, I must pay for them." She would as soon as she received her money.

"I don't ask for payment. The parish has needed a decent school for a long time. I'm pleased that you and your husband are taking an active interest in the area."

"As we should."

"Aye, you grew up here."

A thought crossed her mind. She hadn't intended on going in this direction. However, he was someone she trusted. She closed the book on her lap and said, "May I discuss something that has been weighing on me?"

"Of course. I'm available to you, my lady."

She looked up at him, realizing that he would be the first person to hear her secret. And then she realized she had already confided in him many a time before. When she would visit to borrow a book, she would share how much she missed her mother, and sometimes talk about Helen and her stepsisters. He'd always given her encouragement and sound advice.

"MP Holwell is not my true father." She paused a moment to reflect and then said, "There was a time when saying those words aloud would have caused me great distress. Now, thanks to my lord's loving support, this is really nothing more than a statement of fact. And yet, I sense I should feel something."

His brow furrowed, his expression grave. "Such as?"

"I don't know. Sadness. Regret. Relief. I do wish I knew who my real father is. Or was." She looked up at him. "He could be dead as well. I hardly remember my mother." She touched the pearl she wore on its ribbon around her neck.

"You are very much like her."

"You knew her?" He'd never said as much. "I thought you came to the parish after she died."

"Actually, I had met her at my last posting. I tutored her."

This was new information. "Just like you tutored me?" He had come to Lantern Fields and taught her some lessons. "That is an interesting coincidence. And a fortunate one." She ran her thumb along the spine of the book. "My lord said that there might be someone around here who knew Mother and her secrets. That I might someday discover who my father is." She raised her gaze to him. "Would you have an idea?"

A look crossed his face. There was no mistaking that it was regret. She expected him to kindly tell her no.

Instead, he took the book from her and held her hands to help her up. He sat her on a stool so they were almost at the same level.

"I have a confession of my own, my lady. I ask you to hear me out, but first, I must beg you to please not judge your mother harshly."

"I would not."

His watery blue eyes met hers. "You are as sympathetic as she was."

"Please, tell me what you know."

"I'm your father."

It was a stunning admission. At first, she didn't believe her ears. He nodded as if to confirm the words.

She'd had no idea. And Cassandra didn't know what to say.

"I loved her," he said. "Passionately. She was so bright and lovely. Caring. All the things you are. Of course, I was married and already had three of my children." His wife was a stern woman.

"You and my mother had an illicit romance?"

" 'Illicit' is not the right word. I've always regretted what happened between us. It was not her fault. I was the weak one and she paid the price. But I loved her."

He squeezed her hand. "My lady, I realized my sin. No matter how unhappy I was in my marriage, I had betrayed my vows and I wanted to be right with God. I told your mother I must not see her again. I did not know she was carrying you. She never told me, and then her father up and married her to Holwell. When word came that she'd had a child, I knew just from counting the days that Holwell could not be the father."

"Did you take the living here to be close to her?"

"No, I took it to be close to you. Your mother wrote me a letter about how ill she was. She told me about the living here. I grabbed it. Your mother died just days before I arrived. We didn't even have the chance to speak to each other. I officiated her funeral."

He loosened his hold on her hands and sat back. "However, it has been my good fortune to watch you grow into a graceful, intelligent woman. And now, I must ask you never to speak of this to another soul."

Cassandra was stunned by the entreaty. "I don't

know how I feel about that request. We've known each other a very long time."

"Oh, we can have our friendship, but I would not hurt my poor wife any more than I already have."

"Did she know about you and Mother?"

"I don't know, but I do carry a weight of regret in my heart. I love my children, my lady. I have found peace in my marriage. It is unfortunate that I married the wrong woman; however, I doubt if Elwood Bingham would have let Pen marry a village priest."

Pen. Her mother's name had been Penelope. Cassandra had never heard her referred to by a nickname, by a lover's name.

Nor did she know what she would do with this information Mr. Morwath had just shared.

"Do you understand what I am asking you, my lady? To keep this between the two of us? I'm trusting you with this."

"I will share with Soren. Have no worry that he will bandy it about. But I cannot bear this secret alone."

"I do not wish to have him think ill of me. What happened between your mother and me may sound tawdry to the outside world, but it wasn't. We were in love. It made complete sense to us. It was the very best my life has ever been."

Cassandra stood. She needed Soren. He would help her sort this out. She held out a gloved hand.

"Mr. Morwath—" She could not call him Father. "I thank you for telling me. I now understand why you made sure I had books to read."

"It was a way of reaching out to you."

"A good way. If you will excuse me, I believe I should leave."

"Do you want me to carry these books out for you?"

"I might have to come back for them," she answered, needing a bit of space from him to reason through his confession.

"I make no claim upon you, my lady. I've actually waited for the day when I could tell you. You have heard that Lantern Fields was to be sold?"

"Sold?"

"Aye. They say that Holwell is done up. Apparently, paying your inheritance has left him broke."

Should she lie? No. She was done with lies. She spoke her truth. "I didn't receive an inheritance, sir. MP Holwell spent it unwisely."

"We all wondered."

"If only I had been that aware—" She stopped. "No, my life is exactly as I would wish it. I pray whoever purchases Lantern Fields will be good people."

"That is a good wish, my lady."

It would also mean she need never fear having her path cross with Holwell's. "What will become of him?"

Mr. Morwath shrugged. "He'll stay in London until his term has ended and probably retire here or someplace else."

"He'll go someplace else," she predicted. The man who had pretended to be her father was too proud to humble himself after such a downfall.

He walked her to the pony cart. "I will keep the books you chose ready for when you need them."

She nodded. In the past, she'd always shaken his hand before she left. She didn't know what to do now.

For the first time, she noticed the resemblance between them—the height, the eyes, the set of her mouth. Why, she even looked very much like his daughter Beth, whom she had seen at services from time to time.

He answered the question for her. He leaned forward and kissed her on her cheek as if in benediction. Without a word, he turned and walked back around the rectory to resume his task of conquering the hawthorn.

She drove home, her mind somewhat numb . . . and yet, she had a sense of finally feeling complete. The truth could do that.

The stable lads took the pony cart from her.

She was most anxious to find Soren, but she noticed a strange horse in the stables. "Do we have a visitor?"

"Yes, we do," the head lad said. "A lone rider. My lord knew him well."

Soren might have been familiar with the guest, but he had not been expecting him. He would have said something to Cassandra.

She marched up the path to the house. She took the back entrance so that she could speak to Mrs. Branwell and Cook before presenting herself to her husband and their guest.

Logan was in the kitchen eating a bun fresh from the oven. She stopped, watching him, her heart full of love.

He caught her eye, and popped the last of the bun greedily in his mouth, unabashedly grinning with satisfaction—and in that moment, she silently thanked Mary's spirit that lived in her son. Logan was a gift in Cassandra's life and, in honor of his mother's memory, she would do all in her power to nurture his proud independence. She wanted to believe that is what her own mother had wanted for her. Gentle, loving guidance. She was thankful for what Mr. Morwath had been able to offer her.

Mrs. Branwell was happy to see her. "Lord Dewsberry wishes you to meet him in the library."

"And what of our guest?"

"I have taken him to his room. Lord Dewsberry said he will be here for several days."

"Who is he?"

"A Mr. Ewing."

The name meant nothing to Cassandra. She headed for the library, untying the ribbons of her bonnet as she went.

Soren was at his desk, counting a stack of gold coins.

At the sight of her, he rose and raced to greet her. He lifted her by the waist and swept her around the room with such energy, her bonnet fell to the floor. He stopped at his desk. "Look at them. Do you know how much is there?"

Cassandra had to catch her breath. She pulled off her driving gloves and picked up one of the coins. It was thin but heavy. "Where did you find these?"

"Mr. Ewing delivered them."

"Our mysterious guest?"

"A man in my employ. My business partners in Upper Canada sent these. They are my share of the earnings of our investments. The shipping company is still alive and well. In fact, Mr. Ewing believes we will survive the war. The trading post and store continue to grow. I knew I had the right location for them. My partners sold some of the land we had purchased. Cassandra, how many books would you like to buy? A dozen? Ten dozen?"

Her response was to the throw her arms around his neck, and the two of them hugged each other tightly with relief. Their fortunes had just changed.

"I was hoping for some luck," he said, "but I never expected this. We are going to hire a steward and we'll build a building for your school and buy sheep and cattle—*this* is what we've needed, Cass. According to the letter my partners sent with Ewing, we should only grow."

She looked at him. "So, you really didn't need to marry an heiress."

"No, I needed to marry *you*."

And in that moment, she knew the money had never mattered. Not to Soren and not to her.

Nor would the vicar's confession have any impact on her life. Who she had been was of no importance. It was who she chose to become that gave her life meaning.

And that choice was this man's wife.

They had each other and a future bursting with possibilities. And life was exactly as she could wish it.

Author's Note

Dear Readers,

I believe the only hallmark of a good life is how well I love and how well I am loved in return. Love is *all* that matters. Money will come and go . . . and if I am not careful, so will love. It is a precious thing and must be recognized and valued.

But then you know that.

You are like me. You believe love isn't an illusion.

I don't know why love is not easy. We all want it. Many of us have searched most of our lives for it. Some have found and nurtured it while others have tossed it away. And there are too many of us who have discovered that what we thought was love turned out to be the exact opposite. We've nursed our broken hearts, but hopefully not broken spirits.

Cassandra and Soren have found their magic. Their love strengthens them.

Or perhaps the two of them are so stubborn, they won't give up. They will go on through thick and thin, and there is a grace to that as well.

Yes, Cassandra will have many children. In fact, she is already pregnant. She just doesn't know it yet. But I can share that secret with you.

And what of Willa? She's to be a duchess . . . but will she find love? You know that answer, and I think you'll "love" her story.

All my best,
Cathy Maxwell
October 20, 2017

NEW YORK TIMES BESTSELLING AUTHOR

CATHY MAXWELL

The Match of the Century
978-0-06-238861-2

Every debutante aspires to snag a duke. Elin Morris just happens to have had one reserved since birth. But postponements of her marriage to London's most powerful peer give Elin time to wonder how she will marry Gavin Baynton when she cannot forget his brother, Benedict.

The Fairest of Them All
978-0-06-238863-6

The penniless orphan of a disreputable earl, Lady Charlene Blanchard picks the pockets of unsavory gentlemen to survive. But due to her extraordinary beauty and prized bloodlines, she is chosen as a potential bride for the Duke of Baynton. Except the duke turns out to be the tall, dark and sexy stranger who just caught her red-handed as a thief!

A Date at the Altar
978-0-06-238865-0

Struggling actress and playwright Sarah Pettijohn is absolutely the last woman Gavin Whitridge, Duke of Baynton, would ever fall in love with. However, there is something about her that stirs his blood . . . which makes her perfect for a bargain he has in mind: In exchange for backing her play, he wants Sarah to teach him about love.

Discover great authors, exclusive offers,
and more at hc.com.

CM6 0118